Mourning Twilight

By Kevin F. Branley

Jorge,

Thanks for all the lessons & advice... It was a pleasure & an honor to work w/ you & call you friend. God Bless...

Ken

Ken F. Branley

ISBN 978-0-9848315-0-0

www.mourningtwilight.com

Dedicated to the men and women in the world of Law Enforcement, the prosecutors who see cases through to the end, and the victims they seek justice for.

This book would not have been possible without the guidance, advice and editing of Judith Tarr, and her ability to put the book in it's "Sunday's best suit." Thanks for everything Judy.

"The dead are not far from us...they cling in some strange way to what is most still and deep within us."

--W.B. Yeats

April 25, 1975

The April sky was a seething mass of bruised clouds and piercing cold rain. Storm drains vomited up the excess, flooding the streets, as the wind screeched into yet another gear. It stripped the freshly sprouted leaves from the trees and whirled them into the gale.

The Mystic River swelled over its banks, and the marshlands that bordered it were overrun. Overturned canoes, loose oars, dock posts, and downed trees were sucked under the whitecaps, only to reappear one hundred yards down river.

Vehicles that were unfortunate enough to be caught in the freak storm jockeyed for position under highway overpasses and off ramps. Tree branches and downed wires littered the streets amid the banshee wail of emergency vehicles. Accidents plagued the roadways, but not a soul ventured out into the fury of the storm. The morning commute was stuck, motionless.

At the local high school, a senior was struck and dragged one hundred yards by one of her classmates who was frantically attempting to get his father's new convertible out of the storm. Blood and brain matter seeped from her body down the entrance ramp to the school, as if the car itself was bleeding.

The screams of the students who witnessed it were audible only between the deafening cracks of thunder. Even before the heavy rain had scoured the site clean, the driver of the vehicle had slipped into catatonia.

"She was in his biology class," said those of his classmates who could talk at all.

Elsewhere in the city, two elementary students were electrocuted when flash flooding pooled underneath the tree where they had taken shelter, and an electrical wire snapped in the wind and dropped into the water. They were fried instantly, along with the Good Samaritan who ran to their aid. One of the children's mothers was caught in storm-created traffic just a block away, somehow sensing that something was terribly wrong.

Golf-ball-sized hail bombarded anyone who made the mistake of assuming it was just another freak storm in New England. Car windshields spiderwebbed under the force of the barrage. Citizens were knocked to the ground, sliced and left bleeding.

Any attempt to rescue a victim meant the same punishing sentence. The storm raged completely out of control, worsening by the second, as day turned black as night. The air was cold, damned cold; at least twenty degrees colder than it had been only a few minutes ago.

A feeling of eeriness was present with every gusting current of air, and the smell of death seemed to be emanating from the bowels of the earth itself, its strongest stench rising up from the sewers. Those that were not vomiting up rainwater seemed to be emanating a thick, black, mudlike substance that looked like nothing so much as a mixture of blood and human feces.

Trees swayed in unison, synchronized like dancers. If the good people of Medford, Massachusetts had not been so caught up in their little human tragedies, they would have noticed that the darkest clouds and the most frequent and ferocious lightning gathered over the woods just a few miles to the north, an area known as the Middlesex Fells Reservation.

#

In the west of the city, a Medford Police Department chaplain stared into the storm's fury from his living-room window. His heart raced with anxiety, but he did not know why. He usually welcomed and enjoyed a good storm, but somehow, in the pit of his stomach, he knew this was something different.

A heavy purplish fog settled over the city, turning the morning light to an ominous darkness. His whole body prickled with goose bumps, as bursts of thunder rattled the glasses and plates in his kitchen cabinets.

He stepped away from the picture window, not trusting the storm's fury to stay safely outside the glass. His services as a chaplain would surely be needed after this. The sick feeling sank deeper, and a chill crawled up his spine.

He shook his head and silently blessed himself. He had seen much death in his life, and had experienced many, many different things, both good and bad. This morning, witnessing the storm's ferocity, he knew only one thing. This was no ordinary spring storm. It was a harbinger of something else. Something terrible.

#

Within the Fells Reservation, animals, reptiles, and insects of all kinds fled in search of shelter. Mothers of every shape and species gathered their young and broke for home. The woods were alive with fear.

It was as dark as night, and there seemed to be no relief forthcoming. Huge pines were snapped in half and torn from their roots as barrages of lightning hammered the high ground. Hillside footpaths quickly turned into veins of rainwater and fed the pond below. The pond's occupants took refuge in the depths. Everything and anything that valued existence sought shelter from the storm.

Far off, at the highest point of the reservation, a lone coyote struggled to keep her balance on a rock that overlooked the woods. Lightning danced around her, but never touched her. She stood with her chest sticking out and her tail hanging straight down, as if summoned by the storm itself.

She was not large for a coyote in these parts, but her coat was still thick and full, which made her look heavier than she was. The fur on her back bristled; her eyes glowed in the flicker of lightning.

The next burst of wind hit hard. She swayed with it, in perfect harmony with the storm's fury.

She scanned the wooded area below, searching, looking to the bottom of the hill as if she were going to leap off the rock. Then, arching her neck straight back, she filled her lungs and let out a piercing howl.

Thunder split the sky. Lightning cascaded over the city. Coyote's haunting wail echoed long after the thunder had rolled away.

Night Screams

We double-checked our gear, then checked it again. We were traveling light. Canteen, two days' ration, compass, poncho--got to have a rain poncho in the Highlands--knife, ammo. Lots of ammo. It was always better to have and not need than to need and not have.

Every Long Range Reconnaissance Patrol member, or LRRP, knew that. There was no room for mistakes out in the bush.

The chopper pilots walked toward us from the mess tent. They would be taking us to our insertion. There were two of them, and as they got closer I noticed that the one with the U.S. Cavalry hat, the kind that Custer used to wear, was sporting a pearl-handled .38 on his hip. He had a dark brown handlebar mustache and a pair of aviator sunglasses.

The other pilot had a jungle hat with a similar pair of shades, but he didn't have enough facial hair to match his comrade's mustache. With any luck at all, he would live long enough to grow one . . . if he made it out of the 'Nam.

They both wore combat fatigues and boots and the customary yellow handkerchiefs around their necks. They were older than us. Twenty-three, twenty-four, maybe.

We knew all about the Air Cav. They were badder than hell, and had certainly taken the heat off us on a number of occasions.

There was also a door gunner accompanying us on our trip. He would lay down machine-gun fire in the event we needed any. He looked kind of old to be a door gunner with the Cav, but hey, what did I know?

He was a muscular black dude, about six feet tall, in sun-faded fatigue pants and combat boots and no shirt, with a white flight helmet that had kills nicked in on one side and the words "Head Hunter" on the other. He wore a single dog tag around his neck, and looked like he had been traveling with the Cav too long.

He stood next to the Huey's open door, examining the machine guns. As we approached with our gear, he looked up at us through his dark sunglasses, then looked away. It was better for him not to know us as people, in the event we didn't make it back.

Neither he nor the pilots ever spoke to us. They didn't need to. Everything they needed to say was painted in white italics on the back end of the chopper: "Yea, though I walk through the valley of the shadow of Death, I fear no Evil . . . for I am the meanest motherfucker in the valley."

They had our immediate respect. It was a good vibe to know that the best of the best was inserting us into our mission. A real good vibe. Everyone was fired up, highly motivated, and you could almost smell the blood in the air.

Something big was going down tonight, and we were the creators. Life takers . . . heartbreakers . . . God-damned killers! And we knew it.

The engine of the Huey whined to a

higher pitch as it lifted slightly off the tarmac and began to hover. While the Cav did a final check on their instruments, we took our customary positions inside the chopper. Ramirez blessed himself with the sign of the cross like he always did, his way of saying, "Let the games begin!"

The Huey banked hard left and began to climb steadily east, picking up speed as it dropped its nose forward and took us over the concertina wire and away from the safety of the Fire Base.

My stomach dropped before it recognized the familiarity of the chopper's behavior. We were on our way.

Four other members of the LRRP Team and me had been briefed on a mission, which suggested heavy enemy activity in the Central Highlands. The place was crawling with the enemy, and it was considered strong Charlie country.

The enemy was confident on the ground leading to and coming from Cambodia and Laos, and because of this they would do dumb things, like using trails, walking in

11

single file without flank security, and never bothering to set up booby traps in their own area.

We naturally used this to our advantage, and the gooks hated us for it. They had bounties on every LRRP's head--dead or alive.

We captured a North Vietnamese Army Regular one time, or NVA as we called them, and brought him back for intelligence purposes. When he was being interrogated, he stated that the feeling in the jungle was that "the Ghost Soldiers were only friends with the shadows of their own nightmares."

As soon as the interpreter translated this, it spooked the shit out of me. I don't know why, but I couldn't get that one statement out of my head.

The rest of the team thought it was great and loved it. The NVA looked frightened to death, eyes darting in all directions. I'm sure he thought we were going to kill him, but we didn't.

We were professionals. Killers yes, but professionals nonetheless. We sent him to

Saigon for further debriefing and re-education . . . if there is such a thing.

Now we were on a new mission, or maybe the same old one, new chapter. HQ was looking for a fight, and sent us in to gather intelligence.

Our orders were to gather info and avoid contact. We would have to see about that.

It was a hell of a night for an ambush. The sky was clear, and the moon would be out.

The Huey leveled out to cruise altitude. We were traveling at about one hundred twenty knots. We could see other units off in the distance, engaging in firefights.

The pilot in our Huey changed frequencies, and we struggled to listen to the battle over the roar of the chopper's engine. The NVA were dug in deep. Our guys were taking heavy casualties.

Everyone on the ship was deathly quiet. That could easily be any one of us.

I could see morale slipping away just when we needed it most. I edged my way to the pilot, and was about to ask him to put some motivational music on when he changed the frequency.

The Cav's Special Ops Unit was notorious for fucking with the enemy's mind by cranking loud music over an enhanced PA system during an attack. The CIA had implemented the program to get the enemy spooked, so that he wouldn't fight. Sometimes we would have a Vietnamese interpreter speaking over the PA system telling the enemy to surrender or the Ghost Soldiers would come in the night and kill them.

It could work the other way, too--de-spook our side and get it back in a fighting frame of mind. No sooner had I reached the flight compartment than Jimi started playing Purple Haze. The Huey's engine seemed to give him his due respect, as it was much easier to hear than the previous transmission.

In a few minutes we were out of visual contact of the battle, and I could see the team coming back to themselves again. I let out the breath I'd been holding. That was a close one.

The chopper descended quickly, bounced off the jungle floor and gained altitude once again. This was repeated several times, and everyone's stomach had to readjust as it did. Even knowing what was up, we still got taken by surprise.

The enemy were forever putting spotters in likely American landing zones, in hopes of ambushing the ambushers. Unfortunately, it often worked. Hence, the touch and go procedures, to keep the enemy on their toes.

Soon enough the real LZ approached, and we all jumped into six-to-eight-foot-high elephant grass. The chopper took off just like all the other times. No problems. No ambush.

Now the sound of the chopper had dissipated and we sat silently in the elephant grass, praying that we hadn't been made a target. Our hearts raced like many times before, and we listened for any sound that did not fit with the staccato of the jungle.

After a long twenty minutes I took the

point and began our trek to the first rendezvous as the other four members of the team fell in behind me, approximately ten feet apart.

The air was oven hot as usual, and our camos were already soaked through with sweat. The packs were loaded down with ammo and C-ration, and just trying to breathe through the bug-infested air was a challenge in itself.

Sweat dripped off my headband and stung my eyes. The insects were always a friggin' nightmare and the bug repellent wasn't worth the container it was kept in. My neck and hands were already developing welts from the insects. We were going to get mauled by them when we sat stationary for the ambush.

The jungle was noisy with the chatter of birds, the buzz of insects and the hissing of reptiles. That was a good sign. Dead silence in the jungle could often lead to death itself.

Oftentimes, fleeing birds or animals would announce the arrival of an approaching enemy column. This was one of the reasons why it was absolutely essential to stay quiet and stay camouflaged when setting up an ambush.

We continued to move until we came across a heavily used trail. It was only three feet wide, but the light red-brown dirt stood out like a fluorescent slash in the overwhelmingly green jungle.

There were not a lot of trails this far into the bush, and this was worn down several inches into the earth, which told us it was a high-speed trail. We looked at each other, nodded. We were on the right track.

The rest of the team set up security while I checked for signs of recent activity. There were numerous boot prints along with deeply trenched bicycle tracks that told me the bikes were loaded down with supplies and equipment.

Boot prints meant NVA regular Army--the Viet Cong always wore sandals. The footprints walked heel to toe and made a considerable depression in the ground, indicating that each soldier was also heavily laden.

It was bad strategy for any soldier to use a clearly marked trail. This told us that the enemy was comfortable in this particular area. It also told us that they were probably unaware of our presence.

The squad saddled up and moved back ten feet off the trail. From there we would walk parallel to it until we reached the area Headquarters said was active--in layman terms, the ambush site.

In the early afternoon we stopped, set up a small perimeter and dug into rations. The sun was at its hottest, and triple-canopy jungle provided little relief. The insects were feasting as usual, and everyone was itching to get to the site.

Suddenly, a Vietnamese voice called out in the distance. Without a pause or a word, we scattered, ready to set up a hasty ambush, which basically meant get in some kind of firing line and bushwhack the enemy before he discovered us.

The voice grew louder. Then there were two. Now someone was laughing. Another was singing.

Holy shit! How many of them were there? My heart was beating so hard I was afraid the enemy would hear it and rain holy hell on us.

This was the hardest part: just staying abso-fucking-lutely still. There must be a whole shitload of NVA, because it took balls to be this noisy. They came by us in sets of five with a three-minute lapse between.

I was the squad leader, which meant all eyes were on me, waiting for me to give a command. But there were just too many of them, and we hadn't even had a chance to set up our goddamn claymores.

The enemy were cocky though, and we wanted to hammer them. For now, we counted, because it was just as important to know when not to shoot. We counted and made note of certain types of weaponry, food ration, number of personnel, the direction they were coming from and the direction they were going.

The first chance we got, we would radio the intelligence back to HQ and continue with our mission. We had discovered a major supply route, and the enemy would pay hell for it with an arc light B-52 bombing mission.

We gathered data for the better part of two hours. I was starting to worry that we wouldn't make our objective by nightfall; but it finally seemed that the column had passed. We descended another thirty yards off the path, and sent the dispatch.

Once it went through, we knew the B-52's would make a strike sometime during the evening. By then, we would be far enough away from the danger, but close enough to enjoy the show. It should be a good one. This looked like being one of our greatest missions yet.

We went back to our position ten feet off the path and began our drive to the ambush site. Everyone was juiced up with adrenaline and dying to let out a scream, but training held. Nobody said a word. I could feel the swelling in my hands and neck from the insect bites, but for the first time in a while, I didn't really give a fuck. We were on to something big.

We came within twenty meters of our ambush site just before dark. We waited ten minutes, getting the lay of the land, and then moved into position, setting up claymores and determining fields of fire.

It was dark by the time we gave the site our full approval. Now all we had to do was wait.

We were set up alongside a ten-foot berm, overlooking a river which was about as wide as an average one-way street in the city and only a foot deep. A small path covered with scrub brush was directly across from us.

We were in a U-shaped ambush formation, and if all went according to plan, the enemy would walk right into the mouth of the open part of the U. Then, the trap would spring.

The front of our formation was rigged with three sets of claymore mines with a kill radius of fifty yards. That covered our perimeter. Our flanks were also rigged with a claymore mine each in the event the enemy came from an undiscovered path or a different location. The path across the stream was rigged with claymore in daisy-chain fashion to prevent any enemy heroes from entering our perimeter before we wanted them to.

Any way the enemy wanted to play it, we were ready. At the very least we could cause enough disturbance to get the fuck out of there if need be.

Everyone knew the game plan. I, as usual, would initiate the contact by blowing the front claymore mines, and then it was a free-for-all.

The night air was damp and cold, and everyone was wet with sweat from the journey through the jungle. We cautiously rubbed ointment on our insect bites, careful not to make too much movement and give our position away. We waited and waited and waited, not knowing if the column we had seen earlier was our objective and they were ahead of schedule, or if there were more to come and we would get to taste blood. Either way, our objective was completed as far as HQ was concerned, but we were not satisfied.

At 0430 hours, as night fought the oncoming daylight for control of the day, we had our first piece of contact. The camouflaged NVA regular entered the river warily, looking in all directions. We knew there were more behind, but we didn't know how many, and we sure as hell didn't want to start anything we couldn't finish.

My heart raced with adrenaline. My eyes kept going wide, then I'd remember to squint so the enemy couldn't spot the gleam.

This guy was a veteran. He made almost no noise, and barely disturbed the water as he made his way across the shallow river. He carried a heavy pack of supplies on his back, and was hunched over from all the weight.

At one point I thought he'd made us. He stopped a little more than halfway across the river and took a look around, as if sensing something. Then he turned back toward the direction he came from and hand-signaled for his comrades to cross.

Two enemy soldiers came out of the bush, pushing bicycles heavily laden with supplies. About ten yards behind the two was another enemy soldier, carrying a similar pack to the first one. I almost couldn't control myself with the energy that was pumping through my body.

It was morning twilight, the time when the night met the morning. We used to joke and call it mourning twilight, for all the gooks we killed then. They would be mourning for each other, and we would slither back into the jungle looking to kill some more. It was invigorating . . . addicting.

I looked over at Ramirez, who had a clear view of the path. He signaled with two fingers and a horizontal sweep of the eyes: he couldn't see any enemy soldiers past the fourth.

I waited until the first enemy soldier was just about across, the second two were in the claymore kill zone, and the last one was entering the water.

Decision time. Should I wait to see if there were more? Or should I let them have it?

A Jimi Hendrix tune pounded through

my head. *Purple haze in my brain . . .*

It was show time.

I blew the claymores in the river first. Water and unidentifiable pieces of NVA sprayed everywhere through a cloud of gray and black smoke.

Then, in seconds, a chain reaction: I blew the path across the river, in case there were more of the enemy. *Boom! boom! Boom! boom! boom!*

The jungle lit up. The squad was laying heavy fire into the bush. The first NVA across the stream got his head torn off by the machine gun.

Every fourth bullet was a tracer round. Flesh tore, bone smashed, blood sprayed. In the thick smoke from the claymores, it looked like abstract art from hell.

Ceasefire was automatic without return fire. We watched and waited as the smoke from the explosion filled our lungs, danced through the trees, and then drifted downstream just inches off the top of the water.

The stream itself had turned to blood.

Miscellaneous pieces of skin, brain and bone matter escorted the smoke downstream until it became too heavy for the bloody water and sank beneath the surface, as if consumed by the river itself.

Total silence had fallen. An eerie feeling swept over me.

Something was not right. It didn't feel like other ambushes.

In the perfect stillness, I heard B-52's off in the distance, dropping bombs.

We all looked at each other. Every one of us had the same expression, and the same thought. Arc light mission! They're too close! <u>Holy shit!</u>

The ground shook underneath us. Three miles away, give or take.

They had to be off target. The enemy had long since left the area.

Someone at HQ had screwed up. And our ambush site was right in the line of their destruction.

The bombing came on like rolling thunder, closer and closer, until we were literally being bounced off the ground.

Nobody could hear a thing, we were all deafened by the noise, but I was howling in my head.

This is it! Motherfucker! We're done!

The bombs were less than a mile away now. I saw blood pouring from Ramirez's eyes and ears. His body literally shook and quivered inches off the ground.

This is it! It can't end like this! I'm the squad leader! I have to make a decision! I have to save the team!

Too late to radio HQ. Who could hear to do it, anyway?

Motown struck up the beat inside my head. *Nowhere to run to, nowhere to hide.*

I crawled toward the rest of the squad. We huddled together, so that we could die together.

The one with our names on it came whistling in. *Wwhhhhhhhhhiiiiiiii . . .*

#

BA-BOOM!

I awoke, startled and disoriented. The

glow of my gun's night sights streaked across the room, searching for a target.

The .45, or "hush puppy," was cocked and ready to rock n' roll. I ran a fast mental assessment of the situation.

I was in my apartment, not in the bush. No blood. No bodies. Heavy storm outside.

Thunder. Friggin' thunder. That was all.

I was sweating profusely and shaking like a drunk that has gone too long without a drink. The curtains around the open window were flapping madly, and the rain poured in.

Nika, my faithful Siberian Husky, stared at me from the foot of my bed with a look that said, "Go back to sleep. You're having a nightmare. Again."

That was the key word. <u>Again</u>. The dog didn't appear alarmed, so I knew there was no reason for me to be.

My one and only friend. What would I do without her?

Thunder crashed again. She looked toward the window with her ears at attention, but she seemed more curious than frightened.

I was still rattled. I struggled to find my composure. The rain sluiced down like the monsoon back in the bush. No wonder I'd had that particular nightmare.

I had a lot of those--woke up a lot in a cold sweat, screaming. Some of the nightmares were real, others were figments of my imagination; or at least I think they were. It was hard to tell.

Not all of the night screams, as I'd begun to call them, were bad. Every time I thought I had had enough, and didn't think I wanted to live any more, my grandfather would come to me.

Even though I was sound asleep, I knew that I was not dreaming. He was really there. He suppressed many of my malevolent nightmares by merely appearing. And when he did, I never wanted him to leave.

I always had questions for him, and he always answered them with stories that took me days, weeks or months to figure out. Some, I never figured out at all.

Not yet anyway.

I wished he had shown up for this one. I

could have used him.

I loved my grandfather. He raised me, and when he died when I was seventeen, I was devastated. Even now, eight years after his death, he was constantly on my mind.

Nika cocked her ears toward the window again. I could have sworn I heard the wailing of a coyote.

#

I took my homemade prescription for nightmares: the television and half a joint. I watched live footage of a packed American helicopter lifting off the top of the U.S. Embassy in Saigon. Other footage showed aircraft being tossed off the USS Blue Ridge to make room for yet another incoming refugee helicopter.

Lovely war.

The storm outside fit the news too well. I wished I hadn't seen the broadcast. I'd be night screaming again tonight, after that.

No sooner had the thought taken shape than a bolt of lightning and an accompanying crack of thunder blew my electricity, and the war on the TV faded to black.

Maybe this wouldn't be such a bad day after all. The VA had set up a job interview for at the Fells Reservation State Mental Hospital. There were supposedly a lot of veterans there, but the VA hadn't told me if they were staff or patients.

It didn't matter to me, and I could use the bread. The storm continued to rage, and I puffed on a joint while I waited for it to be time to head out for the 11 a.m. interview.

Death Storm

Just a short time earlier, the Preacher, as he was known to the hippies and police, set up shop in front of Medford City Hall. The teenaged boys and girls who hung out there knew it more commonly as "The Pit."

It got its name from its 360 degrees of descending steps with a monument in the middle dedicated to "those citizens who gave the ultimate sacrifice in World War I and World War II." There were going to be quite a few more names from the Korean War, a little over twenty years before, and the dreaded Vietnam War which was just now coming to its conclusion.

The monument consisted of a 180-degree semicircle with the names of the brave ones inscribed on bronze walls cemented into the rest of the structure. It stood approximately ten feet high with an American Bald Eagle in the center, wings spread proud and wide, gripping the American flag in its talons. At the bottom were the most uncomfortable cement benches that any ass had ever sat on, also made in the shape of a semicircle.

The Preacher pulled his shoulder-length black hair away from his eyes as he began his ascent of the monument. The smirk on his face broadened to a sinister smile as he decided which verse he would read from his Bible this afternoon.

There was an early crowd hanging out already. They would gather to hear his sermon, as the hippies would call it later, while they passed their joints around the circle: two girls, three boys, all about eighteen to twenty-one years old, with long hair, bell-bottom jeans, and psychedelic shirts. All five wore dinky little John Lennon sunglasses and talked like a chorus from "All You Need Is Love."

The Preacher looked down at them from his perch atop the monument and wished death upon them all. But for now, he needed them for witnesses.

They looked up at him and nodded and smiled like toy dogs in the back window of an automobile. Probably too stoned to speak, thought the Preacher.

He wore his customary black jungle combat boots that Uncle Sam had sent his mother after his brother Paul was killed in a place the peace freaks had never heard of, a corner of hell called Khe Sanh. He used to read the letters his brother sent home, saying he was in a safe part of Vietnam and not to worry too much.

The Preacher's mother would sit in front of the television every evening, hoping to catch a glimpse of her elder son. Then after the news was over, she would cry for the better part of an hour, until his father slapped her out of it.

"He'll come home if he's man enough to make it!" he would holler. "You spoil those two boys rotten."

Then the old man would unleash a little whisky-fueled aggression on young Tommy, too. Especially when he pissed the bed and his mother tried to hide it, but the old man found out anyway. Then he made them both pay.

"I'm going to cut your dick off!" the old man would yell, snapping a pair of hedge trimmers in Tommy's face. "See if you piss the bed after that!"

While big brother Paul was there, the old man hadn't been so violent. Although Paul got his share of beatings, he had learned how to fight back effectively. It was only a matter of time before he got the upper hand.

Now that Paul was ten thousand miles away, the old man could unleash his fury at will, always with that cute little cliché of his: "Sometimes people get what they deserve."

And the old man would make sure that everyone got theirs.

#

The more his mother cried, the harder the drunken bastard hit Tommy. But it wasn't until March of '68 that his mother and he gave up hope.

A Marine came to the door while they

were watching the news. They knew what that meant even before he opened his mouth. Eighteen-year-old Paul Joseph Neveska had been killed in action defending a position in the Khe Sanh fire base.

At first Tommy and his mother just stood there, staring in disbelief. The young Marine, not wanting to stay any longer that he had to, started down the stairs.

Before he got all the way down, he met Tommy's father coming up. The old man was a policeman in Medford--which was its own kind of sick joke.

The Marine stopped, because the old man was blocking the way down. "I bet I know why you're here," the old bastard said. "The little pussy got himself killed, didn't he?"

Tommy's mother let out a wail of pure grief. Tommy was still struck to silence, but he saw how the Marine stared the old man down. There was a world of pity and contempt in that stare, and bitterness so deep that no amount of whisky could drown it.

At that point Tommy lost all hope and faith. He had known from the start, deep inside where the darkness was, that when his brother Paul kissed his mother good-bye just days before being sent to Vietnam, they would never see him again.

Tommy didn't get a kiss. He was too big for that. He got a smile and a peace sign, and a set of orders. "Take care of Mom till I get home. You're the man of the house now." Because they both knew they couldn't rely on that asshole father of theirs.

Tommy howled inside, but outside he laughed, gave his brother a hug and watched him drive down the street with a couple of other young men from the neighborhood who had been drafted. Before they went out of sight, Paul yelled out the window, "I'll bring you back a souvenir from Vietnam!"

Tommy got a souvenir, all right. His dead brother's combat boots, uniform, dog tags and medals. Tommy kept the boots and the dog tags, which he wore around his neck at all times, and his mother got the uniform and medals.

She never understood why Tommy wanted the boots. He never tried to explain. The first time he strapped them on, a thought came to him: "A lot of blood was shed while my brother wore these boots. A lot more will be shed by the time I take them off. That, I swear." It was on that evening that the Preacher was born.

His mother died less than nine months after Paul was killed in action, of what was officially diagnosed as congestive heart failure, but Tommy knew it was out of grief from the loss of Paul. She was buried on April 25, 1968, and on that day it seemed as if the heavens themselves were crying for Mary Neveska.

At the cemetery, while the cold rain poured down, Tommy observed how pleasant his father was to everyone. He thanked them for attending the services of his "dear wife." He declared that he would do his best to raise his only son--playing on their emotions, milking their sympathy, spilling out crocodile tears.

Little did they know that the fat pig known as Officer Tony Joseph Neveska wouldn't give the sweat off his balls if someone in his family was dying of thirst. Friends of the family were all sad and sympathetic, patting him on the shoulder and looking at "poor young Tommy" where he sat upright and still in a corner. The old man nodded and sighed and twisted up his face in what passed for concern.

But Tommy saw it for what it really was. The face of a monster. An uncaring son of a bitch who was a disgrace to the police uniform. A man who chose alcohol and sleeping with whores over his family. Tommy had heard his mother night after night, accusing her husband of cheating on her, crying about how she could smell the scent of the sluts' perfume, and on occasion spot a trace of lipstick.

The argument was usually put to bed when Tony had had enough of her crying and started whaling on his wife. But the sympathetic, more like pathetic, people around Tommy and his father were blind to the reality of what the old man was.

He was sure some of them meant well. Those were his mother's friends, the ones his father allowed her to see anyway. And Mary even shunned those friends after she ran out of excuses, or maybe her friends stopped believing her about how it was the funniest thing, how she got this black eye, or the strangest thing happened, and now she had bruises all over her body.

Even all these years later, he knew that their tears were sincere, because they were the same tears they'd shed with her when the Marine brought the news that Paul had been killed in Vietnam. When the time came, Tommy would be sure to spare them.

Just before they all fled the cold rain at the graveside for the wake at the V.F.W. hall, Sergeant Foley, one of his father's superiors, came up to Tommy and pulled him aside under a dripping umbrella. "I've known your father for a lot of years," he said, "and I'll tell you the truth. I don't have any respect for the guy at all. He's a poor excuse for a man, and he's even worse as a cop." Then he bent in closer. "I'm real sorry about the loss of your mom and your brother. Your mother was a beautiful person, and she done a fine job of raising her two boys. What she ever saw in your father is beyond me. No one would ever believe that you three were even related to him." Tommy sat back in awe. He couldn't believe what he was hearing. Someone had actually seen his father for whom he really was, and better than that, he was voicing his opinion openly.

Sergeant Foley continued, "I know it doesn't make you feel any better, but he's the same kind of mean son of a bitch to most of the kids he encounters on the street. Some day he'll have to face the Creator and answer for his sins. But until then, Tommy, try to keep the faith. I know it's not easy, and you haven't been dealt very good cards in life, but everything happens for a reason. If there is anything I can do to help you, or if you just want to talk, here's my home phone, and you know the number for the station house. Anything we talk about will of course be between us men."

He palmed Tommy's head like a basketball and shook it, mussing up his jet-black hair, then slipped a twenty-spot into his hand and looked him in the eye. "Anything at all you want to talk about. I mean it." Then he walked away.

It wasn't until they got to the V.F.W. hall that Tommy found out that Sergeant Foley was the department's Catholic deacon. Tommy was Catholic, too--his mom had raised him in the Church, and he and his brother Paul had attended weekly Catechism class after school.

At the hall, after people finished filing in and started in on the funeral buffet, Sergeant Foley asked for everyone's attention while he prayed for Mary Neveska, Paul Neveska and the only son Tony had left, young Tommy Neveska. Everyone looked at Tommy when the prayer was finished. Some were pitying and some were just curious, and some didn't really seem to care at all.

Nobody had much to say about Tommy, that he could hear, but some of the women got to talking about Sergeant Foley. He had served in the infantry during the Korean War, and supposedly he had seen a lot of action, and had won medals for bravery--they argued over which ones and how many. When he got home, he married his high-school sweetheart, whose name was Rita, and eventually went to divinity school and became a deacon.

Tommy didn't care too much about that, except as information to be stored away. What mattered was that Sergeant Foley had seemed sincere in what he said, and he openly disliked Tommy's father. That was enough to win Tommy over.

He looked down at the boots that had belonged to his brother. He loosened the laces, and then tied them tighter. He could feel the power there.

"Someday your father will meet his

Creator," Sergeant Foley had said. Tommy smiled. Tonight would be a special night.

#

After several hours of drinking beer and shots of whiskey, a marked police cruiser came by the V.F.W. Post to drive Tommy and his father home. The cruiser pulled up to the house just before 8:00 p.m., and Tony stumbled out of the car and into the house, with young Tommy close behind. He had seen his father in this condition before, and was careful not to piss him off.

Tony headed straight for the refrigerator and got himself a cold beer. On his way back to the living room and his favorite chair, he grabbed a bottle of Jack Daniels. He turned on the television, sat back in his chair, took a hit off the Jack D. and chased it down with beer. He performed this ritual with two more beers until he passed out.

Tommy waited to see if he was really out. When the old man didn't move,

Tommy shook his shoulder.

Tony jerked awake. "Don't touch me, you piece of shit! I'm awake! Why aren't you in bed?"

He didn't even look at Tommy while he said that, just snarled out the words with his eyes fixed on the television. He never even saw the police-issue .38 revolver come up and take aim.

"Did you know it's cold in Hell?" Tommy whispered in his father's ear.

Before Tony could have comprehended what he'd just heard, Tommy pressed the barrel of the gun to his father's temple and squeezed.

Blood droplets exploded all over the room and sprayed Tommy's face. He didn't even blink. He stood and watched while the blood spouted from his father's head like water from a garden hose, and even more poured from his mouth and nose.

There was much more blood than he expected, but somehow that was OK. He placed the gun in his own mouth and watched, a bit cross-eyed, as the hammer went back in slow motion, like the second hand of a clock.

Then it dawned on him. He didn't need to kill himself. His problems were over.

He snickered to himself as he realized this. Surprising himself with calmness, he placed the gun on the floor next to his father's slumped body and reached down to run his hands through the hot, thick, frothing blood that pooled on the floor. He smeared it all over his face, enjoying the moment, which he knew would be brief.

His heart raced. He took off his combat boots, and then his socks, wiggling his toes in his father's warm blood. When they were all smeared and dripping, he put the boots back on. He wanted blood all over the inside of them, so that he would always have a souvenir of that memorable night.

What a sensational feeling, he thought. And what a brilliant idea.

His father's suicide. It would surely be blamed on the tragic loss of his wife and his son, and excessive amounts of alcohol.

His fellow police would regret forever that none of them hadn't stayed with him that night, but they would all agree--Tommy could practically hear them saying it to one another. "He was drunk, but there wasn't anything unusual about that. He seemed all right. Normal. No different than he ever was."

Tommy had to act quickly now. The houses here were close together, and many people would have heard the shot and would want it investigated.

None of them would come and investigate for himself. No way would they risk the wrath of Tony Neveska, especially on the day when he buried his wife. There would be questions, lots of questions, but if Tommy's father had taught him anything, it was how to be a cold-hearted hateful person.

His only regret was that he should have thought of all this a long time ago. Sister Margaret in Catechism class used to say, "Sin opens the door to evil. Honor sin and you will honor Satan himself."

Now, as he heard the sirens approaching in the distance, he knew she was perfectly right. He only wished he could have mutilated the bastard's body; cut his tongue out, punctured his eyes, stuffed his balls down the throat of his decapitated head . . .

But that was out of the question. He had an act to put on, and it had to start now. He reached out through the blood and hugged his dead father around the neck, and screamed loud enough for the neighbors to hear.

Then, surprising even himself, he began to cry uncontrollably. Not because he felt any faintest hint of sadness, but because he never, ever remembered being so happy in his life.

He was crying as the first cop came through the door. Next day the newspaper would describe how much tragedy the family had endured, and how it ended with a local police officer shooting himself in the head with his service weapon as his only son watched, close enough to have blood splattered all over his body.

#

Seven years later, as he sat on top of the war memorial in the center of the Pit, Tommy still felt the pure happiness of that moment.

Now, at twenty-one, he was somewhat of a local celebrity. The cops had begun to call him the Preacher, because every afternoon he came out here and delivered a sermon.

They were harmless speeches, he'd heard them say. All about righteousness, punishment and true justice. Nobody much paid attention to what he actually said, except the hippies, and they were too stoned to care.

None of the cops tried to break his balls. He'd gone through enough, they figured. He had stayed with a local foster family from the time he was fourteen until he turned eighteen. It wasn't a bad place. His foster mom was elderly, kind and seemed to understand kids pretty well. Tommy let her think she understood him, too.

There were other kids there, but Tommy usually kept to himself. When he came home from school, he holed up in his room and read book after book. He had already experimented with evil on more than one occasion.

As he got older, he kept more and more to himself; hardly ever speaking, and never looking someone in the eyes when he did. He let his hair grow long, and with his dead-white face and bone-rack body, he looked like a walking corpse. Some kids at school messed with him, calling him "Eddie Munster," but he didn't pay them any attention.

By his senior year in high school he had put on some weight and picked up a new extracurricular activity: weightlifting. It started at the end of his sophomore year when one of the gym teachers, Mr. McKeagan, who had always looked out for the underdog, the weird, the quiet, or just the ones who would never fight back, took an interest in him. He pulled Tommy aside after class one day and said, "Any kid that could live through what you have without being a little fucked up must be pretty strong on the inside, even if he's quiet and keeps to himself on the outside. I know about that, believe me. I was that kind of kid, too."

Tommy wasn't exactly sure about that, but he smiled. Mr. McKeagan smiled back. "I'm going to be here every day teaching summer school. If you want to use the gym when I'm here, I'll give you a pass. No strings attached."

Tommy wasn't going to take him up on it, but something made him go up to the high school the first day of summer school. Mr. McKeagan showed Tommy a few basic routines to get him started, and talked to him, too, while he puffed and sweated and made himself dizzy at first, trying too hard.

Mr. McKeagan's voice kept him moving, telling his story in bits and pieces and between classes. When he was growing up, his younger brother had a stutter. Andy McKeagan always found himself coming home from school with a ripped shirt, dirty clothes or a black eye.

The McKeagan family wasn't much for height or weight. Andy's father was just barely middle-sized, and his mother was much shorter than that. But during those days in which he stood up for his younger brother he realized one thing. The more he fought, the better he got.

#

The morning after his first workout, Tommy was in such pain all over his body that he couldn't believe that weightlifting could possibly be good for you. But he thoroughly enjoyed the feeling of pain. He half ran, half walked, all limped to Sam's Smoke Shop in Medford Square to buy a muscle magazine.

Weightlifting became his new obsession. He worked out all through the summer, and was quite happy with the small gains he made. Mr. McKeagan was also pleased, and when the school year started up again, any time Tommy had a study period, Mr. McKeagan would write him a gym pass so Tommy could spend his time in the weight room.

After all, Tommy heard him say to one of the other teachers, the last thing this kid needed to do was study. He was always studying.

That's right, Tommy thought. Always reading. Reading or working out. Working out or reading. His grades spoke for themselves.

By senior year he was not only weird, he was six feet and a hundred and eighty-five pounds of weirdness. Not huge, but quiet, unpredictable and just . . . strange.

If anyone had bothered to ask him why he was so into his weightlifting routine, he would have told them that he was preparing himself for the battles to come. That would have gone over just fine, because he was a fucking weirdo anyway, and no one would have really cared. For now, everyone just avoided him. No one called him "Eddie Munster" anymore, at least not to his face.

#

After graduation, he packed the few possessions he cared about, left a brief thank-you note for his foster mother and went down to the Oak Grove Cemetery. According to the job-placement board at school, they had a job open, and the guy doing the hiring had served in the Marine Corps with his brother Paul. Tommy got the job on the spot.

The work consisted of cutting the lawn, trimming tree branches, backhoeing graves and other basic maintenance. Even better, there was a back room in one of the garages where Tommy could set up a cot and have a place to call his own, no strings attached.

He worked mostly Monday through Friday, spending his evenings reading books from the library, sitting on a desolate hill on the north side of the cemetery. If time permitted he would read there during the day, especially in the winter when it got dark early.

There were several graves on the hill, but two brought him to this specific location where he could read without being disturbed. Sitting down, he would put his back to a large maple tree and face the headstones that lay approximately twenty feet away. He would read until it got dark, and then go back to his makeshift room in the maintenance garage.

#

The garage itself was built of mortared stone. It had two white garage doors sat side by side, and another, smaller door on the left-hand side that served as an entrance. Inside was a riding lawn mower, a backhoe and a hardware store's worth of gardening tools.

In the back was a tiny room originally intended as a washroom, but his boss told him he could use it for a place to crash. It was hardly bigger than a closet, but it was strategically placed behind the heavy equipment, so he could have a bit of privacy.

There was no heat in the room, but there were electrical outlets if he wanted to bring in a heater. He set up a cot in the far corner and tucked his bag of worldly goods underneath.

It was dark and smelled heavily of gasoline, and there were only two light bulbs. That didn't matter to him, because there was more than enough light to read by.

He would often stop reading in the middle of a sentence and think of his mother and brother Paul. Would they be alive today if he had done away with his father earlier? Then he could go back to reading, because it was too late for them.

He read books on bodybuilding, on draconian law, on how to build booby traps. But his favorites, always, were the ones on devil worship and serving the

Prince of Darkness. When he read those, he cranked the 8-track with Black Sabbath and Paranoid--always and forever preparing himself for the inevitable.

Sin had given him freedom, and he had come to honor it. What better place to work at it than here, in a cemetery?

It was almost too good to be true. But in the end, Tommy thought of it as just one thing: destiny. He was free to commit Sin, and he could dispose of anything he wanted--in a grave, no less.

There would always be time for play. Right now he needed to concentrate on this very specific work.

#

Now, in the twenty-first year of his life, the time was near. As he looked down from the monument at the peace freaks, he found himself getting aroused. They had absolutely no idea of what was about to be unleashed.

He only had to wait for the cops to show

up to get things started, and he had put a guarantee on that that one. If all went as planned, his father's old partner, Lou Barretto, would show up personally, with force, and he would be livid.

#

It had taken Tommy weeks just to plan that part. Louis Barretto had been a cop for a lot of years. He thrived on being a cop, taking advantage of any situation that came his way.

Almost all of the Medford Police were down-to-earth, hard-working, honest and God-loving cops, but as in every department, there were always one or two guys that would mess things up for everyone, and Lou Barretto was one of them. Even his co-workers thought of him as a scumbag. The only cop who got along with the fat bastard was Tommy's asshole father.

Tommy would see to it that both of them would meet again in Hell, this time with Tommy as the ruler of the house. He had watched Barretto's every move for almost a month: where he ate breakfast, how he took his coffee, where and at what times he became a bigmouth drunken idiot, what type of slut he preferred, and most importantly, where he bought and what kind of food he gave to his K-9 partner.

This was a crucial part of the plan. The German Shepherd was a smart dog, and Tommy knew he would have to be more cunning than this adversary.

It was almost a shame to kill the dog; Baron was a vicious animal, and Tommy had seen him go to town on some of the peace freaks on more than a few occasions. He was jet black with a slight tinge of red, and he had to be at least one hundred twenty pounds. Even more striking were the bright yellow eyes that appeared to burn like fire from within his skull.

Tommy had respect for Baron and his ability to attack without discrimination, but he had no respect for Officer Barretto, and it would surely strike a nerve if he found his only friend dead.

#

Every evening after work, usually around 5:30 p.m., Barretto left Baron's doggie door open so that he could reign free inside the house and outside in the fenced yard. Tommy knew that good old Lou would not be home until at least 11:30 p.m., because Tuesdays were dart night down at the bar and he always stayed out late on dart night.

One Tuesday night, Tommy hid in a tree in a nearby patch of woods, close to Barretto's yard. When it got dark enough that a nosy neighbor wouldn't be able to see, he would throw small pieces of raw hamburger into the yard.

The house was on a dead-end street at the end of Stickney Road, and although it was surrounded by other homes on three sides, the miles of woods known as the

Fells Reservation bordered the fourth side.

It was a small bungalow with red shutters and white siding, but it was more than big enough for a small family. Even with a swimming pool, the yard was a decent size.

He had watched Barretto train his dog using raw meat. He had also read in one of his books that raw meat tended to make a dog more vicious. The dog's mind made a comparison between eating raw flesh and sinking his fangs into an uncooperative.

Tommy didn't know how true that was, but it certainly couldn't hurt to try. Tommy wasn't sure the dog would eat the meat he threw without his master's permission, so he tried to throw it into an area where the fat fuck had last been training him. He'd even bought the hamburger at the same grocery store as Barretto. He'd planned everything down to the bone--no pun intended.

Bingo! The dog ate the meat immediately upon finding it.

After that, Tommy continued to feed around the same time so the dog would make it part of his routine. After several days came the grand finale: poison in the precious hamburger.

Tommy had packed the meat with the chemicals they used to poison the rats and possums that frequented the cemetery. Some of those rodents were a good size, and the poison did a number on them. Tommy was sure that it would have the same effect on Baron.

The dog was tough; much tougher than Tommy had anticipated. He vomited for an hour after eating the burger, but he would not die. As it got dark, Tommy decided to finish off the old soldier in a hero's way. After all, he was no stranger to death.

He slid down out of the tree behind Barretto's back yard. Adrenaline pulsed through his body with such force that he almost passed out from the head rush.

The last time he'd felt like this, he'd just killed his father. He stood still for a moment, took a deep breath to catch his balance and silently swung over the fence.

He found himself eye to eye with the

dog. Baron rose weakly to all fours and let out the faintest possible growl.

"You know why I'm here, don't you, Baron?" Tommy said. Baron's growl was a steady roll as Tommy slowly walked closer. "I'm here to kill you. And tomorrow I'm going to kill your master."

Baron wobbled, and his back legs collapsed. Tommy drew the Bowie knife from its leg sheath and looked the dog in the eye. "Did you know it's cold in Hell?"

#

Lou Barretto returned home at midnight from the Glandore Irish Pub in Somerville. He was royally drunk, and had apparently picked up a slut from the bar.

Tommy watched them from his hiding spot as they snickered and giggled their way out of the car and stumbled toward the house.

"Yo, Michelle," Barretto said. "Do you like dogs?"

Michelle simpered at him, wrapping

herself half around him, but Tommy noticed how she didn't trip in her sky-high stilettos. "You have a puppy? I love puppies!"

"You'll love this one, whore," Tommy said to himself.

"He's no puppy," Barretto said. Then he paused.

Tommy held his breath. Barretto must have sensed that something was wrong, because Baron had not barked since his arrival. Although the dog would not bark at the sound of his master's voice, he would certainly have something to say about the stranger.

Barretto left his date swaying in the middle of the walk and charged the front door, calling Baron's name. No response came from inside.

Tommy smiled.

Barretto fumbled for his house key. Finally he found it, and spent a gratifying amount of time trying to jam it into the lock, then get the door to open.

He went in like the cop he was, slowly.

He didn't look quite so drunk now.

His date caught up with him inside. Her voice floated out the open door. "Do you have any beer or wine?"

Barretto's whisky rumble ran right over her nasal whine. "Baron. <u>Baron</u>! Where the hell are you?"

Tommy waited, counting seconds. It shouldn't take more than a minute for the bastard to find his way to the kitchen.

The scream that ripped out of the house wasn't a man's. Michelle must have got ahead of him and found the present Tommy had left.

He closed his eyes. He could see it the way she must be seeing it. Yellow walls, wooden table with two stools, wooden cabinets, fairly new stove. It was cleaner than she might have expected, considering Barretto was a lifelong bachelor, but it certainly could use the touch of a woman.

Then she saw the refrigerator. It was bright white, and when it started, it was perfectly clean.

But not any more. It stood in a puddle

of blood, half wet, half coagulated. Bloody drag marks ran from it all the way across the floor, right to their feet.

Written in blood on the smooth white door was a single word: *PREACHER*.

Michelle's scream cut off. Either she had controlled herself or Barretto had shut her up.

There was a pause. Tommy crouched perfectly still. In his head he saw Barretto charge the fridge the same way he had charged the outside door, and fling it open with such force that he slipped and fell into the pool of blood. As he rose up onto his elbows, he looked up. He saw the dismembered body of his one and only friend, stacked up neatly on the shelves. The head lay in solitary glory on the top shelf, staring at him with dead eyes that had once burned as bright as fire.

His howl of grief and rage and loss was loud enough to wake the whole neighborhood--but not the dead. Then he began to sob.

That was the moment Tommy had been

waiting for. It was so perfect, so purely wonderful.

He had to leave. The cops would roar in any minute, looking for him.

He would dearly love to walk in on Barretto and finish him off, but that was not part of tonight's feature. He had to stick to the plan if he wanted to stay in control.

He slid down out of the tree and crept silently into the woods.

He would have to hide until showtime tomorrow. He could still hear the woman screaming and the alleged tough guy bawling.

Tommy began laughing uncontrollably as he ran through the woods. He could not go back to the cemetery to sleep, because the cops were sure to look for him there. He would hide in Panther's Cave just a short distance through the woods.

It wasn't really a cave, just two giant rocks pitched together in the middle, surrounded by a small hill of other rocks that formed a tentlike opening. But it had always been called Panther's Cave.

When he was younger, he and his brother Paul used to play Army up there with other neighborhood kids, and use the cave as a fort. They always fought over who was going to be the good guys, because the good guys always got the fort and the bad guys always got killed attacking it.

He wished his brother Paul was here now. Thinking of him made all of tonight's pleasures drain away. Now Tommy jogged through the woods, praying to Satan for daylight to come quickly, so that he could commence with tomorrow's festivities.

Sweat beaded on his forehead and soaked through his shirt. The night was cool, and he was glad he had hid a blanket in the cave before he started out on his mission. As he got closer to safety, he could hear the sirens closing in on Barretto's house. Everything was on schedule.

#

Panther's Cave was cold and damp inside, but Tommy did not care. He was not planning on getting any sleep tonight. He would have to stay alert, in case the pigs got smart and searched for him in the woods.

In the distance he could hear the peace freaks singing around a campfire in a place they referred to as the Dump. They called it that because of the large number of stolen automobiles that had been stripped and left there. The hippies had taken out the seats and set them up in a circle around the firepit.

The Dump was deep enough in the woods that not too many cops bothered them. The cops knew where they were, because most of them had spent some of their youth there themselves. The theory was that it was better to know where the peace freaks were than to chase them around the city all night.

Out of sight, out of mind. Tommy hoped the pigs would not trek up there tonight, because the cave was too close to the

Dump for comfort.

Tommy felt his eyelids growing heavy. All the adrenaline had worn his body out. He tipped over sideways and fell asleep, drawn up in a fetal position.

#

The next morning Tommy woke with a start. He scanned the cave quickly, searching for signs of danger.

All was quiet. He hadn't planned on falling asleep, but he was glad he had. His watch showed 8:00 a.m. Perfect.

He would have to use extreme caution in maneuvering to the Pit in front of City Hall. If the pigs spotted before that, they would surely kill him, and he needed the peace freaks for witnesses before he could allow that to happen.

He left the blanket in the cave, knowing that he would never need it or any other blanket ever again. He stayed in the woods as long as he could, until it was time to make his way to the Pit.

He cut through back yards the whole way, never traveling in a straight line, in case someone called the cops. By 8:25 he was looking at City Hall from a nearby back yard.

There were no police in sight, just the burned-out peace freaks. He made his way to the monument in the Pit, and got a nod of approval from one of the hippies who was hitting on a joint.

What the freak approved of, Tommy did not know. The hippies were probably expecting another sermon from the Preacher. They didn't know the Preacher had died last night, and there was a new sheriff in town.

From the top of the monument, on his pre-set stage, Tommy stared into the eyes of the peace freaks and was lost for a moment in his own world.

The sight of the first Medford Police cruiser approaching the Pit brought him back to reality. That was quick, he thought. Someone must have spotted him cutting through yards and phoned the police.

After the first cruiser came another and another, and then the paddy wagon. He smiled when he saw Barretto get out of the last one.

Showtime.

He took a deep breath and sent his voice rolling out across the Pit. "Peace freaks, pigs and other despicable drug addicts, sex fiends and scumbags! It is a beautiful day to die."

From down below, at the head of the charge, Barretto hollered, "Oh, you're going to fuckin' die all right, Preacher. I'm going to see to that personally."

Tommy smiled at him, as sweet as sin. "Your dog cried like a bitch when I killed him. Are you going to cry when I kill you?"

One of the cops behind Barretto was Jimmy Landers, one of Tommy's high-school classmates. He looked scared. Not of Tommy, but of Barretto.

Barretto's face was beet-red with rage. He lunged toward the monument, reached up and grabbed Tommy by one of his boots. Tommy did not fight but continued to smile, taking great pleasure in the moment. Barretto hesitated for a split second, as if he had a touch of sympathy for a lost soul.

Just for a second. That was all he had to give the Preacher. Barretto yanked Tommy from the top of the monument and caught him on the shin with his nighstick.

The stick cracked like a hockey stick smacking a slap shot. The hippies cried out in horror. Tommy fell from the monument and landed on his back. His head bounced off the cement with the sound of a golf ball ricocheting off a brick wall.

The hippies swarmed toward Tommy. Barretto's fellow officers shoved them back.

Tommy lay where he had fallen. The sky that had been cloudless blue was rapidly and mysteriously turning black. The thick clouds rolled in with supernatural speed, as Barretto's nightstick came down again and again.

The sound of stick striking bone was loud and sharp at first, but after a while it started to sound like a baseball bat slapping off a side of beef.

Tommy's smile never faded. With each blow of the stick, the clouds became angrier, pelting them all with torrential rain.

Thunder rolled. Lightning cracked. "You're killing him!" Jimmy Landers screamed, shrill like a girl.

Two of the other patrolmen pulled Barretto off Tommy. Jimmy Landers just stood there, staring at Tommy's body with a shocked look on his face.

One of the cops grabbed Tommy by his pant legs and dragged him into the back of the wagon. The rain scoured away the trail of blood.

Tommy was alive and still conscious, bleeding profusely from the head. As lightning shredded the sky, Barretto jumped in beside him and wrapped his hands around Tommy's throat. "Die, you dog-murdering motherfucker! Die!"

Tommy's eyes rolled up till only the whites showed. He was still smiling that eerie, serene smile.

As the last ounce of life left Tommy's body, a sonic boom of thunder rolled over the city, accompanied by massive bolts of lightning and a barrage of hail. In its wake came the distant, haunting wail of a coyote.

Barretto threw himself out of the paddy wagon just as the rookie cop, Jimmy Landers, slammed it into gear. He drove into the blinding storm, swerving through traffic and bouncing off parked cars, aiming as straight as he could for the hospital.

Adrenaline Rush

Officer Landers didn't stop, couldn't stop. He had to get Neveska to the Hospital.

His mind was in panic mode. He babbled nonstop at Tommy through the small sliding window that separated the cab from the prisoner area. "Hang in there, Tommy! I'm taking you to the hospital. You're gonna be OK, man! Just hang in there!"

The storm's darkness clouds made everything appear in silhouette, with details only revealing themselves through brief slashes of lightning. He couldn't see where Barretto was, but he was sure he would be following close behind in one of the cruisers.

He had to get Tommy to the hospital before Barretto could get to him again. He couldn't believe what he had just witnessed. He and the other officers had known Barretto was fuming mad, but nobody thought he was going to try and kill the kid.

A thunderclap made Officer Landers' heart jump as he sped the wagon around the rotary toward the Lawrence Memorial Hospital. He wasn't cold, but he shivered uncontrollably as he exited the rotary and headed for route 93, the quickest way to the hospital. The blue lights and siren struggled desperately to be seen and heard over the storm's fury.

"Almost there, bro!" he said to Tommy. "Almost there!"

In the brief lightning flashes the city looked like a war zone, with cars crashed into each other and downed trees and electrical wires everywhere. The really strange part was that every time the lightning flashed, it did so a split second before Officer Landers could crash the wagon into an object that had been invisible in the darkness.

Finally he reached the highway. Through the next flash he saw that the road appeared clear up to the hospital exit, approximately two hundred yards away. Hail pounded the wagon like stones being shaken around in a Coca-Cola can and exploded like bombs off the windshield. In the rearview mirror he glimpsed trees, telephone poles and electrical wires littering the road behind him as he raced to save Tommy Neveska's life.

He pulled off Exit 33 onto the Roosevelt Circle rotary and headed toward South Border Road and the Lawrence Memorial Hospital. Lightning continued to guide his path. He had a feeling in his gut that he had succeeded. His wild driving had saved Tommy's life.

As he reached South Border and passed the Bellevue Pond, he started to turn left onto Governors Avenue. A fresh flash of lightning made him stand upright on the brakes. The wagon skidded sideways.

He could hear and feel poor Tommy's body slam around in the back of the wagon. A sob burst out of him. "Sorry, Tommy! I'm sorry, bro! Dear God, please help me get him to the hospital."

The top of Governors Avenue and the route to the hospital had been completely blocked off, as if God Himself had constructed the barrier. The Hudson Bus that traveled through Medford lay sideways across the street. Other drivers, not as lucky or as fast with the reflexes as Officer Landers, had crashed into it on all sides. Two huge maple trees had come down on top of them, crushing anyone who might have made it through with a dented fender.

Some of the victims were screaming in agony. Others lay deathly still on the ground. Their voices overlapped each other like a chorus of the damned. "Help us! Help! We need hel--send for hel--hurt bad . . ."

But Jimmy Landers had already been chosen for a mission. A renewed burst of lightning revealed a sign on the right-hand side of the road, partially concealed by branches.

Commonwealth of Massachusetts Department of Mental Health - Middlesex Fells Reservation - State Mental Hospital.

Jimmy whooped like a loon. "Yes! Hospital! Almost there, Tommy! Almost there!"

There was a medical ward at the good old Cookie Factory. It might not be Lawrence Memorial, but it was something. There was hope for Tommy yet.

Jimmy backed up the wagon, made a hard right into the mouth of the woods and aimed straight for the Mental Hospital with lights and siren wailing at full blast. He hoped that would make up for the fact that the wagon was not fully equipped with one of those two-way radios like some of the other radio cars, so he couldn't call ahead and tell them to be ready for the injured party.

As he headed deeper into the woods, lighting continued to guide his path, and trees continued to crash down behind him like a house of cards falling in slow motion. In the back of the wagon, Tommy Neveska's lifeless body rolled back in forth on the blood-soaked floor.

High above, standing on the rock that

overlooked the reservation, the coyote watched the flashing blue lights of the police transport wagon as it raced through the woods toward the hospital. Her eyes gleamed in the flash of the lightning.

It had begun.

#

As Officer Landers approached the front entrance of the hospital, he looked up at the metal-screened and steel-barred windows. Mental patients gaped down at him. Their faces were gaunt and deathly white, as if they hadn't seen the sun in years.

The storm seemed to lose its ferocity as he came closer to the hospital. He could see more clearly now, though hail had spiderwebbed his windshield. Although it was still eerily dark, the thick purple clouds seemed to be dissipating. It was still raining heavily, but not half as torrentially as it had been just a short time ago.

He was alone. None of the police

cruisers had managed to keep up with him.

He was both relieved and scared. Relieved because he didn't want Barretto anywhere near him, never mind near Tommy Neveska. Scared, because now he had to open the back of the wagon by himself to check on Tommy, and he wasn't sure if Tommy was going to come out fighting.

He had seen the crazy look in Tommy's eyes when Barretto attacked him, and he had heard Barretto raging about the vicious murder he claimed Tommy had committed. The fact Tommy hadn't moved or spoken since he went into the wagon didn't necessarily mean much. He could be crouched inside, lying in wait.

Officer Landers took a deep breath and walked around to the back of the wagon. Thunder and lightning rumbled and flickered in the distance, but right overhead the clouds let more and more sunlight through. He listened carefully through the fading drizzle, straining to hear any movement.

He knocked on the door. "Tommy," he said, his voice shaking a little. "It's Jimmy Landers. I brought you to the hospital."

There was no response.

Landers' hand shook as he reached for the handle. He held his breath. It was deathly quiet.

He unlatched the door and pulled it open, darting to the side in case Tommy charged out. If he was well enough to run, so be it. Jimmy Landers was not about to give chase.

Nothing. He peered around the door of the wagon.

It took him a few moments to realize that the dirty laundry piled up against the back was Tommy. Blood soaked the floor and dripped down the rear of the wagon-- more blood than any one body should hold.

The sight and the smell of all that blood made Officer Landers want to vomit. He sagged against the wagon, head on forearm, fighting to keep his stomach where it belonged.

A hand touched his shoulder.

He nearly shit his pants. He whipped around, hands up and ready to fight. "Whoa! Get your hands off me, man!"

A man in a hospital orderly's uniform stood back out of reach, looking from the officer to the wagon. "Are you all right? What the hell happened?"

#

The orderly yelled for a gurney. Two more orderlies came running as he nerved himself up to climb into the back of the wagon and check the body for any signs of life.

It looked dead. Felt dead. They loaded it onto the gurney, ignoring the young cop. He stayed where he was, looking lost and sick, until one of the nurses came out and walked him, zombie-like, into the hospital.

#

This main part of the hospital was strictly administrative, but an elaborate network of tunnels connected all the buildings to each other--almost five miles' worth of twists and turns. From the first floor, a visitor, or three orderlies with a loaded gurney, could take the elevator down past the basement and into the labyrinth.

Tommy's body raced through the tunnel from the bottom of the administration building to the Jefferson medical building. These orderlies worked the most dangerous psychiatric units on the grounds; they knew all too well how to get to the medical unit. Whether it was a patient-on-patient attack, or a patient attacking a staff member, injury and even death were not uncommon in this hospital. They averaged at least two deaths a year.

After a number of lefts, rights and straightaways, the orderlies came to the elevator in the medical building. By pure luck or Divine intervention, it was open and waiting.

They came out into sunlight. Less than fifteen minutes ago, holy hell had raged outside. Now they were bathed in heavenly light and warmth. They raced through it into the Code room, where the trauma staff waited.

Dr. Weinhart was the attending that day. He shook his head when he saw the patient. The young man had obviously been dead for some time. But there was always hope, he liked to say.

They ran an intravenous and started CPR. They shocked his heart. They worked on him furiously for twenty minutes.

Finally they covered him with a sheet and pronounced him dead, thirty minutes after arrival. Severe head trauma was the cause of death, with excessive blood loss.

Interview

The rain stopped and the clouds rolled out as quickly as they had rolled in. The eerie, purplish, heavy fog seemed to be lifting.

An hour before my 11:00 interview, I decided to be a little early. I grabbed my keys to the jeep and whistled for Nika. She loved going for a ride, and she would especially like running around in the woods while I went in for the interview.

It had rained so hard that the seats in the jeep were soaked. It had a canvas top, but I had taken the doors off the previous week, and the wind had blown the rain in.

I went and got a painter's drop cloth from the garage and spread it on the driver's seat. It should keep my ass dry long enough to drive to the interview and back. With Nika sitting comfortably beside me, I backed out of the driveway and made my way down South Street.

South Street paralleled the Mystic River and gave quick access to Route 93. I was surprised to see how swollen the river had become in such a short time. It reminded me of monsoon season in Vietnam.

While I drove, I saw how much damage the storm had done to the city. There were maintenance, utility work crews, ambulances and fire department personnel out everywhere.

I got on 93 and got off just as quickly at the Fells Reservation exit. Signs pointed toward the mental hospital, but I did not need them. I had spent many days and nights in these woods with Nika after I came back from Vietnam. Even in winter I would warm myself in front of a campfire, surrounded by snow, in the middle of the woods, comfortably isolated from outside influence. It reminded me of my childhood home in Maine.

As I passed the Belleview pond on my right, I came to the top where Governors Avenue met South Border Road. There were a number of emergency workers here also, dealing with a mess of overturned bus, crashed vehicles and fallen trees.

I stopped to watch for a minute, and then took the hard right on the dirt road to the State Hospital.

I ran over the directions in my head, the way I'd give them to someone who didn't know the area as well as I did. Go straight until you hit the fork in the road. In the middle of the fork is a place called Panther's Cave. Take a left at the cave and go straight. That will take you up to the guard shack, and you can get a pass to enter the hospital.

#

As the jeep turned into the woods from South Border Road, the coyote observed it from beneath a freshly fallen tree. The man driving the jeep did not know it yet, but his path was blocked ahead.

She sprinted from her hiding place and ran parallel to the jeep, keeping herself concealed in the woods. She ran for about three hundred yards until the jeep stopped in front of a fallen tree. She paused to catch her breath, watching to see what the man would do next.

She could sense that the dog was aware of her presence. It pricked its ears her direction, sniffed the air and growled.

"What's the matter?" the man asked. "What's out there?"

The dog ignored him. Her growl was low and steady. Anything that came at him, that growl said, had to come through her first.

#

Just a short distance into the woods, there were a number of Medford Police cruisers abandoned on the side of the road. Someone must have snapped up at the psych ward, and they'd had to call the troops to calm things down. Probably the storm, I thought. That would set the crazies off.

The M.D.C., or the Metropolitan District Commission as it was called, had men with chainsaws making short work of the pines and maples that had fallen victim to the storm. It looked like the road would not only be cleared by nightfall, there was going to be plenty of firewood for next winter. I pulled the jeep off the road and into the woods, and Nika and I began our trek to the hospital and my job interview.

Chainsaws buzzed all through the woods, and sawdust was everywhere. The workers did not look up as we walked by, and I did not attempt to make eye contact. I felt like a ghost walking through the barren landscape.

Some distance up the road, we came to the part that hadn't been cleared yet. The amount of damage from the storm was incredible. I couldn't even see where the road was supposed to be under all the trees and downed branches.

Strangely, the trees had mostly fallen on the road. When we stepped off the side of the road into the woods, we found the way to be a lot easier: a lot fewer downed trees, and a lot clearer going. But Nika wasn't any more comfortable there than she'd been since she left the jeep. She kept staring into the trees ahead and to the sides, and she never stopped growling.

She seemed spooked, and that was totally unlike her. She was an amiable dog, a stray that I had picked up at the Greyhound station just after coming back from Vietnam. She looked more intimidating than she really was.

I had never seen that dog afraid of anything before in her life. She usually went bananas over the opportunity to go for a walk in the woods. Now her tail was clamped between her legs, and the farther in we went, the harder she shivered.

The air had become quite cold. The sky began to darken again.

Nika stopped and stared straight ahead. She'd finally stopped growling. She whimpered softly, picking up one foot at a time, shifting her weight, as if she was going to bolt at any second. She was sniffing the air for a scent, but I could tell that if she smelled one, it was not familiar to her.

"Nika! What's the matter, girl?" I reached down and wrapped one arm around her body and the other around her neck, and gave her a big squeeze, like I always did. I wanted to let her know that I felt everything was cool, and as long as she was with me, things would be all right.

It worked for her, mostly, but now I was starting to get spooked myself. I shivered even harder than she did. The air began to grow stale and foul, as if the storm had broken a sewer pipe somewhere.

First the nightmare, and now my dog was all messed up in the head. "Maybe I shouldn't have smoked that weed before I came out here," I said, trying to make light of it. But the words fell flat in the dead air.

We walked on, with her looking up at me periodically for reassurance. I tried not to let her know how spooked I was. She was a smart dog, and could read me as well as I could read her.

I picked up a stick off the ground, and her ears perked up slightly. I tossed the stick about ten feet ahead of us, and she followed it with her eyes until it fell to the ground. Then she stopped, looked at me dead in the eyes, and gave me a stare that said: "Are you shitting me? Do I look like I want to play fucking stick right now?" I swear she was pissed that I even tried to pull that one over on her.

As we got closer to the hospital, we both became a little more apprehensive. The woods were eerily quiet. I began to walk faster.

Up ahead I thought I saw the silhouette of a person slipping in and out of the trees, heading in the same direction we were. The air now smelled so putrid that I covered my mouth with my shirt as not to breathe it in. My skin was all over goose bumps, and my dog kept looking up at me as if she was saying, "Let's get the fuck outta here!"

I peered through the trees, trying to get a better view of whoever was ahead of us, but they seemed to have disappeared. I could hear the rustle of leaves, and I knew I wasn't imagining it, because Nika's ears perked toward it.

I stopped to see if I could hear better, but the rustling footsteps had stopped, too. Then I saw the shadow again, but it moved in total silence. It was if whoever it was was floating through the woods, inches above the ground.

If we'd been back on the reservation, Grandpa would have been able to explain this. But we were not on the reservation, and Grandpa's body had died a long time ago.

Nika whimpered. She was shaking so hard she was almost falling down. The only earthly thing that held her here was her loyalty to me.

I seriously contemplated turning around and blowing off the interview. Then, all of a sudden, a warm breeze gusted through the woods. The sun parted the clouds. The cold was gone as quickly as it had come.

Nika shook herself all over and yawned hugely. She was still shaking, but not nearly as hard.

I stood in the sun and concentrated on just breathing. I felt as if I had experienced something spiritual, powerful, and evil, all at the same time. It scared the hell out of me.

#

A red-tailed hawk soared gracefully overhead. Its shadow briefly blocked the sun's rays, the way an airplane does when it flies at the perfect angle. The hawk's screech echoed through the Middlesex Fells Reservation.

The coyote looked up at the sound. So did the cops gathered at the hospital. For that instant, the entire woods were silent.

#

The hawk's cry seemed to clear the air. Nika and I walked for another fifteen minutes through normal if somewhat damp and muddy woods, until we heard voices up ahead.

Nika picked up the pace and began to trot slightly ahead of me, but still looking back for reassurance.

As we got closer I could see that the voices belonged to the police officers who had left their vehicles back on the road. There were about eight of them, and they were talking loudly among themselves.

Seeing them made Nika feel better. She lifted her head a little bit, but her tail was still curled between her legs.

Hawk or no hawk, something was still not right. I had a feeling of despair that I just couldn't shake. A feeling of sorrow, as if I should be mourning something, or someone.

I stopped, and Nika stopped, too, without looking back. I began to feel that I was going to regret ever coming here, and I almost turned around and went home.

Instead I found myself walking toward the building and the police officers, as if my feet had a mind of their own. Again without looking, Nika walked just ahead of me. We were both caught in this trap, whatever it was.

#

Behind the man and his dog, the lone coyote crouched in the cover of the woods, peering through the brush. She had observed every step they had taken toward the hospital, and would be sure to follow every step back out. She was as defiant now as she had been during the storm, and she was gathering strength and confidence by the minute. The journey was about to begin.

Birth of a Preacher

Two of the three orderlies who had rushed Thomas Neveska's broken body into the Code Room wheeled it out again shortly after he was pronounced dead, and rolled it back down the corridor and into the elevator. Now that he was a corpse instead of an emergency patient, there was no rush to get him down a level to the morgue.

A white sheet covered his bluish naked body, and a plastic tube protruded from his mouth. His clothes, boots and personal belongings lay at his feet on the gurney, stuffed in a plastic bag marked *Patient Belongings, Destination Morgue.*

The building was very old, and the elevator itself was practically antique. The door had a six-by-six-inch window with metal wire crisscrossing the glass interior, and it had to be slid open manually. Inside of that was a metal cage-like folding door that had to be secured to its magnetic border before the elevator would work properly.

It was poorly lit, and neither of the orderlies said a word to each other as the car jumped and bounced down to the basement. The air in the elevator was strangely chill. One of them shivered and rubbed his arms.

The elevator bounced one final time and came to rest an inch or so below its destination. The orderly who had felt the cold so strongly heaved the inner door open, and then the outer. They both had to pick up the gurney over the lip the elevator had left between the car and the floor.

The basement was also poorly lit, as anything destined for this particular area did not require light. The lights that did work took turns flickering on and off.

The orderlies had performed this ritual on a number of occasions, and it was as if the squeaky-wheeled gurney was on autopilot. They walked a short distance down the hallway, still feeling the chill, and stopped at the first set of double doors on the left-hand side. A sign painted in thick black letters hung over the door: MORGUE/PATHOLOGY.

They stopped, spun the gurney sideways and proceeded through the doors. Once inside, one of them finally spoke. "Did you see all the cops outside?"

It was more a statement than a question, and he only said it to break the eerie silence and dispel the unexplainable cold presence.

"Yeah," the other orderly said. "I wonder what the poor bastard did to deserve a trip to the morgue."

"I don't know, but somebody laid a heavy beating on this cat."

"Yeah, you ain't shittin'."

#

The morgue properly consisted of two rows of eight three-and-a-half-by-three-foot square steel doors, making a total of sixteen trays, eight on top of eight. The body trays were lined up on the left as you walked into the room, and opposite the trays were tables where autopsies were performed.

Just beyond the autopsy tables were stainless steel cabinets that looked as if they hadn't been cleaned or disinfected in years. The cabinets contained the necessities for the completion of any pathology procedure: scalpels, scissors, suture thread, saws--both manual and power--and a variety of odd-looking instruments that were spring-loaded and resembled giant, razor-sharp vise grips. These were used to cleanly amputate anything that needed it.

The doors on the morgue had the same meat-locker-type handle as the police wagon. The orderlies looked at each other and shivered--though neither could have explained why. Handles were handles. Weren't they?

The orderlies wheeled Tommy's body headfirst against the steel doors, and the one nearest to the door popped it open, pulling the tray out parallel to the gurney.

The other orderly stood on the other side, and with the ease of long practice, they pulled the sheet up from under the body and turned it into an instant hammock.

They slid the body off the gurney toward the steel bed, lifted it ever so slightly and laid it on the tray. Then they shoved the tray back in and shut the door, making sure it was locked good and tight.

They left the gurney where it was, flipped off the light and hurried out, eager to get back up to the fresh air and the sunlight. As they pulled the doors of the morgue shut behind them, they could feel the cold air trying to escape from the room behind them.

They exchanged deer-in-the-headlights glances and beat feet for the first floor. Neither of them had the intestinal fortitude to brave the elevator again. They headed straight for the stairwell.

\#

Tommy Neveska was in a place that in

the past he had only dreamed of. It was cold, very cold, and it was dark. He could not see through the darkness, but as he walked through it, he could sense hands reaching for him from every direction.

There were voices in the blackness, low, muffled cries of anguish and despair. Tormented souls, he thought, unable to form coherent words, as if their tongues had been cut out.

Now and then there were screams. Horrible, agonizing screams that echoed all around him, coming from above and fading away into the void below.

As he walked on, his sight gradually improved, as if his eyes had adjusted to the darkness. Hands reached up from below, straining toward his feet--not to grab or pull him down, but to honor and worship him as if he had been their king.

Some of the hands were attached to bodies that looked both pink and black, completely hairless and without ears or eyelids, as if they had been badly burned in a fire. Others looked as if they had been mauled by a pack of vicious animals. Their eyes were full of terror, and they bowed their torn and bleeding heads as he passed by.

There were no walls and no ceiling in this place, and it seemed there wasn't even a floor. Beyond the bodies was simply blackness.

It was cold, but he was not uncomfortable. Not in the least. He had not been this happy since he blew his father's head off, and walked barefoot through the old man's blood. He could even feel it seeping through his toes and sliding under his feet. The tortured souls below, he realized as he went on, could not see him through the darkness. They merely felt his awesome presence.

Angry purple clouds swirled over him, like the ones that had boiled overhead before that pig Barretto smashed his skull in. Thunder cracked. Lightning struck again, and then again.

This was no ordinary lightning. It struck fast, it struck hard, and it split a darkness so deep it had never known the light of day.

In between the lightning and the darkness, he saw a narrow footbridge high above him. It looked like a railroad track held together with rope instead of iron, or a footbridge that one would see in the jungle in a Tarzan movie.

The bridge swayed wildly with each crack of thunder and flare of lightning, and the Preacher could see two lines moving on it, one yellowish blue and the other a reddish black. The reddish black line seemed to be tumbling off as the bridge swung, but the yellowish blue held on, disappearing into the clouds on the other side.

The lines were people. The colors he saw were auras, the reflections of their souls. The lighter ones made it across the bridge into whatever was beyond. As the darker ones fell, they screamed, until they crashed into the darkness below.

The tormented souls that he had first encountered, the ones that worshipped him, attacked the freshly fallen souls with startling speed and agility. They bit and scratched and pulled at every hair and piece of flesh. There was no God in this place to help them. For that is what Hell is: an eternity empty of God.

#

Tommy walked on, and the path became narrower and deeper. The putrid, horrible smell of decaying flesh and feces wafted up from below. A river of death ran directly below him. Condemned souls reached up out of it, groping blindly at his feet, dead eyes darting, straining to see through what to them was absolute blackness. But for Tommy who could see, there were shadows above them, flitting through the darkness. Those were the gatekeepers, he thought, the guardians of this place.

He could sense that they were also watching him, but he felt no danger. They moved quickly back and forth, swooping down as if on giant wings and soaring back up; he felt the breeze of their passing against his skin. In time he hoped to be able to see them clearly.

It was exhilarating. It filled him with immeasurable happiness.

The staccato of screams grew louder and more agonizing, and there seemed to be an endless supply of dark auras to feed the condemned souls below. Looking down at himself, he realized that he was completely naked.

He knew then, with soaring certainty, where he must be. He was in Hell, and Hell had risen up to worship him.

"I'm home," he said. "I'm finally home."

At the sound of his voice, the cries of anguish and torment swelled to a crescendo.

Tommy fell to his knees in this glorious garden of death. The ground was piercingly cold and wonderfully comfortable. He would rest, he thought, just for a minute, here in the depths of Hell.

#

As we approached the entrance of the hospital, Nika, still visibly apprehensive, attempted to follow me through the front door. But she knew the rules. She had to wait outside.

She crouched and whined and tried to guilt me into making just one single little exception, but I was hard-hearted. "Down," I said. "Stay."

I asked the closest cop if he could tell me where the personnel building was, but he, like all the rest of them, ignored me as if I wasn't even there.

I pushed through the front door. Just before it closed, I looked back at Nika. She gave me her most piteous, abandoned, hopelessly forsaken look.

It worked: I did feel guilty. But I didn't call her in.

Once I was inside, I intersected a dude dressed in white pants and a white shirt-- probably an orderly--and got him to tell me where to find Personnel.

He didn't even pause on his rapid way to wherever he was going, but he told me what I needed to know. "Back out the door, down the hill, second building on the right, first floor, third office on the left."

Nika was thrilled to death when I came back out. The cops, not so much. They were still whispering among themselves and paying no attention to anything or anyone else.

Another cop came out of the woods, puffing a bit as if he'd been hiking at speed. The cops who were there already actually relaxed, and one or two called out to him: "Sergeant Foley!"

More interesting to me was Nika's reaction. She stood up straighter. Her tail came up and started to wag, tentatively at first, then with more confidence.

He had singlehandedly taken the eerie presence out of the place. There was only one dissatisfied customer: a cop in his forties, overweight, with black hair, greasy and unkempt, and oily skin. His uniform looked disheveled, as if he'd slept in it. He was what, in layman's terms, I would have called a real scumbag.

He was swearing softly to himself, pacing back and forth and darting venomous glances at the other cops. "Nobody say a fuckin' word to Foley," he said loud enough for them to hear, but too soft for the man who was still making his way up from the woods.

He caught me staring at him. "What are you looking at, Geronimo?"

Under any other circumstances, I would have beat his head in, but this was not the time or the place. I kept my eyes on him as I made my way down the hill, getting a good look at his face. I'd be sure to recognize him the next time we met.

He looked away first. He'd be telling himself he had more important things to worry about, starting with the police sergeant who had almost come up level with him.

"You do that, white boy," I said under my breath.

Nika's cold wet nose poked into my hand. She was trotting beside me, looking and acting like her normal self. Whatever fear had possessed her was apparently gone.

Now she had my attention, she angled away from me and headed back toward the sergeant. Her tail wagged vigorously.

She went right up to him. He thumped her good and hard, the way a real dog lover knows how to do. She leaned into him, loving the way he was loving on her.

Nika was a friendly dog, but I had never seen her take to anyone so quickly. Foley caught my eye and nodded slightly. Nika gave his hand one last, approving lick and bounded back toward me.

There was something good about this man, I thought. Something that could make evil disappear. That must be a useful skill to have, in his line of work.

On Campus

The grounds of the mental hospital were really quite beautiful. There were low rolling hills of green grass, and three-story-high brick buildings scattered through the long fields. It looked more like a college campus than a mental facility.

You could tell which floors were the psychiatric wards by the steel bars and heavy screens on the windows. Patients stared out of some of them, and some of those waved to me as I went by. Maybe they thought that if I waved back, a piece of them would be as free as I was, walking down the dirt road in the sunlight.

#

Nika was actually all right with waiting for me outside the personnel building. Up in the office, I gave the receptionist my name and reason for being there.

"Barry Redcrow," she said, checking me

off on the appointment calendar. "Hello, Barry. I'm Loretta. Mr. Haskell is running a little bit late due to the crazy stor--did I say crazy? Sorry, we really must watch our terminology while we're 'on campus.'" She set the words off with air quotes, and giggled. "Wasn't that a wild storm?"

"Sure was," I said. I didn't want to tell her that I was sorry to have missed it, as I was in the middle of a fucking nightmare. That would have gotten things off on the wrong foot to say the least.

"Anyway," she said, "Mr. Haskell called to say he was delayed, and we were cut off in the middle of our conversation. The storm must have taken down a phone line."

She seemed a little crazy herself. She looked like a stereotypical secretary: older woman, schoolteacher glasses, dowdy dress, but her smile was just a shade too bright. And there was that giggle. I got the feeling she'd been working here just a little too long.

She handed me a clipboard and an

application fill out. "Redcrow," she said as I sat down and started in. "That's kind of unique, isn't it?"

"Not where I come from," I said.

"And where might that be? Are you American Indian?" There was that giggle again.

"As a matter of fact I am," I said.

And there was the smile. "Oh, how interesting! I don't think we have anyone on campus who is of American Indian heritage. How very interesting. You know--"

Whatever she was about to share with me, I was saved from it by a tall and very well-built black dude a few years older than I was.

"Mr. Haskell," Loretta said, barely missing a beat. "This is Barry Redcrow. He's an American Indian."

"Is he?" Steven Haskell said. He didn't seem to find that nearly as interesting as his secretary did. "Come on in, then. You can finish the paperwork while we talk."

Loretta winked at me. "Oh, he likes you.

You go ahead. You'll be just fine."

Then she giggled. Which made me wonder just how much I should trust her judgment.

#

Sergeant Foley found Officer Landers in the head nurse's office, hunched over in a chair, holding a styrofoam cup of coffee between his knees. A motherly-looking nurse rubbed his back. He barely seemed to notice her, or anything else that went on around him.

"Officer Landers does not wish--" the nurse began.

Jimmy looked up. At the sight of Sergeant Foley, he let out a breath he must have been holding since he got there. "It's OK," he said. "This is one of the good guys."

The nurse didn't look as if she quite believed him. "Are you sure? Because if you're not, I'll have him escorted straight off the premises."

Jimmy's lips twitched. In another existence, it would have been a smile. "Yeah, Mrs. Fletcher. I'm sure. Thanks very much for everything, and please don't say anything about this to my mother. She'll have a conniption."

"I promise," the nurse said. Sergeant Foley wondered if the hand he couldn't see, behind Jimmy's back, had its fingers crossed.

She left without acknowledging him, though they'd met more than once in the line of duty. That was odd. But then everything about this day was odd.

Foley shrugged it off and concentrated on the job at hand. Officer Landers had the greenish pallor of a man who had been or was about to be violently nauseated. His brown hair was disheveled and his blue eyes were bloodshot. His blue uniform shirt was halfway unbuttoned and his tie hanging off to the side. There was dried blood all over his hands.

"How are you feeling, son?" Foley asked him.

Landers stared at him as if he'd gone around the bend. "That fat scumbag Barretto killed the kid! That's how I'm feeling. I'm feeling like I want to bash his brains in with a friggin' nightstick."

Sergeant Foley blinked. The skin of his cheeks felt faintly scorched by that blast of completely uncharacteristic temper.

He closed the door in the faces of a small platoon of nurses and orderlies. "Well," he said in his driest, calmest tone, "as much as I would like to do that myself, it's just not an option right now."

Sergeant Foley despised crooked cops. He had known two in his career. One had blown his own head off years ago, and the other one was standing in front of the hospital at this very moment. "If we're going to get the scumbag, we have to do it by the books. In the end, I promise you, it will be better than beating his head in with a nightstick."

Jimmy looked up with eyes red from crying, and laughed bitterly. "I don't know, Sarge. Guys like that always seem to get away with shit. If I go against him, everyone will come down on me. You know how it is out there."

"I know that if you don't stand up and tell the truth, the fat bastard will take you and everyone else down with him."

Jimmy shook his head. "I'm not sure I even want to be a cop anymore. If that's what being a cop is about--"

"Being a cop is about standing up and doing the right thing," Sergeant Foley shot back. "It's about honor and duty, and defending people that are too scared or incapable to defend themselves. You knew that when you took this job. The people need guys like us. Do you want that fat fuck Barretto to run the show?"

His jaw snapped shut. He'd surprised himself with his own bad language, but his emotions had got the better of him. Jimmy Landers was a good, hard-working, honest cop, and Foley didn't want to lose him. He'd lost too many others to Barretto's tough-guy act and downtown connections.

Jimmy sighed, and shuddered as if a goose had walked over his grave. But his eyes had cleared. He looked like brave young Officer Landers again. "You're right," he said. I'm just talking shit because my head is all messed up. I need some time to sort things out. Would you mind helping me with the report? I want to make sure that bastard gets what he deserves."

"Of course I'll help you," Sergeant Foley said. "We'll get him, don't worry. Starting right now. Tell me exactly what happened, from the beginning."

#

Outside, Barretto was conducting damage control. He paced back and forth in front of a dozen or so police officers. "That punk Landers better keep his mouth shut. You guys all seen what happened, right? Neveska killed my dog. My police dog. A member of the force. Did he think we were going to let him get away with that? Then he came after me with a knife.

You seen that, right? Right?"

He looked each one straight in the eyes. They all knew the code. Baron might be a dog, but he was, to all intents and purposes, a cop. And the boys of the Medford Police Department were not going to let one of their own go down without someone paying a heavy price.

Barretto had fucked up. He admitted that to himself. All cops know that there's a certain way to handle situations like this. He should have waited until they could get Neveska alone. Then the little bitch would have just disappeared.

He wouldn't have been the first, and certainly would not have been the last. But Barretto had blown up too soon. There was going to be hell to pay for this one, and anyone caught in the crossfire was going to need a blood transfusion.

He zeroed in on the two weakest links. "Maloney? Scagliani? You guys are with me, right?"

The two officers shuffled their feet and said nothing. They were fairly new on the job, just a couple of years on, and knew better than to tangle with a senior officer. Both of them were Vietnam veterans, so were well accustomed to sudden death, but being on the job in Medford was a lot different than being on the job in Saigon. It was a good gig, and they wouldn't want to go down in a blaze of fire so early in their careers.

Barretto pushed in close to the younger, bigger one. "You better write it down just like I said, Maloney. There'll be hell to pay." He stood inches away from Maloney's face, bouncing his index finger off Maloney's badge. Everybody knew what that meant. "You'll lose everything if you fuck with me."

Spittle was flying in Maloney's face. Barretto's temper was close once again to spinning out of control. He wrapped Maloney's tie around his left hand and twisted, and raised his right hand for a full-on slap.

"Officer Barretto! What the hell do you think you're doing?"

Sergeant Foley came on at a fast march, side by side with Officer Landers. Their steps were in perfect, and military, cadence.

Officer Landers had cleaned himself up, buttoned his shirt and replaced his tie. His back was straight. He had his confidence back, and they could all see it. Most of them were visibly relieved.

"Get your hands off that officer immediately!!" Sergeant Foley barked.

Barretto did so, but he took his time. He let Foley see just how much he respected Sergeant Goody-Two-Shoes, the Straight-Arrow Cop.

Maloney had had enough of being bitched around. He shoved Barretto's hand off him and gave him a look that said, "Don't fuck with me." It would have worked better if he hadn't turned around and looked to the Sergeant for support.

Sergeant Foley marched straight up to Barretto, got in his face almost the exactly the way Barretto had got in Maloney's and said, "You want to try that with me? I'll tear you a new asshole."

Barretto went beet red and started to sputter. "No, no, Brian, I was just--"

"That's Sergeant Foley to you, dickhead!"

When Sergeant Foley wasn't around to hear, Barretto called him the Holy Man and sneered at him for a self-righteous asshole. However, he was smart enough to know that Foley was one tough bastard, and would surely eat him up and shit him out.

Barretto ducked and flinched like a dog that had been smacked upside the head a few times too many. "I'm sorry, Sarge! Sorry!"

Sergeant Foley pulled Barretto's service revolver from its holster and unloaded it right in front of him. "You are suspended pending further investigation."

Barretto should have known that was coming. But he had had just about enough. He snapped. He stabbed a finger at Jimmy Landers. "What did that little punk say to you?"

Before Sergeant Foley could open his mouth, Landers looked Barretto directly in the eye and said, "I told him what a scumbag murderer you are."

The silence was thick enough to chew. "You better watch what you say, kid," Barretto said. "Everyone here knows what happened. You'll be on your own."

Jimmy kept his head up. At six foot two and a hundred-ninety, he towered over Barretto, and he was fitter than the fat bastard had ever been in his life. "I'm not worried," he said. "You're a scumbag, and you'll get yours."

While Barretto glared the kid down, Sergeant Foley lifted Barretto's nightstick from his duty belt. "Evidence," he said in Barretto's ear. "You're done. Don't even think about coming near the station until you're properly notified."

Barretto looked from Foley to Landers, then raked his arrogant stare over the whole group of officers. "You guys better do the right thing," he said to them. "I'll be watching."

"Is that a threat?" Sergeant Foley demanded.

Barretto laughed out loud, put his hands on his hips and rotated slowly toward Sergeant Foley. "Yes, it is, <u>Brian</u>. Yes, it is."

He turned back around, still laughing, and began the trek out of the woods.

#

The Preacher woke to total darkness. He could no longer see, and the power surge that had animated him was gone. It was quiet: too quiet for his liking. He was completely alone.

The air was still cold. He felt it, enjoyed it, gained strength from it.

He lay motionless for a few more moments. He was still naked, and it felt as if he were lying in a pool of cool water, wrapped in a wet sheet. He couldn't have strayed too far off the path, then, when he decided to stop and rest.

When he attempted to sit up, his head

hit something with a hollow bonk. Whatever the ceiling was, it was extremely low and extremely cold, and it felt like metal.

There was metal all around him, on all sides. He seemed to be encased in some sort of steel box or--casket.

He began to shiver. He told himself that he was only a little cold, and not scared-- for he feared nothing. But he knew it was not the cold that was making him shiver.

He screamed with such fury that he surprised himself, a scream of tremendous power and anger, echoing in the steel box. His body surged with rage.

He pushed up with all his strength and kicked wildly. A frenzy of power vibrated through his body. Somewhere around his feet, something popped.

Warm air trickled up past his ankles. He wiggled his way toward it. Something heavy and crackly obstructed him. Plastic- -a bag.

He kicked it out of his way, and apparently out the chamber door. He heard it land with a thump a short distance outside. There were boots in it--he had felt the shape as he kicked and pushed. His boots.

He slid out the rest of the way and dropped beside the boots, and lay on the cold floor. Slowly it began to come back to him. Baron, Barretto, the pit, his death.

Yes. His death.

He had walked the path to Hell, and gained great power from it. He had proved himself worthy. Now he yearned to exercise that power.

He rose carefully, pausing to get his bearings, then walked slowly around the room. Even in that dim light, he could see clearly.

He knew where he was. He was in the mental hospital, in the morgue.

"The morrrrrrgue," he said aloud, lingering over the word. His laughter echoed through the basement.

He pulled out the tray on which he had been lying, and saw that it was full of his own blood. His hands worked with supernatural speed.

When he had finished painting the truth for the world to see, he knew exactly where to go. Down. Down below where the voices were whispering, waiting for his arrival.

Yes. He would go down.

#

Through the window of Haskell's office I could see that the police just above the hill were slowly but surely starting to leave, and the sun was shining brightly. The storm seemed to have dissipated.

"Have a seat," Haskell said. "That was some storm, huh?"

My eyes slid briefly away from his. I wasn't about to tell a potential employer I'd missed the storm of the millennium because I'd been in the middle of a friggin' nightmare. "Sure was," I said. "Freaky."

Haskell studied me for a few seconds, as if he suspected something, then said, "You got that right. Let's get right to it, shall we?"

He looked down at the file in front of him. "Let's see. Your military file says you were with the 75th Rangers. Long-Range Reconnaissance. Damn proud outfit." He nodded. I nodded back. I wondered if I should stand up and salute, but he might not take that so well. "Two tours in Vietnam, three Purple Hearts, two Silver Stars and a Bronze Star. Pretty impressive."

"I surrounded myself with good people," I said. "They made me look good."

"You're being modest, to say the least. It says here that you were in from '67 to late '69. Those were some pretty heavy years to be earning medals in Vietnam, man."

"Yeah, no shit." I said, and bit my tongue. Damn. Had I blown the interview already? "Sorry, Mr. Haskell. That sort of just slipped out."

Haskell laughed. "Steve. Call me Steve. Everyone does--except for Loretta, and I'm not even going to go there."

He laughed again. I laughed with him.

The air got a little easier to breathe, though I was still nervous.

"What took you so long to get out?" Haskell asked--no; I'd better learn to call him Steve. "I mean, damn! That's a long time in-country."

"Believe it or not, I probably would have stayed for another tour, but a snake about this long"--I held my hands about fifteen inches apart--"put an end to that. I was searching a tunnel, and it bit me. Next thing I knew, I was in a hospital bed in Japan."

I could see it. Smell it. Feel the shock and the anger, and the disappointment. I would have stayed. I was addicted to searching those damn Viet Cong tunnels. It was like it wasn't even me, like it was someone else doing all that killing, up close and personal. I could taste the gunpowder in the air--and in my lungs, a lot of death. I saw in flashes, faces of the young men I had killed in those labyrinths.

Haskell was talking to me. I snapped out of my trance. "Viper? Barry?"

I stared at him. "Bamboo viper?" he repeated patiently. I wondered if he knew I'd had a flashback. If it would cost me the job.

"Bamboo viper," I said. "Extremely venomous snake. One of the deadliest. We called them 'one step' or 'two step,' because that's how many steps you took before you fell flat on your face." I frowned at him. "You've heard of them?"

"Oh yeah," he said in a tone that told me he knew them up close and personal. "I was in Vietnam myself."

"I figured you must have been," I said. "Who were you with?"

"1st of the 5th Air Cavalry." He pointed to a picture on the wall behind me. I turned around in my chair to see a picture of Haskell and a handful of Army buddies posing by a Huey. Haskell was clearly older than the soldiers around him. He was posing next to a machine gun with no shirt on, and I instantly thought of last night's night scream.

On the nose of the helicopter were the

words <u>Head Hunters</u>. That rang a bell. "Damn fine unit," he said. "Great bunch of soldiers. We kicked a lot of ass over there. Took some hard hits, too. Ia Drang Valley. Nasty place."

I nodded, my respect for him ramping up a good few notches. The Ia Drang Valley was nasty, all right. Everybody who'd ever been in Vietnam had heard about it.

"The whole country is a nasty place if you ask me," I said.

Haskell studied me again, briefly, before he said, "Enough about the 'Nam. There'll be plenty of time to talk about that."

I sucked in a breath. "So I got the job?"

Haskell smiled. "If we veterans can't look out for each other, then who will? I just want to ask some questions, get a feel for you, and make sure you are the right kind of person to have work in the psychiatric ward. If you're uncomfortable with working on the ward, we can put you into the maintenance department. But to tell you the truth, I could really use a guy on the ward."

"No problem," I said. "Perfectly understandable."

He started off with pretty normal questions: where I lived, how long I'd been living there, whether I liked it, and why Medford?

"Because the Veterans' Administration said there was a job out this way," I answered that one.

"You live near the river?"

Now that was a left-field kind of question. I answered it, because I didn't see the point in refusing. "The river is in my backyard," I said. "Good bass fishing."

"Oh, you're a fisherman?" he asked.

"Of course. I'm American Indian, for God's sake!"

We both laughed. Haskell looked back down at the file. I caught myself hoping that he didn't have a lot of juice over there, because there was some personal stuff in my full file that I wasn't comfortable talking about. Certain operations while in Vietnam.

Hopefully someone had just given him

the rudimentary file.

"It says here you are originally from Maine," he said. "Passamaquoddy Reservation. People of the East . . . People of the Dawn. When Loretta said you were American Indian, I didn't think she meant right off the reservation."

I was slightly impressed that Haskell actually knew a little history of my people. People of the East, People of the Dawn, were our ancestral names, from before the white man came. I wondered how much more he knew, but decided I would wait to ask.

He'd already moved on, in any case. "Why the Army? What made you leave the reservation? Me, I got drafted, I didn't have a choice, but you'd have been exempt. What made you go, when everybody else was trying to get out of serving?"

"It's a long story," I said.

Haskell was not going to let me off the hook that easy. "I've got time," he said.

"I was afraid you were going to say that." I said with a slight laugh. I took a breath. "All right then. My parents were killed in a car accident. After that, things weren't the same. I wanted to get as far away from the reservation as I could. I had my grandfather sign the enlistment papers for me when I was seventeen."

That was the part I could tell Haskell. I couldn't tell him what had really happened. That when I was fifteen years old, I had become very sick. For days I couldn't even get out of bed.

My mother, father and grandfather were very worried. My grandfather was the reservation medicine man, or shaman as some people would say. A shaman was a great spiritual leader, one who was able to walk and communicate in the spirit world, who possessed great healing power, and who could control nature itself. He could envision things before they happened, sometimes very accurately.

I couldn't tell this man about my grandfather's powers, or the meaning of what he was. I had been running a high temperature, and hadn't eaten in several days. Everyone thought I was going to die, and nothing my grandfather could do seemed to help.

I remember him telling my parents that if I did not die, I would become stronger, and that Mother Earth surely had plans for me. Everyone waited to see what was going to happen.

After seven days or so, my parents decided that they would leave the reservation and seek outside medical help. I remember Grandfather advising them not to, and telling them to let the illness take its course, and that I was going to be all right.

They were not convinced my grandfather believed that. He had been acting strangely the entire time I was sick, as if he knew something but was unwilling to share it with the rest of us.

I was too sick to move, so they were going to try to bring someone back to the reservation. Grandfather was adamant about them staying on the reservation. "It's a dangerous time to leave," he said over and over.

My mother kept saying, "Don't worry, Dad. We'll be back soon. Just keep an eye on Barry until we get home."

"Please," he said. "Stay."

"Dad," my mother said, "you're scaring me. Is everything all right?"

"I do not know," he said. "All I know is that I feel you should not leave."

It was spring then, late April, and it was an unusually hot Saturday, especially for the northeast of Maine. My parents left that morning in an old, broken-down jeep. It was a two-hour trek to the nearest medical facility. The roads were all dirt, and took a terrible beating year-round from the logging trucks.

Some time after they left, I could hear the other kids my age splashing down in the lake. They sounded as if they were having a lot of fun, and it was so hot. I got the urge to go down to the lake and swim in the water.

I was still feeling sick and weak, but I felt that something was telling me to swim in the lake. It was really strange. Just thinking about it afterwards gave me goose bumps.

My grandfather asked me where I was going. I told him that the lake was calling me.

It was like a dream. My grandfather looked worried. He must have thought I was sleepwalking, or in delirium. He tried to walk me back to bed, but I insisted that the lake was calling me, and that I needed to go.

He felt my forehead. "You're very hot," he said. "Maybe a quick soaking in cool water is not a bad idea."

We walked together down to the lake, with me leaning on him but trying not to. He had brought a blanket with him. I remember that clearly.

Many of my friends were down there swimming, and they were happy to see me feeling better, though I really wasn't. But I couldn't tell them what had really brought me down here.

There was a rock by the lake, and a

long rope that hung from a tree high above it. All the kids would climb on top of the rock and swing from the rope into the water. "Come on!" my friends called. "Come for a swing!"

"You'd better just wade in," my grandfather said. "What if you swing too far out? You won't be able to swim back to shore."

He gave me a tight, powerful hug, as if saying good-bye for the last time. This freaked me out, because he was a man who showed little emotion. But the lake was calling me.

I pulled out of his grip. "I'll go on the swing," I said. "It's something I have to do."

He looked terrified, but he didn't try to stop me. It wasn't until I let go of the rope and landed in the water that I figured out why.

#

Sergeant Foley and Officer Landers went back into the hospital with a plan.

With the help of Nursing Supervisor Fletcher and a camera belonging to the Nursing Department--because it would be an hour at least before an official evidence camera could make its way through the storm's destruction from the station--they descended to the morgue to collect a little more evidence.

It wasn't that they didn't trust the Internal Affairs detectives to handle the investigation. They are all good, by-the-book, honest cops. But one never knew what Barretto might try to do to cover up what he had done. Foley and Landers agreed: it would be good to have a separate set of photographs of Neveska's broken, beaten body.

One of the orderlies took them down the stairs, since the elevator, as he put it, "was acting a little kooky when we took the body down."

The orderly was young, maybe eighteen to twenty years old, with shoulder-length brown hair. He looked like a nice enough guy, Foley thought, but definitely left the impression that he had spent more than a few hours around the community water bong. He looked vaguely spooked, but he had guts enough to lead them down the dimly lit stairs. An aura of dampness breathed up from below.

The steps were steep and narrow, and the police officers held tightly to the metal railings. The orderly bounded down without touching them, as if he did it several times a day.

He stopped in front of a door with a sign over it that said *Basement*, though the stairs kept on going.

"What's down there?" Officer Landers asked.

"Tunnel," Sergeant Foley answered. He had been to the morgue before.

"It's for moving patients from building to building without exposing them to the elements," the orderly said.

While they talked, they made their way down the hallway to the morgue. The door when they came to it was not only unlocked, it hung partly open.

"Uh-oh," the orderly said. He looked even less happy than he had upstairs. "Someone is in deep shit. This door is supposed to be locked at all times. I know I locked it behind me after I delivered the body."

Sergeant Foley stepped past him toward the door. As he did so, he observed the faint imprint of a bloody boot mark leading from the morgue down toward the hallway. He pushed the door open, found the switch and flicked the light on.

It flickered overhead, not quite managing to come to full brightness. It provided enough light to dimly see about half of the room, including the empty morgue tray that had been pulled open.

The morgue smelled like a morgue--the distinctive smell that anyone who had been in one would recognize. But over and above that, it smelled of copper: the one smell that only an experienced person could immediately identify. From the puzzled look on Landers' face as he sniffed the air, he was not familiar with it yet, but after today he would never forget it.

Sergeant Foley knew exactly what it was. He had smelled it far too many times in Korea. It was the smell of blood. Lots of blood.

The light was too dim and unsteady to show where the smell was coming from, but the orderly had seen and smelled enough. "This is not good. I'm out of here, man!"

Sergeant Foley caught him as he made a break for the exit. "Hey!" he said. "Calm down."

The orderly struggled wildly. He was in a complete panic. "I knew there was something messed up about that dude! This is so messed up, man!"

Foley twisted his arm up behind him and shook him hard. "What are you talking about? What dude?"

The orderly wheezed with the pain of his twisted arm, but he still tried to lunge against the sergeant's grip. "*Your* dude, man! The dude that guy over there brought in with the paddy wagon." He jabbed his chin toward Officer Landers. "That dude was messed up. We brought him down here, and the elevator was acting freaky, all weird and cold inside. The cold followed us all the way down the hallway and all the while we put that dude in his drawer. That drawer," he said, pointing to the one that was open and obviously empty.

"That one?" said Landers. "Are you sure? There are a lot of doors here."

"Of course I'm sure!" the orderly said. "Let me go, man. Let me out of here."

The door creaked open behind them. Sergeant Foley startled so hard he let the orderly go. The kid jumped even higher and dived for the opening, ricocheting off Nursing Supervisor Fletcher and disappearing down the hallway.

"What's going on in here?" Mrs. Fletcher demanded.

"That's what we're trying to find out," Sergeant Foley answered.

She glanced past him and gasped. He turned to see what had taken her so completely aback.

The lights had finally come up to full power. As Foley took in the sight, Officer Landers spoke for them all. "Holy shit."

The morgue tray was spilling over with blood: wet, dried and coagulated, mixed together and spread over the stainless steel body pan like a macabre display of abstract art. Bloody handprints were clearly visible on the side of the tray, as if the corpse had pulled himself out of his own deathbed. There were footprints in blood on the floor, as well. Bare feet.

After several long moments, Sergeant Foley broke the silence. "There has to be a logical explanation." He meant to sound reassuring, but it came out more like a plea. "Medical Examiner? Could he already have come and taken the body?"

"He hasn't even been notified yet," Mrs. Fletcher said, "and even if he had been, we would have known about it. This door is always properly secured."

"Barretto?" Officer Landers suggested. He sounded sick. "This guy was dead, Sarge. Surer than shit."

Sergeant Foley knew exactly where the kid was going. He said it for both of them. "No body, no evidence to prosecute the son of a bitch."

"Oh. My. God."

Foley started to say something about it happens, some cops are like that, we'll get the bastard somehow, but the nurse was not talking to him at all. Her eyes were fixed on the wall.

It was made of brick and painted white, the better to show the words scrawled on it in letters two feet high. *DIE PIG! DENY YOUR MAKER!*

The words were written in blood, as thick as if slapped on with a brush, but Foley could just make out the print of a hand and the swipe of fingers that had shaped the letters. The excess dripped down toward the floor, as if the bricks were bleeding through the whitewash.

The words were only the beginning. Next to them were three 6's joined together at the top, forming a circle. As his eyes followed the bloody footprints on the floor, they found other 6's scattered everywhere over the walls and the floor.

"The sign of the Antichrist," he whispered.

Lower down on the wall was an arrow pointing in the direction of the footprints, and a line of smaller, almost illegible words: *The Beast is always watching.*

No one person could have done this. There was just too much blood, and too much writing, smeared and scrawled everywhere. But there was only one set of footprints, and they all clustered in one area, trampling around and around, until they broke loose and headed for the door. By the time they got there they were faint but still discernible, and they passed through the door and out into the hallway.

Sergeant Foley followed them, looking carefully for any evidence that suggested the body of Tommy Neveska had been tampered with. There were no signs of the door being forced open, but that didn't mean anything if Louis Barretto had something to do with this.

On the outside of the door, Sergeant Foley found what he had been looking for. There was a fingerprint on the handle. Smudged, but maybe, just maybe, enough to obtain ridge detail and link Barretto to the scene. With a little luck, they might be able to pull a fingerprint off the catastrophe on the wall, too, and then they'd have him.

"Son of bitch," Sergeant Foley said under his breath. Then louder: "Jimmy, take Supervisor Fletcher upstairs, and see if any of the telephones are working. If they are, notify State Police Crime Scene and tell them to get their asses down here. If you see any of the other guys up there, send them down to help secure the scene. I want to know where Barretto was during the entire time he's been on the hospital grounds. Also, Marie," he said to Mrs. Fletcher, who was still staring in blank horror at the bloody wall. She did not even blink. He raised his voice. "Marie!"

She jumped and shuddered, and pulled her eyes away to fix on him. He spoke firmly, as if to push the words into her head and fasten them there. "Get me a list of every orderly or any other person on duty that may have had access to the morgue at any time after this body was placed here."

She nodded jerkily. She was a seasoned nurse, but this had to be above and beyond anything she had ever seen. "Jimmy will take you upstairs," Foley said as gently as he could. "I'll stay down here to make sure nobody else disturbs the scene."

They left with relief so strong he could taste it. He was not so happy to be left behind, but someone had to do it.

"I hope Barretto is responsible for this," he said to the bloody walls. "Because if he isn't . . ."

If he wasn't, then someone, or something, else was. Something connected with the freakish, vicious storm. Something outside of human understanding.

He blessed himself with the sign of the Cross: Father, Son and Holy Ghost. He clasped his hands together and began to pray in a soft clear voice: "Hail Mary, full of grace, the Lord is with thee . . ."

As he prayed, the sound of flies gathering within the morgue grew louder, rising to drown the sound of his voice.

#

Barretto made to the entrance of the woods, where all the police cruisers had been dumped and the trek to the hospital had begun. Most of the road had been cleared, and workers were cleaning up one last remnant of the storm's fury right by the hospital grounds.

He could still hear the chain saws working, but they were not as angry as they had been just a short time ago. He jumped into his cruiser and started the engine, but as he was about to drive away, a thought came over him. He left the cruiser running, took his Buck knife off his gun belt and walked over to Sergeant Foley's cruiser.

He knew it was Foley's, because it was clearly marked *Sergeant* on the rear quarter panel, and because Sergeant Foley always had a pair of rosary beads hanging from his rearview mirror.

Barretto slashed all four of Sergeant Foley's tires. "I'd shit in the front seat, if I could force myself to go right now," he said to himself, and then laughed at his own joke.

This would have to do for now. He was going to tie one on tonight for sure. Then he would come up with a game plan to get back at anyone who wasn't going to play ball with him.

"Louisssss . . ." Barretto heard his name being called as if from very far away, carried as a whisper on the wind.

Then again, louder: *"Louisssssss . . ."* It seemed to come with the breeze that gently brushed through the trees, soft as a snake's hiss. It was eerie, with a suggestion of the supernatural.

"What the fuck is it?" Barretto called out. His heart was thudding. He was all alone out here, surrounded by police cruisers, but still vulnerable.

The woods were suddenly cold, and clouds darkened the sun. It was not the cold of an earthly wind. It was raw, dead, almost pressurized, all around him, as if a winter night was closing in.

He checked his watch. His wrist was shaking almost too hard for him to see. It was still late morning--but of what day? What year?

"Where the hell is everyone?" He tried to shout, but his voice fell flat. It was so cold now, he could see his breath.

The darkness closed in. It was a left-over pressure system, he told himself, or a pocket of the storm.

He lurched toward his cruiser. Just as his hand fell on the handle of the door, a voice yelled his name almost next to him. He nearly found the shit he had been going to leave in Sergeant Foley's cruiser.

"LOUISSSSSS!" A sinister, hissing laugh echoed behind it: low and long-drawn and menacing.

Barretto was starting to get less freaked and more pissed. Landers or one of those other fairies must be fucking with me, he thought.

He hauled the door open and dropped into the driver's seat. The motor was already running. As he slammed it into gear, he glanced up, into the rearview mirror.

The horrible, death-blue, bloodied and bruised face of Tommy Neveska stared back at him with pure white eyes and a sweet, sweet smile.

"Louis," Neveska hissed in his ear.

Barretto screamed like a girl and threw himself out of the car, reaching for the service revolver that Sergeant Foley had relieved him of just an hour ago.

The car, still in gear, rolled past him and slammed into a tree. It was completely empty.

"Mind," he said, gulping air. "Playing tricks."

He approached the cruiser cautiously and bent down to peer into the back.

Nobody there, but there was something smeared all over the seat. "Is that blood? One of the guys must have got some of Neveska's blood on himself on the way up here."

But the blood was much too fresh for that.

He backed away as fast as he could without falling flat on his ass. There was another cruiser a little ways up the hill. They all took the same key; if he got dinged for taking the wrong car, he'd say he'd made a mistake.

The air was still weirdly cold, but he was perspiring heavily. He puffed and struggled toward the car, intent solely on getting the hell out of there.

A dog barked nearby. A big dog, like a German Shepherd. Then it started to whimper. The sound echoed through the woods.

It sounded just like Baron.

He knew better, but he couldn't help himself. "Baron?"

Of course it wasn't Baron. Baron was

dead, mutilated and shoved into a refrigerator, and Barretto needed to get out of there.

He fell into the cruiser, jammed the key in the ignition and sped out of the woods.

#

I let go of the rope and hung suspended for what seemed like an eternity. A million thoughts at once shot through my head. I regretted letting go, but did not know why.

I looked directly into my grandfather's eyes. Everything around me was in slow motion. I got the feeling, suddenly, that something terrible had happened to my parents, and that the same terrible thing was about to happen to me. It had already been ordained. There was no way to stop.

I saw the truth of it in the tear that ran from my grandfather's eye, right before I hit the water. Even the tear was in slow motion, but I could see it clearly, as if it were only inches away. It was the first time I had ever seen him cry.

156

Even while this was happening, the activity around me carried on as usual. Only my grandfather and I were in slow motion. I knew something was terribly wrong, but it was as if I had to carry out my destiny by jumping in the lake.

#

The entire memory ran through my head in seconds. I didn't dare tell Haskell what had happened. If I did, there would be a couple of guys in white suits waiting for me when I left his office.

But I wanted to tell him. I wanted to tell someone. It was so clear in my mind, and I had never told anyone.

It was as if I hit the water in slow motion, the whole time staring into my grandfather's eyes, and his eyes staring into mine, as if we were the only two on the lake. Neither one of us blinked. I saw my grandfather's tear hit the ground in the same moment that my feet touched the water.

The lake swallowed me: my feet, then my waist, up to my chest, my neck, and finally over my head. The water was cold and black. Black as midnight and cold as ice.

It was only three or four feet deep at that particular spot, but it felt as if I were sinking into a bottomless pit. I seemed to have been falling for minutes, as fast as if I had weights tied to my body, but somehow I had not lost my breath.

The water grew colder by the second, and still I sank. I reached up, thrashing in panic, but there was no one to catch me.

I fell for what seemed forever, until finally I closed my eyes and gave up. As soon as I did that, as if they had been waiting for it, I felt cold, dead hands scrabbling at me. At first I thought it was my grandfather or some of the kids at the lake, but these hands were coming at me from below--grabbing, pulling, scratching and tearing at my skin. There seemed to be hundreds of them, digging into me with their fingernails.

I tried to scream, but nothing came out. My heart was trying to batter its way out of my chest. I must have been under for an hour. Why had no one come for me?

Then I heard my name. It was a voice I had never heard before, and I never wanted to hear it again. It was clear as if someone was whispering directly into my ear.

I opened my eyes. I was still under water, and I was not alone.

This was the presence of evil. Years later, when the memory of so much else had faded, I could see every detail. Its jet-black hair streamed back from its head. It stared at me with white, dead eyes, the pupils barest pinpricks, the face blue and bloated, as if it had been submerged for days.

Terrible gashes scored that face, some so deep that I could see the skull beneath the skin. The lips were swollen and cracked and as blue as the face, death blue, as it hung suspended in front of me.

It wrapped both hands around my

throat and squeezed, pushing me straight down into the endless depths. The fingers were icy and the grip unforgiving. It smiled a sick, evil smile as it stared into my eyes, as if memorizing every hidden part of me.

I stopped breathing. Everything went black.

Then, as suddenly as it had begun, I could see daylight through my eyelids. I could feel air rushing through my nose and into my lungs, I could hear the sounds the wind makes when it whispers through the leaves of the trees--and then a long, powerfully sad cry echoed across the lake and through the forest.

I opened my eyes. A distant vibration hummed through my body, as the Boston/Maine cargo train roared down the track, blowing its whistle from across the lake. It sounded like a cry of agony and deep sorrow.

I turned my head. I lay on the shore of the lake, with my grandfather gripping my right wrist, by which he had pulled me from the water. My body felt lifeless, as if I had no energy left to stand.

He lifted me in his arms. My head rolled slackly until he braced it in the crook of his elbow, the way a mother cradles a baby. Fresh tears streamed from his eyes.

I focused on the blanket he had brought. It lay crumpled on the bank just out of reach. My eyes filled with it, until everything else disappeared.

It was suddenly deathly quiet. Not even a bird dared to sing. The wind had died, and the air was unnaturally and unexpectedly cold.

My friends ran out of the water. I heard their shivering, and their chattering teeth.

This was no nightmare. I knew exactly what it was.

I looked from the blanket to the circle of kids around me. They were all silent, staring at my body and legs.

"Snapping turtle," one of them said.

I barely had enough energy to lift myself up and look, but somehow I managed it. Arms, legs, chest--I was covered with claw marks and fingernail scratches. I looked as if something had dragged me through a hundred yards of thorn bushes with no clothes on.

I hurt bad, but all I could think of while my grandfather wrapped me in the blanket and carried me home was my parents. I knew, somehow, that they were dead.

#

"Barry? Barry! Earth to Barry Redcrow!"

It was Haskell, pulling me out of my trance--again. "Are you all right?"

I shook the memory out of my head. Haskell was staring at me--sympathetic, not suspicious. That was good. I hoped. Considering what kind of hospital this was, maybe it wasn't.

"Sorry," I said. "It's just--you know, long story. When I was fifteen years old, I woke up one morning and told my grandfather I'd had a terrible nightmare, that my parents had been killed in a car wreck. 'That was no nightmare,' he said."

"How did you know?" Haskell asked.

I shrugged. "I'd been sick, and hadn't eaten for days. I had a high fever. By the time I woke up from the coma, my parents had been dead for a couple of days. Everybody said I'd had a 'vision.'" I air-quoted that, which made Haskell's lips twitch. "They said I'd been chosen in the old way: fasting, dreaming, seeking a spiritual guide, all of that. My people place great honor in vision seeking. I was sick, and didn't see my vision coming, or go looking for it, either. I wish it never had."

Haskell watched me steadily, studying me, waiting.

Why not? I thought. Why not trust him? The worst he could do was book me into the next available bed in the crazy ward.

"Believe it or not," I said, "visions aren't all that common. Sometimes the elders go looking for them, with chemical assistance, but it's not the same. The last person who had an actual vision before me, in fact, was--"

"Your grandfather," Haskell said.

163

I raised my eyebrows at him. "You're quick," I said. "You sure you're not Native American yourself?"

Haskell grinned, but then he sobered. "Call me intuitive," he said.

Intuitive. Whatever. I still had more story to tell. "My grandfather wanted me to be there for my parents' burial--and as it happens, I came to on the morning of the ceremony. You know about that, right?"

He lifted his hands. "Maybe. Why don't you tell me anyway."

"All right," I said, closing my eyes so I could see it. "We bury our dead with gifts-- dig a hole in the earth, and sit the corpse upright in a chair and lower the whole thing into the grave. We buried my mother and father together, sitting across from each other in that cold, damp hole.

"My parents were very much loved and respected. Everyone came to the ceremony, from all over the reservation, and the gifts overflowed the grave and tumbled out across the cemetery. There was gold and silver jewelry, and other things that were less valuable maybe on the open market, but they were priceless to the people who gave them: things of spiritual value. Common things like knives, blankets, smoking pipes or handmade tools. Things that told stories, or symbolized honor to our people.

"We measure wealth by how many friends and how much family one has. My parents were very, very wealthy. The grave was filled with flowers, one from each member of the tribe, to help my parents on their way to the spirit world." I paused to pull myself together. Haskell was tactfully silent. "I . . . didn't handle it very well. Like I said, I was only fifteen."

Haskell nodded slowly. "I'm sorry," he said. "Sorry I asked."

"Now you know," I said. I wasn't angry. I was more tired than anything.

What I had told him was true, but it was only half of what really happened. I didn't dare tell him the rest. He was a good guy, and damned intuitive. But not good or intuitive enough to handle the whole of it. I wasn't even sure I could, and I'd been living with it for years, as vivid in my mind now as on the day it happened.

Medicine Man

After the people had left the ceremony, but still a few hours before nightfall, Grandpa led me to a field just across the way from our house. He wanted to show me something, he said, and asked me to gather cedar branches from the forest to build a small fire.

Cedar was traditionally burned during religious ceremonies. That made me nervous. I knew I was going to participate in a ceremony reserved for senior members of the tribe--and we were alone. No one else had come to out to see what we were doing, as if they sensed that this was a private ceremony.

When I came back, my grandfather was dressed in the traditional garb of a shaman, that even I had rarely seen. His glance warned me not to stop or ask questions, just do what I was told.

He drew a large circle in the dirt around the spot where I had begun to place the wood for the fire. When the circle was drawn, he began singing softly to himself.

I had seen him do this many times, and knew not to disturb him. This time however he did something different: he drew a small piece of something green and pungent, about the size of a dime, from the small fur bag that hung from the belt at his waist. "Hold it under your tongue," he said between verses of the chant.

I obeyed, though my fingers shook. He did the same. The stuff felt weird; almost as soon as I put it in, my tongue went numb.

Grandpa knelt beside the small bundle of firewood I had arranged, reached into his pocket, then began rubbing his hands together. Fine powder, lighter than sand, fell from between his fingers onto the cedar boughs. The wood began at once to smolder. In a few moments, a flame flickered up from the bottom and fed on the pile of kindling.

The burning cedar smelled sweet. Its purpose was to guide the seeker back to the people if he became lost in his vision.

Like every medicine man, Grandpa knew the name of the fire, and could summon and control it at any time. His glance told me to sit down close by the flames. I had no trouble doing what he said.

I was beginning to feel very comfortable with myself. The green paste under my tongue must be peyote--not the kind most people think about when they hear the word, that comes from a desert cactus, but a mixture of herbs and roots gathered from the forest. It opened the way to the spirit world and let the shaman walk among them as well the living.

Deep down inside, I was terrified, but the peyote pushed all that out of the way. My head was light, my body was numb, and I felt as if I was floating. I was keenly, almost painfully aware of the world around me.

Grandpa's song went on and on. He drew a flaming stick from the blaze, showing no fear of the fire at all, and began drawing in the dirt. Every so often he paused, raised both hands over his head and turned his face to the sky, and his song grew louder.

He spoke in the ancient form of our language. I couldn't understand exactly what he was saying, but I thought I recognized some of the words, including <u>resurrection</u> and <u>soul search</u>. I was getting scared again, but I trusted my grandfather to keep me safe.

After the third or fourth invocation of the sky or the spirits that lived in it, he drew symbols on my face and forehead with the burnt end of the stick he had used to draw in the dirt. I felt pretty good by then, and laughed for no reason. The ashes felt warm on my face as he drew on it, and I wished I could see to see what the symbols were. But there wasn't any mirror, and my legs were too rubbery to let me stand and go tottering back into the house.

Grandpa went on like this for over an hour, till daylight drew its last breath. Then as the song of birds and the chittering of the red squirrels and the creaking of crickets rose to a crescendo, he finished his song and sat beside me with his eyes closed, as if exhausted.

After several minutes had gone by, he spoke to me in our language. "Look to the west."

The last shreds of sunlight were settling over the tree line, and it looked as if the sky was melting into the blackness of the forest. The sky was lit with beautiful bright shining stars, and as I looked upward, a meteor streaked across it. I almost thought I could hear it.

I looked down at my arms and hands that were covered with scabs from my episode in the lake, and they began to wiggle like worms on my skin, slithering down off my body and across the clearing. Somehow I was not afraid. I searched the woods for what I supposed to be looking for, but there was nothing out of the ordinary.

Then I saw it. Movement in the trees, just at the edge of the field. My heart jumped.

It was low to the ground and heading in our direction. As it moved closer, I could see that it was a coyote, slinking noiselessly through the grass. Then I saw another, and another, until there were several.

Coyotes are very elusive, and rarely let themselves be seen in the forest. But here was one not thirty yards away, and a pack hovering behind it.

Something very small stirred between the first coyote's feet. A pup, probably just days old, walked with what appeared to be its mother. The two approached and stopped within ten feet of where we were sitting.

Grandpa remained where he was, with his eyes closed. The mother coyote sat on her haunches just outside the circle he had drawn in the dirt, as if she sensed its presence.

The others ran along the border, but it seemed they dared not cross into the circle. They growled deep in their throats and showed their long teeth, which gleamed in the firelight. Their slanted yellow eyes never left us.

I was suddenly very scared. I wanted to get up and run, but the coyotes would make quick work of me. Somehow I knew that I would be safe if I remained inside the circle with my grandfather.

The coyotes raced around us in every direction, as if they were looking for a way into the circle to attack us. The mother coyote and the pup sat directly in front of us. She showed no sign of fear. Nor did the pup, who began to dance around its mother, as if unaware of our presence.

Grandpa opened his eyes and stared at the mother coyote. She stared back. As they locked gazes, the other coyotes circled faster and faster, howling and yipping in a deafening chorus.

As the dust from the circling pack rose to blur the stars, I wished some of the tribe would come out and break up the ceremony and scare the coyotes away. But I had the distinct feeling that nothing on

Mother Earth was capable of scaring these creatures tonight.

The wind began to pick up, whistling through the trees. Down past the field, where some of the neighbors kept a couple of horses, I heard pounding and squealing. Something else in the world was aware of this attack, at least, though no one came out to check on the horses.

Grandpa and the mother coyote never moved. I could sense that she was strongly aware of me. I could smell the stink of my own sweat. So, from the wrinkle of her lip, could she.

The wind grew even stronger, and began to dim the flame of the campfire. Dust swirled up all around us, climbing into a whirlwind. I could no longer hear the horses, only the wail of the coyotes yearning to attack, and the howl of the wind.

Grandpa stood perfectly still. The campfire was completely out, and I had to shield my eyes from the dust and smoke. The wind slammed into me. I had to duck my head and protect my eyes. I could barely see, but I knew one of the coyotes had entered the circle. The wind must have blown the perimeter away.

I strained to see through the dust and the wind. The coyote was very small, just a potbellied ball of fluff. Its eyes were curious, not filled with hate as were the other coyotes'. It snarled briefly to make sure I saw its teeth, but they were much too small to be really dangerous.

It walked straight toward me, unafraid. The other coyotes' wail rose to a shriek, but even that barely carried above the wind. It blew so strongly now that I had to cover my eyes with both hands.

My last vision was that of the coyote pup walking up to where I was sitting. The whirlwind tugged so hard I could barely sit up, stinging my exposed skin. The end would be quick, I thought. The other coyotes would move in quickly for the kill. I waited for the first set of teeth to sink into me.

Then there was nothing. No wind. No

coyotes. No cries for help from the horses. Only Grandpa singing softly, barely to be heard.

My grandfather knew the name of the wind. As I lowered my hands from my stinging eyes, I saw he was sitting in the same position he'd been in when he started, slowly rocking back and forth. The campfire was once again lit, and the flames burned brightly, filling the air with the scent of cedar. Away in the forest, the crickets were chirping, as peaceful as if they had never been interrupted.

Had the whole thing been a hallucination? I looked down at my arms. The scabs were completely gone. Only fresh pink skin remained.

I was still tripping from the peyote, but not as intensely as I had been a short while ago. I felt as if many hours had passed, although I knew it couldn't have been that long.

I looked and listened all around me for the presence of the coyotes, but heard nothing. Then from a distance came the cry of a coyote; then another, wailing from a different direction. They were calling to one another through the forest as they often did before a hunt.

"Go now and rest," Grandpa said. "I'm afraid you've already experienced too much; you may not be strong enough for any more."

I opened my mouth to protest, but he stopped me. "You are young. Your understanding is weak. In time you will know what has happened, and its meaning will be clear to you--but not for a long while. In the meantime, rest, and be reassured. Dark spirits will not trouble you, but always be aware of their presence. They are ever present and always watching."

This scared me more than anything else I had been through that day and night, and brought the weight of that tragic week crashing down upon me. But my grandfather took my hands and held them tightly, until I stood steady. In that warm, strong grip and in those eyes that looked so firmly into mine, I understood that he had performed that ceremony for my protection.

All my people were around me then, though none of them had been physically present for the ritual. They were all there, the young, the old, the dead and the living, surrounding me in a complete and embracing circle. They were everywhere: in the woods, in the stars, in the shape and form of animals on the earth. I could feel their power within me, as if we were one.

In the soft light of the campfire, I saw a single tear well from the corner of my grandfather's eye.

#

Once again the forest was quiet. On our way back to our now lonesome home, a messenger from the spirit world met us, a wise and friendly spirit, an advisor and giver of warnings to our people: a great horned owl, coming to rest on our roof. It stared at us as we approached, with its yellow eyes burning bright.

I knew, looking at it, that the worst was yet to come. The owl was a messenger of death. It brought messages of deaths to come, and deaths that had already taken place.

My grandfather spoke to it in our ancient language. The lingering effects of the peyote made me think it would answer, but it simply watched, perched like a sentinel on the top of the roof.

Just before the night met the morning light, we walked past the Messenger and entered our house to rest. As the sun began to rise, I finally was able to cry myself to sleep.

Spooked

The top of Governors Avenue was still partially blocked by the overturned bus, but the trees had been cut and laid on the side of the road. This made it a whole lot easier for Barretto to get home.

His own car was parked at the police station, but his house was just blocks away from the entrance to the woods. He decided to take the cruiser home and get his car later. Serve that bastard Foley right, anyway. They'd all see who won that war.

Meanwhile he was damned spooked. He needed to get home and have a few drinks.

He sped down Governors Avenue, constantly checking his rearview mirror. No dead face leered back.

He screeched brakes around the turn onto Sampson Road. It was mostly clear, though he could see where the crews had been at work.

The car stereo suddenly came on. The

DJ was going on about the freak storm, sounding too fucking cheerful for words. "*Whoooa!* What a wild storm! That was as far out as I have ever seen. And if you think that was wild, wait until you see what the Preacher has in store for Officer Barretto this evening! <u>Whoooa!</u> I can't wait to hear about that one! He's going to tear your fucking heart out, Louis!"

Barretto lunged at the dials. The power button was off--didn't budge when he twisted it. "What! What the hell?"

He looked in the rearview mirror again. Empty. So was the back seat--he almost went off the road, between trying to drive and twisting around to make sure there was no dead dog murderer back there.

Cold sweat ran down his face. "I'm going crazy," he said. "I'm--going--batshit--crazy."

He swerved off the road and slammed on the brakes. Guns. He needed guns.

He had guns in the house. Plenty of guns. Enough to mow down an army of laughing dead men.

181

He left the cruiser's engine running and the door open.

"A man's home is his castle," he said. "That's right. You better believe it."

A clap of thunder startled him halfway out of his skin. A demonic scream of rage seemed to emanate from the ground below him. All around him, dogs howled mournfully, echoing and re-echoing, as if every dog in Medford had started up at once.

The sound only made Barretto run faster toward the sanctuary of his own four walls. Once he made it inside, he told himself, everything would be all right-- never mind that that was where it all started.

As he got closer, he heard the same whimpering cry that he had heard up by the hospital, coming from the catch basin several feet from the house. It sounded exactly like Baron welcoming his master home.

"Baron," he said, though he knew that was probably not a good idea.

The dog, or whatever it was, barked and then whimpered again. Barretto picked up the pace, running toward the sound. The closer he got, the more joyous it seemed.

He bent over the catch basin and peered in--straight into Tommy Neveska's laughing, demonic face.

#

Sergeant Foley had used most of the film that Nursing Supervisor Fletcher had provided with the camera, except for some that he had saved for the footprints in the hallway.

The hospital's 35mm camera was better than the one the Medford Police had. That was a good thing, one of the few in this whole day. This crime scene was what the department called a "heavy," and there was no room for sloppy evidence retrieval.

"You only get one shot at a crime scene." His police academy instructors had worked hard to impress this on him, and it had stuck.

He took a final picture of the doorknob with the smudged print. The morgue was eerily quiet, except for the buzzing of the flies that feasted on the blood smeared on the walls and the floor and the tray. How so many could have found their way down here so fast was beyond him.

Careful not to smudge the prints, he closed the door behind him, just in time to see Officer Landers coming back down the hallway with two other young police officers.

"Barretto is nowhere in sight," he said, "but I got through to the State Police. They're sending a crime-scene tech. 'Within the hour,' they said."

"Did you tell them what's up?" Foley asked.

"Just that there's a crime scene involving a murder."

Foley nodded. "Good," he said. "Good. We'll have to play this one close to the vest."

Landers flushed a bit at the compliment. "That's what I figured, Sarge."

"Good," Foley said again. He stabbed a finger at each of the other two officers. "You two stay here. Don't let anyone--and I mean anyone--enter this crime scene without me being there. You got that?" He barely waited for them to nod before he went on. "This hallway is also to be considered a crime scene. I know we don't have a lot of control over which direction staff or patients may come from, but preserve this area as best you can, and don't let any civilians down this way."

"You got it," they said in unison.

Foley turned back to Officer Landers. "Jimmy, you come with me. I don't know if whoever came out here was bleeding, or just shaking off Neveska's blood. God knows there's a lot of it."

Landers looked a bit green. Foley hoped he could keep his stomach where it belonged.

They followed the direction of the faint prints down the hallway to a metal door marked *TUNNEL STAIRWAY*. In front of the door the owner of the prints must have stopped: there were tiny drops of blood, as if he'd been bleeding.

Foley had learned in Korea how to tell the direction of travel by the direction of the blood drops. They pointed toward the door.

This time, next to the print of the bare foot was the faint indication of a boot. Sergeant Foley snapped photos of the boot mark and the drops of blood, then opened the door.

A blast of cold, stale air came up from below, as if the tunnel itself was breathing. It smelled as if an animal had died down there: a fading stench, but there was no mistaking it.

"Are you ready for this?" he said to Officer Landers.

Landers swallowed hard, but his answer was firm enough. "I'm ready, Sarge."

Foley unholstered his .38 and scanned the brick steps for additional signs of blood. Landers, seeing this, did the same.

They descended slowly, all their senses

alert, with Landers in front. A few steps down from the door, he swayed and caught himself against the wall. He stared at it as if he'd never seen anything like it before. "Jesus, is the entire hospital made of brick?" His voice sounded both loud and muffled, as if the air was trying to swallow it up.

"Looks like it," Foley said.

"It must have taken years," Landers said.

Foley nodded. The walls arched together overhead, and the stairway curved downward. It was like being inside the body of a snake. There were light fixtures every few feet on the left-hand side, but some of the bulbs had burned out and not been replaced. In between the ones that worked, it was almost pitch black.

Neither of them had a flashlight. Foley cursed himself for not thinking ahead. There was no way they were finding any evidence here, not without light.

He knew he should turn back, but something made him keep on going. The air grew even more stale and cold. They should get some K-9's in there, Foley thought--use the dogs to sniff out the trail.

The stairway ended abruptly in a tunnel that ran off in both directions. There was light here--almost enough to blind him after the dark above. Bulbs were out here, too, but not so many. He could easily see the red-brick walls and floor and the arched ceiling.

There were storm gutters embedded in each side of the floor, indicating that storms outside could flood the tunnel--as in fact the freak storm had. Half an inch of water filled the gutters.

Foley had two pictures left in the camera, enough to get a shot of each direction. As he focused the lens, he saw a symbol drawn in fresh blood on the floor, just underneath one of the lights, as if whoever had put it there wanted it to be seen. It was an arrow pointing down the tunnel, fletched with the numbers 6-6-6.

"'The Beast is always watching,'" Foley said under his breath, snapping a picture of the arrow.

"What?" Landers said. He sounded jumpy.

"Nothing," Foley said. "I have one picture left. Let's see if we can find another sign."

"Do we have to?" Landers said. "Listen, Sarge. You know these tunnels go on and on. We won't be finding anything down here by ourselves, not without light. Let's go back and get the K-9 unit and--"

Foley's thoughts exactly. He stared at the arrow, then at the camera. What was he doing down here, anyway?

He was like a K-9 himself sometimes, so caught up in the thrill of the hunt that he forgot to follow procedure.

Procedure was about safety. He'd been taught that at the police academy, too.

He shot the arrow from another angle. The camera, hitting the end of the film, started the automatic rewind. The sudden whirring sound made them both jump.

He took a deep breath and turned back toward the stairs. "Let's get out of here," he said.

This time he led the way back up through the belly of the snake toward the morgue. A faint but distinct buzzing sound came down from above, growing louder as they ascended. The flies were leaving the morgue and streaming down into the tunnel, following the trail of blood.

#

After I filled out the application, Steve Haskell escorted me outside to have a look around the campus. "We train on the job," he said: "you learn by doing. You'll be assigned to a specific ward, but you'll be called to other wards to assist the staff there with problem patients. You'll get to know those firsthand, but most of them are housed in the rear wings."

"I'm not worried," I said. And I wasn't. I needed the money, and I didn't think the crazy farm could throw anything worse at me than I'd been through in Vietnam.

Haskell might be thinking the same

thing. Or he might not. He walked me all the way out of the personnel building and headed toward the main entrance, which still had a few lingering cops. I looked for the fat Italian pig who'd tried to bust my balls, but I didn't see him. He must be inside.

Haskell's voice droned on in my ear. "This place used to be a whole town in the old days--post office, library, even its own cemetery." That made me twitch a bit, but not enough to interrupt him. "When you get a chance, stop in the library and look at the pictures of the place in its heyday. We had a farm, and gardens--some of the most beautiful perennial plantings this side of the Mississippi."

"Really?" I said, snapping back into focus. "Is there anything left of those?"

"A bit," he said. "You interested? We don't have any positions open in Landscaping and Grounds right now, but if one opens up, I can put you on the list."

I shrugged. I could dig in the dirt; I'd done enough of it in my grandfather's vegetable garden. It might be easier than wrangling crazies.

While Haskell went on with his guided tour, I kept quiet. I was trying to picture it in my head, the way he described it: back in the day.

Back in the Day

"Back in the day," Haskell said, "Middlesex Fells Reservation was twenty-five square miles of wildlife preserve and conservation area, just five miles north of Boston. It was full of whitetail deer, fox, coyote, even the occasional black bear.

"Then in the late 1800s came the state hospital. Back then, the philosophy for dealing with the mentally disabled--plus anyone else who didn't fit the definition of normal--was 'Out of sight, out of mind.' Insane Asylums, Lunatic Asylums, Hospitals for the Insane, sprang up all over.

"Middlesex Fells was one of the largest. Before it was built in 1870, towns and cities all over the state lined up to bid on it, but the state already owned the land here, and with the Hillcrest Reservoir and the woods around it, it was a good fit for the founders' philosophy. They were all about peace, tranquility and harmony with nature. We're not that far from Walden Pond here, after all." Haskell chuckled. I nodded and smiled.

"So in 1874 they finished building the Middlesex Fells Insane Asylum--you saw the sign over the entrance, right? Carved in granite and trimmed in marble, so it's too much trouble and expense to change, even though ten years or so ago we officially changed the name to Middlesex Fells State Mental Hospital. Still haven't changed any of the signs on the grounds, either. Budget, you know."

I nodded again. He launched back into his spiel. "So there it was, brand shiny new: 1200 acres, six hundred patients. You see how it's built, all those Gothic Revival piles, like cathedrals or Ivy League colleges--complete with ivy. They're supposed to look holy and welcoming, and tell everybody, 'Come on in, it's good here, you'll be happy.'

"The architect, Dr. Anthony H. Stoneridge was his name, was a big proponent of moral treatment for the mentally ill. He designed this and a number of other places all around the country to look like havens, retreats, rather than prisons--but don't be fooled. The whole point was to keep the patients in and everybody else out, for their often safety, he'd say, and the safety of the rest of the world, too. So he built the place with its own church, library, post office, laundry facilities, shops, movie theatre, vehicle maintenance buildings, and water supply. There was a farm to help feed the patients and staff, and a cemetery for those who died.

"The church was Dr. Stoneridge's pride and joy. It's good old Medford brick on the outside, like everything else here, but inside is all granite and marble. The floors are solid oak; the fixtures solid brass. See the cross up there on top of the bell tower? Cast iron, painted gold."

"It's landmark," I said. "You can see it for miles around."

"That's the point," he said. "Everyone knows what it is, and orients by it when they're hiking or biking around here.

"So," said Haskell, "that's the history. Here's the setup--back then as well as now: the more secure and quiet patients toward the front, the louder and more disturbed ones in the rear. Each section of a building is called a wing, and each wing houses a specific type of mental illness, criminal deviance, or back in the day, any other so-called abnormality. The point originally was to provide a bed for everyone and anyone.

"You've seen the administration building and the personnel building. The first three floors of Administration feature Admissions, the gift shop, the patient information office, and the library and archive, plus medical records, payroll, and various staff offices. The three floors above that consist of living quarters and offices for doctors and nurses on call. Down below, tunnels lead to the other buildings.

"Now if you look down there past Administration, see that three-story building? That's the medical facility, and also the movie theater. If a patient has a medical problem, or needs his teeth fixed or his eyes checked, that's where we take him."

"And if he needs some cinema therapy, too?" I asked.

Haskell laughed. "Yes, we have movie nights in the theater--and if anybody has a medical problem, he's right there to get patched up.

"Now as we go on past the medical center, these are the psychiatric wings extending out from it like a flying V. If you ever get a chance to fly over it, you can see it looks like a giant bird made of slate and brick and edged with aged copper. Administration is the bird's head and brain, the medical center is the body, and the psychiatric wings on the left and right are the bird's wings. The very tips of the wings hold the most severe cases of mental illness: the most deviant, and the criminally insane. Those are the locked wards. Maximum security, minimum chance of escape."

#

I waited for more, but Haskell's narrative had finally wound down. I looked out over the grounds, and one thing made itself all too clear to me.

"With all due respect," I said, "it appears that the place has deteriorated some since 'back in the day.'"

I meant my remark to be humorous, but Haskell wasn't laughing.

"I'll be honest with you," he said. "Back in the day, this hospital was really something. Good things happened here. Good work got done.

"But that was then."

This is Now

"Now," said Haskell, "this is one messed-up place. I don't know any other way to put it. Strange shit happens here, and I don't just mean in the psychiatric wards. If you're a praying man, it would do you good to say a few extra.

"The State of Massachusetts keeps the woods in pristine condition, but nobody can say the same for the state mental facility. The war in Vietnam cost plenty, and one of the numerous casualties of the war's budget is maintaining the country's mental facilities.

"This hospital is overcrowded and understaffed, and it lacks the funds to improve either condition. There's nobody to hack down the ivy that's strangling the buildings. The perennial gardens are choked with weeds. The farm's long gone--animals died off, crops grew over with grass and disappeared. They sold off the farm equipment years ago, or left it to rot. The church hasn't been used in years; all that beautiful granite and marble and oak is crumbling away inside. The bell in the tower hasn't been rung for decades.

"Back in the day, if you came onto the grounds, you felt this amazing sense of peacefulness and calm. Today, I'm sure you've smelled the stink that comes off the buildings, like something in there is long dead.

"And maybe something is. The war may have stripped the funding from patient care, but there's always a few hundred thousand in the kitty for so-called research on the less fortunate members of society: the lost causes, or the ones whose families and friends gave up on them long ago. You'll hear them in there, screaming while the doctors experiment on them. The worst, the failures and the rejects, are left to die in brick-walled rooms that stink of urine and feces, and when they finally let go, their only remembrance is a round stone set flat in the ground and carved with a number and a letter: P for Protestant, C for Catholic."

"Muslims, Jews, and Native shamans need not apply?" That slipped out before I could stop it. Steve Haskell's honesty, and his bitterness, shocked me more than a little bit. "So why do you stay?"

"Because somebody's got to," he said. "Somebody has to care, even if it doesn't do much good. In a place like this, there's no way you can avoid the sadists: staff members who prey on people's misery, with no one to call on for help, and worse, no one to care. There are just a few of them here as anywhere, but those few rule with an iron fist. Nothing is too sick or depraved for them, even rape of both male and female. But I can try, you know? I can do what I can.

"It's a jungle in there. I won't lie to you. Facilities designed for six hundred patients now hold 1400, with patients two and sometimes four to a single room. Patient-on-patient abuse is epidemic. The weak and the feeble suffer most, and suffer constantly."

If he wanted me to turn around and run like hell, he was doing a good job of it. But I could tell he knew I was made of tougher stuff--like him. Like everybody he tried to bring in, to help as much as they could. I listened and I remembered and I learned. And I kept my eyes open, like a hunter in the woods.

Labyrinth

Tommy followed instinct down the stairs to the tunnel after he left the resting place, or birthing place, of the morgue. He had pulled his boots on, and still wore the blood-soaked sheet his body had been wrapped in after his death, to savor the moment, so to speak. He was aware that the sheet was dripping with blood and leaving a trail. He hoped someone would follow it.

The voices of tormented souls echoed up from the tunnel, punctuated by moans of agony. He flew down the stairs toward them, skipping two or three steps at a time, with never a trip or a stumble. His balance was perfect.

At the bottom he turned left, stopping briefly to leave a message before he ran on. And on.

Finally he reached a crossroads. "An intersection of the abyss," he said, giggling to himself. He turned left again, and as he did, he knew that the hospital was no longer above him.

He was exactly where he was supposed to be. He had executed many terrible deeds to get here, as had been foretold in his dreams.

A hundred yards past the crossroads, he found a manhole cover in the middle of the floor, and heard the roar of water beneath.

He pried up the steel cover with effortless and inhuman strength. The rungs of a steel ladder went down the shaft. He could feel the surge of power through his body as he descended, like the rush of rain water through the pipes.

All of it was in honor of his birth--the storm, the floods, the destruction. God was not happy. And that made Tommy stop, just as the ladder ended on a dry ledge above the flood, and laugh until the tears ran down his face.

When he had run out of laughter, which was a good long time, he peered down the pipe. Shafts of sunlight pierced the darkness, marking the locations of sewer drains high above. They stabbed his eyes with pain, but they showed him what he needed to do.

These pipes must lie underneath the whole of Medford and run straight through to the Mystic River. He could go anywhere they went, and nothing above would know that he was there.

He grinned in delight. His Master had thought of everything.

He would test this means of travel tonight, with a visit to an old friend. But for now, he would just keep fucking with the bastard's mind.

#

A quarter of the way up the stairway from the tunnel, a swarm of fat black flies exploded in Sergeant Foley and Officer Landers' faces. They had had warning, could see and hear the swarm coming, but it came on too fast and hit too hard. They had no time to react.

They fell backwards, tumbling end over end down the stairs, crashing to a halt at the bottom. They lay for a few moments, sorting themselves out and counting scrapes and bruises.

"What in the name of sweet Jesus--" Officer Landers began, then stopped, either because he remembered that his superior officer was a religious man, or because he had run out of words to say.

Sergeant Foley lurched to his feet, braced for further attack. The camera was crushed beyond repair, but that was not a disaster: the film canisters were safe in his pocket. He had what he needed from that.

He wrapped the camera strap tightly around his hand and lunged back up the stairs, with Landers half a step behind. At the top he found the two officers he had left on guard standing in front of a wide-open door. One leaned against the wall with his hands over the face. The other just about leaped into Foley's arms, babbling nine miles a minute.

"We heard this buzzing, Sarge, louder

and louder, coming from the morgue. We thought there was something electrical, you know, and we didn't want it to contaminate the crime scene, so we--so they--they just--"

"Calm down," Foley said. "Take your time. It's not your fault. Just tell me exactly what happened."

The kid swallowed. "The buzzing--it got louder and louder. We opened the door to take a look. We--I can't--I don't--I never saw--"

The other officer lowered his hands from his face. It was dead white. He was in borderline shock, Foley realized. His voice was a flat monotone. "The blood turned into flies. Millions and millions of flies. Turned into flies and flew away. Flew . . . away . . ."

The words trailed off. That was all he would say for hours afterward.

Foley peered inside the morgue. The first officer was still babbling behind him. "Sarge, they burst through the door, there was no way, we couldn't stop them, we tried, they wouldn't stop, they wouldn't--"

He tuned the yammering voice out and concentrated on the evidence in front of him. The drawer was still open, and the lights were all on. Everything was exactly the same--except for one thing. The stainless steel tray gleamed. The walls and floor were pristine. There was not a spot of blood to be seen.

"Let's get out of here," Foley said.

Divine Meeting

As Haskell and I approached the main building of the hospital, he called out to one of the cops still gathered in front. "Yo! Sergeant Foley!"

The cop turned at the sound of his name. He had a grim look on his face--not the kind of expression I wanted to get in the way of.

"I'll just head on out," I said to Haskell, "if you've got business with--"

"No, no," Haskell said. "I want you to meet him. He's a good man and a good friend, and the best judge of character I know. Probably as good as your grandfather."

So, I thought. I was still being interviewed. Would I still have the job after I got vetted by the good Sergeant?

I eyed him doubtfully as he came up to us. He wore a crucifix on one lapel and an M.P.D. pin on the other. The other cops had M.P.D. pins on both sides. Must be a chaplain, I thought.

Well, that explained why Haskell thought this Foley might share some skills with my grandfather. I wasn't so sure. What did these men know about me or my people?

There were people around, cops, orderlies, a nurse or two, but the whole place had gone deathly and eerily silent. Foley's hand seemed to take forever to reach toward mine.

"Brian," he said. "Brian Foley."

"Barry Redcrow," I said.

Our hands met. I felt a spark, a warm, bright, electric feeling running through my body. As my eyes met Foley's, I saw that he felt it, too.

A clap of thunder shattered the clear sky. The silence broke.

A guttural scream of rage burst from the ground beneath our feet. It echoed and re-echoed through the grounds, and then abruptly faded.

Nika shrieked like a man who has been shot. Where was she? God, how could I have forgotten her?

I tried to look away, to find her, but I couldn't unlock my gaze from Foley's. Everywhere, all around us, dogs seemed to be howling in terror.

Finally Foley's gaze let me go. He looked up at the sky, as if he could see the thunder itself. Then he turned back toward me, withdrew his hand from mine and said, "God Bless."

While I stood staring, he bowed his head and made the sign of the Cross and said, "In the name of the Father and of the Son and of the Holy Ghost."

He left me there, and the rest of the cops followed him. I heard one of them, a very young one, ask shakily, "Sarge, what the hell is going on here?"

A flock of mourning doves flew up and over Foley's head as he answered, "Hell is exactly what's going on here."

#

A short distance away, the Preacher lay

in wait, hidden in a storm drain. Instinct had brought him up toward the surface, but he didn't know why.

He could hear the voices of the men above him. They were talking about him, about the show he had put on. He laughed at that. The real show hadn't even begun.

He slithered like a snake through the pipes, flat on his belly with his arms pressed to his sides. Where patches of sunlight marked drain covers, he sped up, in case Someone might be watching.

Two people started talking above him. One of those voices, out of all he had heard, filled him with hate and disgust and inexplicable anger. He had a sudden, overwhelming need to see whose it was, and destroy it.

Just short of the storm drain he stopped and looked up. A black dude stood talking to a man who looked like an Indian. The black dude's voice wasn't the one. Then the Indian answered, and the Preacher went blind with rage and hate.

This man's soul did not deserve to live.

It had no spirit in it. Even the pathetic junkies and scumbag whore hippies had some fire in them. This Indian had none.

The Preacher would take this man's life and send his soul to Hell, where it would be a slave forever. The Master had given him that power: to take such souls as he saw fit.

He would eat the Indian's eyes first, because the eyes were the doorway to the soul. The Preacher slithered closer to the drain cover, studying his prey, but taking great care to stay in the shadows.

Then he saw a third man, a man he knew, and all his glee and his unholy hunger evaporated in a surge of pure fear. "Holy Man," he whispered, or hissed.

Up above, the man said his name, introducing himself to the Indian: "Brian. Brian Foley."

The Holy Man's hand touched the Indian's, and thunder split the sky. The Preacher's raw scream of rage followed hard upon it, echoing and re-echoing, for he had no need to stop for breath.

The tunnels around him vibrated. Creatures of all kinds scurried for cover, from the rats in the sewers to the dogs in the yards above.

Foley was a Power--an Enemy. His spirit burned bright and eternal. He had recognized something in the Indian that the Preacher had not.

Above them all, the evil and the good and the one who, as yet, was neither, a red-tailed hawk shrieked, followed by the wail of a coyote.

The Preacher writhed on the floor of the tunnel and gnashed his teeth. The Indian must suffer. As for Foley--that had not been included in the plan. He would have to await instructions from the Master.

He unfolded his limbs and sprang up like a hound of Hell and sprinted back the way he had come, and then down, clinging to the side of the pipe like an insect. Down as far as he could go, one foot closer to Hell with each step. Cursing the whole way. "Fucking Foley! Fucking Holy Man!"

Home Sweet Home

Barretto reached the sanctuary of his front door in a state of near-collapse, and almost kicked the door in rather than try to get his key into the lock with wildly shaking fingers.

"Once I'm in I'll be good," he said to himself over and over, like a prayer. "Gotta be in to win."

That struck him as hysterically funny-- especially the hysterical part. He cackled like a loon as he lumbered down the basement stairs toward the locker where he kept his hunting gear. He popped it open and pulled out a Mossberg 12-gauge shotgun and a Remington 30-06 rifle.

"You want a battle?" he yelled at the air. "I'll give you a battle!"

He carried the guns and an armload of boxes of ammo over to the bar and loaded them, then went back to the locker for the .45 that was always loaded. He stuck the pistol in his belt and carried the guns

215

upstairs.

He looked out each window before shutting and locking it. With each window he secured, he felt more confident, until the house was locked up tight.

When everything was barricaded against invasion, he went back down to the bar and grabbed a bottle of Jackie D. Tony Neveska, may he rest in peace, had always favored the Jack Daniels. Barretto saluted him with a long slug from the bottle.

Then it hit him. He'd beat the ever-living shit out of Tony's only surviving son. Tony, his partner, his fellow cop. His old buddy. "My God," he said, almost ready to throw up. "What did I do? <u>What did I do?</u>"

He took another blast from the bottle and took it back upstairs, turning on the television to see if he was on the news. Unsurprisingly, the only thing that caught anybody's attention today was the freak storm.

He had almost forgotten that. Almost as if he was the storm, or at least a part of it.

He kept hitting on the Jackie D, feeling

more relaxed with each swallow, reassuring himself that it was all for the sake of his beloved Baron. He kept at it all the rest of the day, except when he mounted an expedition to the fridge for a beer chaser.

Every time he did that, he paused, dreading to find Baron's dead eyes staring at him from the shelf. But the dog's body was gone, buried in the back yard with an empty bottle of Jack Daniels for a headstone.

The more he drank, the clearer his head seemed to get. He brooded over what he had done to the kid, and how he was going to get away with it.

He was still in his uniform with the empty holster that had housed his police-issue .38. The 30-06 rested against his chair, fully loaded, safety off, along with the other guns.

He picked up each one of them periodically to make sure he could see the red dot on the gun, insuring that the safety was off: the rifle, the shotgun, the .45.

"Red is dead," he said.

His eyes grew heavier with each shot of whiskey, until the loaded shotgun rested across his lap and the .45 hung precariously in the holster made for the .38. He remained on watch, waiting. Waiting and wondering who, if anyone, he should call.

No, no. He was not going to call anyone and start whining about angry ghosts. Someone would check in with him. Be sure he was all right. Let him know what he was in for for knocking over that dog-murdering little son of a bitch.

The phone never rang. Nobody came to the door. Louis Barretto was all alone with his guns and his good friend Jackie D.

#

I got a warm feeling when I shook the cop's hand. Friendly, warm, inviting, as if we were destined to meet.

It kind of freaked me out, but when I looked into the cop's eyes--Foley's eyes--I sensed that he had the exact same feeling.

And the thunder. What the hell was that about? There wasn't a cloud in the sky, yet the ground all around us seemed to radiate electricity.

Haskell was talking to me, but I didn't hear a word he was saying. All I could think about was the cop, Foley.

I snapped out of it when I felt Haskell tugging at my arm. "What?" I said.

"I said," he said, "you want me to assign you a bed? Snap out of it, man. Someone's going to think you're a patient."

I looked around. Foley and the cops were gone. It was just the two of us again, in front of the administration building, with a clear sky overhead and no thunder within sight or sound.

By the time I got my head straight, Haskell had shown me around the main entrance and most of the administration building, and I was beginning to think that this might not be such a bad gig, despite the freaky start. Most of the staff seemed extremely relaxed, and I could see that more than a few were stoned up nice from a recent "smoke break."

"It's a lot more active in the day and evening than it is at night," Haskell said. "At night it's real quiet."

"I like it quiet," I said.

We went on from the administration building to the first of the locked psychiatric units. Haskell filled me in as we went: ten wards, labeled A through J; four floors per unit, and the most disruptive patients stowed away in the rear of each unit, for the reasons he'd explained to me earlier.

The guards in the units wore white, buttoned-up, long-sleeved shirts with white pants, black shoes and black bow ties. "Am I going to have to dress in one of those ice-cream suits?" I asked Haskell.

"Afraid so," he said. "All the security staff have to wear uniforms, to keep the patients from impersonating guards and orchestrating an escape. No one in, no one out, without the nod from the ice-cream man."

He laughed. I echoed him, none too comfortably.

The floor we were on at the time was filled to capacity. I began to see what Haskell had been telling me about budget problems, understaffing and patient overcrowding.

The patients seemed to be lost in their own worlds, oblivious to the others around them. One was deep in conversation with the sock puppet on his hand. A woman wandered around aimlessly, repeating over and over, "Oh my God! Oh My God! <u>Oh My God</u>!" Every couple of steps, she stopped and spun completely around.

Electrical burns spiraled down her body from head to toe. "She stripped the insulation off an electrical wire, wrapped herself in it and plugged herself in," Haskell said. "Some of the patients call her the human candy cane."

I could see that. I could also see how very not funny it would be for staff to say the same thing.

I was almost relieved to see a couple of patients beyond her who looked quite normal. One, a very attractive woman, was drawing intently on an artist's pad. Another played a board game by himself. I wondered what their problems were, and why they were in here with all the obvious crazies.

That Night . . .

Sergeant Brian Foley lay beside his lovely wife Rita in their second-floor bedroom. The window was open, and the cool night air swayed the new curtains Rita had put up just a few days before, brushing them gently against the bed.

Rita had long since fallen asleep. Foley drifted in and out, enjoying the opportunity to sleep with the window open after a long, cold New England winter.

It was a very quiet night, as usual in West Medford. In the distance he could hear the long wailing cry of a cat in heat.

There were woods just behind the house, and the Mystic Lakes just beyond that. Animals, domesticated or not, often prowled the area at night. It seemed early in the year for a cat to be in heat, but nevertheless, common enough.

The cat's yearning echoed through the neighborhood. Brian Foley wondered if anybody else lay awake listening and feeling for the poor suffering thing. Each cry was louder, longer, deeper in tone and more drawn out, and it seemed to be making its way toward him. If there had been any other cops here, at least a couple of them would have been making jokes about a pussy looking for some pussy.

It wouldn't find anything here, though the latest serenade seemed to be coming from right next door. Their Rottweiler Miranda had passed away a few years ago, and he and his wife had never had the heart to replace her.

Damn, that cat was loud. It sounded as if it was the size of a puma--and also as if it was howling right outside the window, which was impossible, because the bedroom was two stories up, and there was no roof or ledge for the thing to climb on.

He turned to his wife to see if the caterwauling had woken her up. She was sound asleep, but she pulled the covers up close to her neck as he watched.

He shivered. It had suddenly become a

lot colder. The cat was still screaming outside, loud enough to wake the dead, if not, apparently, the living who were lucky enough to be asleep.

He stood up and crossed the short distance from the bed to the window. A shadow flickered past outside, but by the time he pulled the thin curtains back, it was gone.

The air was downright unpleasantly cold. It smelled putrid, as if something was rotting right outside the window. He bent to peer out, and found himself face to face with the horribly beaten, swollen features of Tommy Neveska.

The vision's eyes were pure white, almost glowing, with the tiniest pinpricks of pupils. The purple lacerations on his cheeks and forehead seemed to wriggle like worms.

"Holy Man," the dead man said in a hissing whisper. He threw his head back and let out the blood-curdling battle screech of a fighting tomcat.

It was a wicked, wild, otherworldly

sound. He laughed crazily, louder and louder, until he broke off abruptly, grinned like a lunatic and yelled at the top of his lungs, *"Holy Man!"*

#

Foley jumped backward in his bed, and fell onto his wife. She woke with a cry. "What is it? Brian--Brian, what's wrong?"

Foley silenced her with a finger on her lips. She was a policeman's wife, she knew what that meant. She lay perfectly silent, eyes wide, while he retrieved his .38 from the dresser and returned to the window.

He was sweating profusely, and his breath came in desperate gulps as if he'd been underwater too long.

Neveska was gone. There was no cat, and no smell of death. The breeze that rippled the curtains seemed warm again.

He left Rita in bed, ran down the stairs and outside to the yard, but there was no sign that anyone had come on the property that night. The neighborhood was completely quiet, only the faint hint of crickets.

Rita caught up with him in the yard below the bedroom window. She was breathing hard, as if she had been running, but her voice was perfectly steady. "Come back to bed, Brian. It was just another dream."

That was what Foley had been telling himself, but he didn't believe it.

But what else could it have been? Nothing could have got up there, unless it could fly. There was nothing to hold on to. It was just house. All house. Straight up and straight down.

Rita wrapped her arms around him and held on tight. He hugged her back. She was holding it together, but he could tell that he had spooked her badly this time. "I'm sorry, honey," he said.

She shook her head and buried her face in his chest. He lifted his face, turning it toward the sky. It was the last gasp of night before the daylight: part dark, part light.

"What happened at that hospital yesterday?" Rita asked him. Her voice seemed to come up from his heart.

Foley felt a rush of utter sadness, and he had no idea why. Something was terribly wrong. He should be in mourning, he thought, but for what, or why, he did not know.

Something felt strange, not painful exactly, but not right, either. He looked down at his hands, turning them palms up. As he watched, a faint purplish bruise appeared in the center of each.

#

I woke in the middle of an enormous lake with my arms wrapped around the neck of a strapping white horse. The horse was swimming smoothly and powerfully toward the shore. Everything around us was dark, but with the approaching dawn, I could just make out the thin line between water and land.

I looked all around at the dark water,

expecting to be attacked from below--by whom or what, I did not know, but just had that feeling of imminent doom. All the while, I clung to this powerful animal that worked so hard to save my life. I could feel the muscles in his neck flexing with every stroke.

Total silence surrounded us, except for the barely audible splashing of water. The magnificent beast seemed to know exactly where he was going. He swam faster than any horse I had ever seen, and I sensed that he was not frightened, only determined to deliver his cargo safely to its destination.

Soon the shore was upon us. I spotted the tiny flicker of a fire just inland from the shore line, and slid off the horse's back onto the beach.

As soon as I let go, the horse broke with amazing speed toward the forest. His glimmering white coat flashed through the trees, and his hoofbeats echoed like passing thunder.

The putrid smell of death assaulted me,

waking memories of the horrors of war. The air was very cold. As I walked forward, the distant fire grew larger, and I came upon the dead and rotting bodies of the people of my reservation.

My people! I was at the place of my birth, and my family and friends lay dead and rotting before me. Slaughtered by evil--for these people had no known enemies.

The hair rose on every inch of my body. My feet carried me forward with no will or instruction from me.

Flies swarmed on the bodies, feasting on their rotting flesh. The houses beyond lay darkened and empty. I moved on past them toward the fire.

There my grandfather sat within a circle of fire. He stared at me but did not speak.

I tried to enter the ring of fire, but as I stepped forward, its walls grew higher, barring my way. Still with his eyes fixed on me, Grandpa pointed toward a house on his left-hand side. I was to enter, the gesture said.

He looked away then and gazed into the

fire. He had not said a word. And that frightened the living snot out of me.

I turned from him toward the house. It had no windows, just an opening where a door had once been. The entrance was dark.

A great horned owl glided silently out of the forest and hovered in front of me like a gigantic hummingbird, body motionless, wings a blur. Its eyes looked directly into mine, and they spoke of great knowledge and mystery.

As swiftly as the owl appeared, it spun and darted back into the forest, and perched on a tree just beyond the darkened house.

There were no rooms inside, only a stairwell made all of red brick, from the dark, narrow steps to the arched ceiling. It descended steeply, twisting and turning. I got the feeling that if I were to lose my balance, I would fall into the abyss.

With great apprehension, I walked down the steps to the darkness. The smell of death and rotting flesh grew stronger in the cold damp air. I could hear the distant humming of flies, so powerful that it sounded like electrical power lines.

As I balanced myself against the wall, I felt something faintly slimy under my hands. Blood.

After what seemed like an eternity, I reached the bottom. A man stood there with his back toward me, dressed in a white priest's robe. The robe shone in that place of darkness. His hands were bandaged, and seemed to be bleeding quite badly: blood dripped from them and fell to the floor.

Flies swarmed in the stairwell, but none came near the man in the white robe. With his right hand he gathered blood from the wound in his left and wrote something on the wall. What it was, I couldn't see.

I looked left and right. An arched tunnel of red brick led in both directions. Every ten or twelve feet, I saw semicircular support arches, also of brick.

I glanced back. The man in the white robe had turned to face me. He held out his heavily bleeding, bandaged hands as if offering them to me.

I saw that his bare feet were also bandaged, and also bleeding badly. He wiped his brow with his sleeve, and the sleeve came away covered in blood.

The man was Brian Foley, the cop I had met at the hospital, the cop who had shared thunder with me. His eyes were greatly troubled as he stepped aside to let me see what he had written on the wall with his own blood.

The words glowed like blood-red neon lights, dripping down the wall. <u>Fear Not Evil. Fear Not Death!</u>

Foley pointed down the tunnel. Shadows closed in, bringing with them indescribable cold and the stench of death.

I wanted to run, but they were closing in too fast. I looked back at Foley. The words were gone, replaced with numbers and a single word, again written in glowing blood: *Psalm 105:4*

Foley looked on me with deep compassion, still pointing down the tunnel toward the shadows. My feet would not carry me either toward Foley or back up the stairs.

The shadows swarmed toward me. I stood frozen in such terror as I had never known before. Out of the advancing darkness, countless voices wailed in torment and suffering.

In the instant before the shadows swallowed me, I woke. It was the hour when darkness fought daylight: morning twilight.

Showtime

Louis Barretto awoke to the sound of scratching on his roof, like a desperate animal trying to claw its way through the shingles. It was cold, very cold, and he could see his breath rising in front of his face.

Barretto sat up straight and scanned the room. All the doors and windows were shut tight, just the way he had left them.

A soft droning buzz swelled around him. A handful of fat black flies circled his head. He swiped at them violently, and the 12-gauge in his lap fell the floor.

The sound of clawing on wood had grown louder. As he strained to hear, a faint but steady *tap, tap, tap* joined it. The air grew even colder; he choked on its foul smell.

"What the hell," Barretto said. He must have been passed out for hours. His head was heavy from the Jack Daniels; as he reached down for the shotgun, it started to pound.

Something was not right. He could feel in the air that he was not alone. On the roof, the sound of innumerable wings joined the clawing and tapping.

Something was about to happen. Barretto wanted to get up and run, but where would he run to?

The unnatural noises kept getting louder. He could feel the cold air penetrate his chest like stake of ice driven right through him. Dread and sadness overwhelmed him. He shuddered. "What did I do . . . what did I do." It was not a question.

The cacophony on the roof vibrated through his body. Then suddenly it stopped.

Before he could sag back in relief, the television turned on by itself, blaring at top volume. A doctor in a surgical mask bent over a patient who lay motionless on the operating table. The grainy black-and-white picture zoomed closer and closer. Barretto leaned forward, craning to see what would happen next--and working up the balls to shut the damn thing off.

The camera focused in closer and closer to the patient's face--closer, closer, so close that finally he recognized his own face. It was Louis Barretto who lay on the table.

His mouth and eyes were sewn shut with thick dark thread. His hands were sutured to the sides of his head, completely covering his ears.

The surgeon pulled down his mask and stared directly into Barretto's eyes. "See no evil, speak no evil, hear no evil." His voice was low and guttural. He laughed crazily, pulled the mask back up and went back to work on his patient.

The television shut off by itself. Barretto pumped two rounds of buckshot into it, sobbing and crying.

Whatever was on the roof went crazy. The flies massed around him. The frigid air stank of death.

A voice spoke, a familiar voice. It did not surprise Barretto at all. It was dark and calm and profoundly malevolent. "Did you know that it's cold in Hell, Louis?"

Barretto turned to face the speaker. In that moment, two things happened. His hair instantly turned snow white, and he never spoke again.

#

Sergeant Foley picked up the telephone just before 7:00 a.m. It was Jimmy Landers, quavering and apologetic. "It's Louis Barretto, Sarge," he said.

Between yesterday's events and the nightmare that had thrown him out of a sound sleep in the dark before dawn, and now this, Foley's temper snapped. "What's that asshole done now?"

"It's not what he's done, Sarge," Jimmy said, even shakier than before, "but what's been done to him."

That chilled Foley's temper thoroughly. Whatever he thought of Barretto, the man was a human being. He deserved at least some consideration. "Is he all right?"

"He's being transferred to the Fells

Reservation for psych evaluation," Landers answered. "He's in Lawrence Memorial now. Somebody done him up real bad. Real, real bad."

The kid sounded ready to crack. God knew how close Foley was to it, and Landers was a rookie. Foley pitched his voice to be level and calm, and said carefully, "Tell me exactly what happened. Piece by piece. Just like in the book."

Landers gulped audibly over the line. Foley braced for hysterics, but the kid had guts. He got control of himself and said almost steadily, if just a little bit too fast, "One of Barretto's neighbors reported hearing gunfire coming from his house. When the patrol units arrived, they found all the doors locked. They kicked the front door in and found Barretto sitting a rocking chair with his eyes and mouth sutured shut and his hands sewn to the sides of his head. And his hair--his hair was dead white." Landers sobbed for breath. He was losing it again. "In a locked house, Sarge. A locked house. And on the fridge--on the fridge--was a message written in blood."

Landers stopped. Foley waited for him to go on, but he seemed to have run out of gas. "Well?" Foley prompted.

"We're going to test," Landers said, "to test--"

Foley cut him off. "What did the message say?"

"It said," said Landers, "<u>See no evil, speak no evil, hear no evil</u>."

"I'll meet you at the Fells Hospital," Foley said.

#

On his way out the door, Foley noticed something strange. A flock of mourning doves sat peacefully on the stack of wood he had been cutting up for the fireplace. There were about thirty of them, and a couple were even perched on the handle of the axe that he'd left sticking out of the last split log.

They didn't scatter as the timid birds usually do. Foley got the feeling he could pick up each one of them if he wanted to. He paused less than a foot away from the ones perched on the ax. They stared up at him without flinching, as if they had known him all his life.

They made him feel warm inside. He blessed himself, and the doves flew up all together and settled in the huge old tree in front of the house. There were others in the tree already--hundreds of them, so many they filled every branch, all the way to the top.

Patient Art

I got the call a couple of hours after I got home from the grand tour, asking me if I was available to work the day shift. "Guess I really did get the job," I said.

The person on the other end of the line didn't laugh. It was a weak joke, anyway. "7:00 to 3:00," she said. "Be on time."

"I'll be there," I said. And I would. I was glad to get the opportunity to make some cash.

#

I'd been told my first day on the job would be in one of the quieter units. But looking down the long hallway at 7:00 a.m., seeing it packed with fruitcakes, I wasn't so sure.

Joe Burke, the orderly I'd met yesterday, was more or less in charge of getting me settled in the job. He took me down the corridor to the recreation room, where freshly medicated patients painted or drew pictures or played various types of board games. They all looked like I felt. I hadn't slept much, again. The nightmares wouldn't let me alone, even for a 6:00 a.m. wakeup call.

Joe showed me around, pointed out the stacks of board games and pointed me toward the display of art on the wall. Most of that wasn't much better than kindergarten level, but some was quite good. A few pieces were even spectacular.

We paused in front of a painting that really was professional quality. A beautifully colored rainbow curved upward over a mass of clouds. A line of people in single file ascended the arch. Angels with glorious wings hovered above them, smiling down. High over them all, the sun shone, casting forth beams in the shape of a cross.

The people on the rainbow's arch were smiling, but the ones on the ground, waiting in line to enter its glow, wore expressions of fear and apprehension. The path to the rainbow led past a pit of red bricks, in which sat the Devil with a pitchfork of fire. His face was a mask of rage and endless misery.

His throne was made of human bodies, some torn in half, some decapitated, and some impaled through the chest by the fiery tines. All of them wore the same expression. They were still alive. They could still feel, and what they felt was torment.

Flames roared all around them, as if the bricks themselves were made of fire. Farther below the Devil and his prey, at the very bottom of the canvas, hundreds of hands made of fire reached for the souls that the Devil had initiated, pulling them down into the bowels of the earth.

The painting was so detailed, it was as if the person whom had painted it had visited both the glory of Heaven and the torture of Hell. Joe and I stood in front of it in uncomfortable silence. While I was still trying to find something to say, the overhead speaker paged Joe to take a phone call.

He turned toward it in obvious relief. "Excuse me," he said. "That's Admissions. Probably a new 'student' on campus."

I nodded. He went off to the nurses' station to take the call. I stayed where I was, studying the painting.

While I stood there, a young woman came up beside me. I remembered her from yesterday: the attractive young lady I'd seen drawing in the day room. She had dark eyes with an air of mystery about them and long black hair, but her skin looked like it could use some sun.

"You don't approve," she said.

"That's not true," I said. "It's just . . . different. It's deep."

"That's the point," she said. "Art is supposed to open your mind and make you think for yourself." She held out her hand. "I'm Jessica Choofane. You're new here."

"I just started today," I said.

I shook her hand. It was warm but not sweaty. Soft and peaceful, but not as if she was medicated out of her mind.

She didn't seem crazy to me, but here she was. I got the feeling she was a kind person, gentle. Warm, like her hand.

"I take it you're the artist," I said.

She smiled. "Yes. Can you pick out anything else by me?"

"I'll try," I said, "but first I have a question."

"You want to know why the Devil in the painting seems so tormented. And frustrated."

She said it with perfect confidence. And she was right. That was exactly what I'd been thinking. Which surprised me.

"He's in Hell," she said. "Not even the Devil is happy in Hell. That's the point of being there."

"Is that what this hospital is?" I asked. "Hell?"

"You'll have to figure that one out for yourself," she answered. "I just provide the food for thought." Her smile faded; her face grew serious. "You'll either be here for a long, long time, or you'll move on right away."

"Is that right?" I said.

"That's right," she said. She followed me down along the wall of artwork till we came to another one that was even more fascinating than the first.

I glanced at her. Hers? She nodded. "Very good," she said.

This was a drawing in pencil, a portrait of a doctor and nurse standing side by side. Both were dressed in surgical gear: masks, caps, scrubs. They held their hands up the way surgeons do, to keep anything from contaminating their gloves. A stream of words emerged from the nurse's mouth: <u>At least we did everything we could, Doctor.</u>

Next to this portrait, on the same sheet of drawing paper, was a second portrait of the same doctor and nurse. Jesus hung on a cross behind them. In this panel, the surgical masks were off, and there were tears in the eyes of the doctor and the nurse. This time, the doctor spoke: *I know . . . but sometimes everything is not enough.*

I felt Jessica looking deep within me, probing my thoughts. I didn't know what to say, or how, except that there was something very different about her work. I wanted to take the drawing down and study it more closely. It spoke to me of great sorrow, helplessness, condemnation, all at the same time.

I took a step closer to the drawing. "Say something," she said.

I opened my mouth, but before I could speak, Joe said behind me, "Did you hear what I said? We got a guy coming in, all banged up in the head. Somebody put a mindfucking on a Medford cop. Sewed his face up with surgical sutures."

That jerked me out of my daze. Jessica was gone; I couldn't see her anywhere. I stared at Joe. "Sewed his face up? What? Shouldn't he be headed for the emergency room?"

"Already done," Joe said. "Poor bastard blew a fuse. Now we get him. We have to go down and meet him at the basement elevator. Hold onto your shorts, bro--this could get messy."

Great, I thought. My first serious crazy. I didn't know if I should celebrate or go hide.

"Just remember," Joe said, looking me in the eye. "Nobody gets refused entry to this campus."

I started to nod, and suddenly there was Jessica again, right in between us, as if she'd popped out of thin air. "Barry," she said, "don't listen to the voices."

"What voices?" I said. Thinking, OK, she's crazy after all.

Or maybe not. Joe had a look on his face, as if he knew what she was talking about. Maybe he was crazy, too.

"You'll know them when you hear them," she said. "Just ignore them and you'll be fine."

That wasn't exactly reassuring. Joe laid a hand on my shoulder. "Come on, Barry. We gotta go."

I wasn't sorry to leave Jessica and her odd warning behind, but it gnawed at me. As I followed Joe down the hallway, I asked, "What is she talking about?"

Joe shook his head. "Don't forget where you are. Some of them can seem very normal, but they're beaucoup messed up in the head."

That didn't answer my question, but it was the best I was going to get. I'd have to figure it out for myself--if there was anything to figure out. If it wasn't just a crazy lady being crazy.

#

The patient waiting for us at the basement elevator wouldn't be causing any trouble for a while. He was catatonic: dead in his own living body.

I didn't recognize him until I heard one of the cops say, "Can you believe this guy had a full head of black hair only yesterday?"

It was one of the Medford cops, the fat asshole who'd tried breaking my balls yesterday. Now he looked shrunken and fragile.

Though his face looked young, his hair was snow white. Suture marks around his eyes and mouth bled tiny dots of fresh blood. He stared off into the distance, drooling from the side of his mouth. He didn't seem to be feeling any pain.

I had seen that look many times in Vietnam. This guy was definitely not going to pose the problems Joe had thought he would.

Footsteps thudded down the stairs. For a second I was in last night's nightmare again, then the world settled back into its morning reality. Sergeant Brian Foley came striding toward us with Steve Haskell and a young cop tagging behind--same one I'd seen with him yesterday.

"We got a guy going bananas over at the J Ward," Haskell said to me. "You might as well come over and get your feet wet. That's where we all spend a lot of time."

I glanced at the man on the gurney. "Don't worry about Barretto," Foley said. "We'll keep an eye on him."

That struck me as a bit strange,

considering they weren't hospital staff, but Haskell seemed good with it. I can't say I was sorry to leave that poor torn-up bastard behind, though whatever J Ward was, it didn't sound too good, either.

J Ward turned out to be in another building, and we would get there through the basement tunnels. But first we had to take security precautions.

J Ward was an Extreme Caution Unit. That meant empty pockets--no keys, no change, nothing an inmate could get his hands on and turn into a weapon. We had to leave all those things at the nurses' station and go in, as it were, unarmed.

Once we were judged safe to go, we went down. Straight through the belly of the snake into the brick tunnels, just like the ones I'd seen in my dream. I kept glancing over my shoulder, looking for the shadows that must be on my heels.

"My Love is Vengeance--that's never free." -The Who

Extreme Caution Unit

Adam Sampson had been incarcerated in the Extreme Caution Unit for approximately five years. He had made a name for himself in the <u>Medford Daily Mercury</u>, and become a bit of a celebrity in the rest of the country as well.

Adam Sampson liked--no, loved--fire. Fire had been his passion since 1965.

In 1965, in a place unknown to the world at large but well known to the men who fought there, a terrible battle took place. The country was Vietnam, and the valley was called Ia Drang. Although there were numerous casualties, it was ultimately determined to be a victory by the U.S. Government. As a result, the U.S. declared Vietnam a war that could be won "helicopter style."

Everything, the powers that be

maintained, would be flown in and out by helicopter. Supplies, troops, attacks-- choppers would handle them all. And the enemy would pay hell for it.

The enemy did pay hell. So did Adam Sampson.

He and a number of other soldiers were engaged in heavy fighting when an air strike was called in close to their position. More than half of his platoon was vaporized instantly by the napalm, and the remaining soldiers wished they had been.

Sampson was badly burned over half of his body, as the flaming jelly seared through his clothing and mercilessly attacked his skin. There was simply no stopping it. No stopping it at all.

It fucked him up in the head real bad, and he had a lot of time to think about that as he lay in a burn unit in Japan. "No stoppin' fire like that," he would repeat over and over to himself.

While the men next to him screamed and burned, his mind spun around and around. Some of them seemed to smile with their charred black bodies and their bright white teeth shining through. None of their teeth had been that white before they were burned beyond recognition.

Funny what a man's mind got to thinking of when Hell came rolling in. The smell. There was nothing like it at all, that Sampson had ever experienced. The smell of burning human flesh. Nothing quite like it really. Especially his own.

Nothing quite like the irony, either, of being able to smell his own burning flesh, and actually live to remember how joyous it was. The nightmares never went away. And Sampson would never be the same.

No ears. No body hair. Lips all but burned away, his nose just a hole. His eyes had made it through unscathed: when the flames rushed at him in seeming slow motion, he had protected them with his arm.

He looked like a human raccoon, with the band of healthy skin around his eyes, and the rest of his face basically not there. His torso was completely untouched, thanks to his flak jacket.

"He's one of the lucky ones," the doctors said.

Sampson never felt lucky. Every so often he spoke aloud to himself, usually the same words. "The cold hard truth."

He looked at himself in the mirror once. Once. After that he smashed every scrap of glass that happened to catch his reflection.

He couldn't go back to Wisconsin, not looking like this. He tried to run away from himself. He traveled around the country, but attracted the same stares everywhere.

Finally he embraced the cold hard truth. He was a part of the fire. The fire owned him--right up until he was arrested.

Sampson loved fire. He also loved churches--and setting them on fire as the parishioners left Mass.

It was beautiful how it worked. A five-gallon can of gasoline, the metal kind you used to see on the back of an old World War II Army jeep, linked with fishing line to a shotgun shell duct-taped to a mousetrap. Someone opened the church doors from inside after Mass, fishing line tripped the mousetrap, mousetrap fired the shotgun shell into the gasoline can, and <u>Boom</u>! People burned.

Not just any people. Church people. People who had no idea how cruel their God could be.

If it were up to him, he would burn the whole fucking world. And if hadn't been for that fuck Brian Foley coming to speak to his friend the priest, Sampson would never have got caught.

Although the word was out that he was a serial burner, as he liked to call himself, he had not yet struck in this area. He figured he could get a few burns in before moving on.

He watched from his hiding place as Foley approached the church doors. Sampson was a hands-on burner: he loved to watch the process from the very beginning. Watching the bomb go off, hearing the screams, watching the ones closest to the explosion twist in a burning pirouette and run, not comprehending what was happening to them as they slapped at the flames consuming their bodies. Watching the ones that the fire hadn't touched, standing frozen in shock. And then, wafting toward him on the breeze, the one and only, joyous smell of burning flesh.

That day, the day it all came to an end, he saw Foley pause by the door, peering at the gasoline cans lined up in front of it. Foley didn't look like much, just a plain ordinary guy in a Sunday suit. Sampson figured he could whoop the guy's ass and still enjoy his fireworks.

Foley turned out to be a tough prick. He gave Sampson a good fight, and got the infernal device disabled before it blew. Which led to Sampson's arrest and incarceration in the psych ward, ripped away from his beloved fire.

Oh, but he had burned many churches and many church people all across the country before he succumbed to the misery of this life without fire, and he knew the fire would once again be at his beck and call.

#

An orderly met Steven Haskell, Joe Burke and me at the door of the Extreme Caution Unit on the third floor of J Building. The place looked like a prison ward, with locks and doors to match. We could hear the clientele screaming from within, and the look on the face of the orderly said it all.

I felt a rush of both excitement and horror as the orderly let us in and then locked the door behind us--barring the only way out.

Our reason for being there was straight ahead of us down the corridor, on the other side of heavy, glassed-in door: a huge man, badly disfigured by fire, swinging what appeared to be a sock wrapped around his hand, with something heavy in it. The smell of fresh blood, and lots of it, pervaded the ward.

Two staff members huddled together just outside the door, obviously scared to death. One of them said, "Sampson wedged a book underneath the door and locked himself in. We can't get it open." He was breathing hard, almost sobbing.

Inside, Sampson swung his makeshift bludgeon down on the head of another patient, over and over again. Even through the door it sounded like a large wad of clay being whipped against a wall. The floor was awash with blood, and there were enormous, bloody footprints everywhere. Sampson's hands were covered with thick wet blood, and his monstrously scarred face was splattered with it.

He stopped once and sat down for a minute. I thought he was done--and started wondering how the hell we were going to get in there. Then he got up and started in again.

"He's been doing that," the staffer said. "Every--five or ten--minutes." He choked, and threw up all over himself and the floor.

The monster in the day room was as big

as Joe Burke. Six foot three, a couple of hundred pounds. Joe gave out the orders. "Get a mattress off one of the beds!"

The two orderlies scuttled off to do as they were told. In a minute they came back lugging a mattress. "We'll try to wrap it around him," Joe said. "At least get his clubbing arm under control."

I couldn't take my eyes off Sampson. His state-issue pajamas looked kid-sized on his giant frame.

He must have felt me staring at him. He stopped and stood up straight, and looked directly at me through the protective glass. His blue eyes burned with anger and pain.

He left the bloody mess that had been his fellow patient and came up to the door, only inches from my face. He wiped his dripping, gory hands across the glass, never taking his eyes away from me. Then he pulled a doorknob out of the sock, dropped the sock and let the knob fall after it. Last of all he turned and presented his massive rear, dropped his pants and pulled a dime out of his asshole.

He dropped the dime on the floor beside the sock and the doorknob. His eyes locked with mine once more, and his mutilated face contorted in what I realized, with horrified fascination, was meant to be a smile.

"Really should be careful what you leave unattended around here," he said. His voice was soft, but I heard it clearly through the glass. His burned off lips not capable of forming perfect words, but understandable nevertheless. "A dime makes a nice screwdriver. Just ask Tomlinson over there." He nodded toward the body on the floor. "I have to say that it's quite an honor to meet you, Mr. Redcrow."

I almost shit when he said my name. His eyes laughed: he was loving it. "I've heard a lot about you," he said.

He stooped down and pulled the book out from under the door. Joe bulled in with Haskell right on his heels.

Sampson paid them no attention at all. His eyes were fixed on me. Even when he lay down, as docile as could be, and put his hands behind his back for the four-point leather restraints and the lithium injection, he watched and watched me.

The swarm of staff that overwhelmed him then was brave enough now that he was helpless, but even now they were terrified of him--and he knew it. So was I, but I figured I had good reason. As they strapped him to the secured bed, he said in a sluggish, drugged-out voice, "Tell Foley I said hello." He closed his eyes and started to sing a song from The Who, ever so softly: "<u>No one knows what it's like . . . to be the bad man . . . to be the sad man . . . behind blue eyes . . .</u>"

They carried him off while a doctor and two nurses certified time of death for a patient named Eric Tomlinson. Cause of death: shattered skull.

Down the hall in the Quiet Room, the orderlies who had wheeled Sampson in came out and slammed the heavy wooden door behind them, locking it with what looked like an oversized skeleton key on a giant ring. The slam of the door echoed through the ward.

All the doors on that hallway were the same: massive, wooden, painted white, but the heavy hinges at top and bottom were black. A single square window, reinforced with wire mesh, offered a view into each room.

"This is where it all happens," Steve Haskell said beside me. "The baddest of the bad. The criminally insane--like your friend Sampson over there."

Monsters, I thought. It was like some ancient castle in a horror movie, where the mad scientist kept his creations locked up away from the world. There were monsters here, too--terrible ones, though they walked and talked more or less like human beings.

\#

Officer Landers and Sergeant Foley had to secure their service weapons in a safe before entering the locked unit to which

Louis Barretto would be admitted. This had been standard procedure since 1969, when a patient relieved a police officer of his gun and ammo and killed the officer and four staff members and wounded a fifth, saving the last bullet for himself.

Barretto looked as if he would be checking into A Ward for a good long time. Foley and Landers stayed with him until one of the nurses tucked him into bed, they hung around for a minute or two, by way of paying their respects. However much of a bastard Louis Anthony Barretto had been, and however much harm he had done over the years, they still pitied him.

"I want to take a look at Barretto's house," Foley said as they left A Ward and headed back toward the entrance. "Tommy Neveska's place, too, out at the cemetery. Crime Scene's been through both by now, but . . ."

"You need to see for yourself," Landers said. "Me, too, Sarge. Me, too."

Meet Gus

Gus had been a custodian at the Middlesex Fells Mental Hospital for over thirty years. He knew every inch of tunnel that ran underneath the grounds, as he had been destined to walk them for what seemed like an eternity. But even Gus would admit that every once in a while he got turned around and had to climb out through a manhole to see where the hell he was. After a few such episodes, he had taken to using the manholes just to save time.

Gus had seen a lot of freaky shit during his tenure at the hospital. He'd been shot once when one of the lunatics wrestled a cop's gun away from him, and shot up the night shift: took a bullet in the chest.

That was no big deal, he said to himself. He'd been shot before, fighting the Krauts in World War II. Gus was a tough old bastard.

But lately things around the hospital

were different. Much different. There were new enemies to fight. Tougher enemies. Enemies that even Gus wasn't sure he wanted to tackle.

He was in the tunnel now on his way to J Ward. Ahead of him he heard footsteps walking fast, then slowing down, then speeding up again: the familiar sound of someone who had gotten turned around and didn't know which way to go. The lights were dim these days, but Gus could see the shadow growing larger as the footsteps got louder.

Gus had always been a churchgoing man. He put on his best suit every Sunday before setting foot in the Lord's house, and the rest of the week he lived by the Lord's rules: kindness and helpfulness to anyone who needed it.

He'd left his mark all over the grounds, from what was left of the perennial garden to the cemetery. Those two things mattered the most to him now, and he almost always made sure to check in on one or the other just before dark. From what he'd been seeing and hearing there and elsewhere, he knew something was brewing. It was going to get ugly. Very ugly.

#

In all the excitement over the new arrival and the incident with Adam Sampson, nobody had time to care if I found my way back to my assigned ward. Joe Burke gave me a quick set of directions, basically "Go down in the tunnels and take this turn and that turn and you'll be back up where you belong."

These tunnels were a lot bigger than the ones overseas, but they had a similar enough feel that I couldn't stop remembering crawling on my belly through tight and airless spaces, waiting for the muzzle flash that would take my life and bury me deep in the jungle floor forever.

I picked up my pace. At every turn and after every transition from dark into light, I expected to see Foley in a glowing white priest's robe, dripping blood from his head, hands and feet.

The tunnel was darker than I remembered from just a couple of hours ago. I kept looking over my shoulder for the swarm of flies, and sniffing for the putrid smell that wasn't ever there. The cold wasn't so bad, either, though it wasn't terribly warm.

Nobody else was down here. There wasn't anybody I could ask for directions. I wished I'd paid more attention on the way out, instead of just following Joe Burke.

I needed to get out of this place. I decided to take the first set of stairs leading up.

The tunnel was completely silent except for the sounds of my footsteps and my labored breathing. The air was heavy; it was hard to get enough oxygen. If I screamed for help, it wouldn't do much good.

My brisk walk turned into a light run. I wished I had my "hush puppy" on me.

#

Sergeant Foley and Officer Landers arrived at Barretto's house to find the Crime Scene Unit still at it.

"Anything?" Foley asked.

"Too early to tell," said the officer in charge. "Spooky, though. The house was locked down tight. Nothing bigger than a fly should have been able to get in."

Foley frowned as that sank in. "Did you recover the sutures that were taken out at the Lawrence?"

"Tagged and bagged, Sarge. Did it myself. Eyes, ears, mouth and chest."

"Chest?" Foley said. Now that was news. Sergeant Foley didn't like news, not when it had to do with a case he was working on.

The officer nodded. "Perp carved the word HEATHEN horizontally across his chest. Sewed it up very professionally too, according to the Emergency Room doc."

"*Heathen,*" Foley said, rolling the word around on his tongue. He couldn't say he much liked the taste.

He prowled though the house with Landers, twitchy and muttering, following close behind. He checked out the chair where Barretto had been found, with the shotgun and the blasted-up television. The bedroom, which was much tidier than one might have expected, considering Barretto's personality and his lifelong bachelorhood. Foley's eyes traveled upward from the narrow bed with its tight, perfectly smooth covers, and stopped cold.

"Sarge?" Landers said. He sounded even more nervous than before. "What's the matter?"

Foley pointed with his chin. The kid's breath caught so hard he coughed.

A crucifix hung upside down on the wall above the headboard.

"Sacred Heart of Jesus," Foley said softly, "pray for us."

The crucifix swung sharply back upright. In the same instant, an unseen force swept Brian Foley up and slammed him to the floor. Sharp pain pierced his side and hands and feet. He lay with the wind knocked out of him, wheezing for air.

Jimmy Landers leaped to help him up. Once he was on his feet, his knees wouldn't hold him. He sank down onto the side of the bed.

Landers hovered and fussed. "You all right, Sarge? You scared the piss out of me."

Foley looked down at his palms. A blood blister swelled up in each, ready to burst. He could feel the same on each of his feet.

He looked up at Jimmy Landers. The kid was seriously scared--and with good reason. This was a lot heavier than a disgruntled cop killing a weirdo.

Foley needed time to think. "I'm fine," he said. "They're not going to find any evidence here--not the kind they're looking for. Let's get out of here and head back to the hospital."

Jimmy frowned. "I thought you wanted to check out Neveska's place."

"I do," Foley said. "That's why we're going to the hospital."

#

The Preacher lay dormant in the farthest depths of the hospital. The place was a labyrinth of passageways and tunnels, one on top of another. Anywhere he wanted to go, he could go, at any time he chose.

The deepest tunnels were cold, damp and dark, but the Preacher could see through any darkness. He smiled as he rested, pleased with his handiwork.

He wished he could have seen the look on the cops' faces when they found that fat scumbag Barretto all sewn up and ready to go. And Sampson--now that was special. Sampson would do great things on the Preacher's behalf, but not until just before the dark met the light.

His smile faded. Why was that?

Then he shrugged. It didn't matter. It just was. The same way he couldn't set foot above ground at any other time, either, for fear of being spotted from high above.

<u>He</u> was always watching. But the Master had taught His servant well. The Preacher had plenty to do, even in the little time when he was allowed to do it. He would play more games tonight.

His laughter echoed eerily through the hospital grounds and through the sewers of Medford. Dogs howled in fear. Humans stopped in their tracks.

He laughed for two minutes straight, and never needed to draw a breath. He laid his hand over his chest where the heart should be beating, and there was nothing. The knowledge filled him with a sense of power.

"No pulse," he said, and hooted in the darkness. No heart, no pulse--but still the adrenaline pumped through him, the way it had after he killed Barretto's dog. His heart had pounded then, too, as he ran toward Panther's Cave, trying to hammer its way out of his chest.

The heartbeat was gone. The adrenaline lived. It felt . . . electrical, like a steady current streaming through his body. He was exhilarated--ecstatic. It lifted him right up off the ground, levitating in the long, narrow basin.

This, he thought, was just the beginning. "There will be power gained tonight," he said. "And then--and then--"

Once more, laughter filled the depths and cackled up out of the sewers.

The Seer

Jessica Choofane was not insane. Far from it. In fact, she was more lucid and saw more clearly than most. She had a gift of seeing things that had occurred in the past, no matter how far away, or that were about to occur, as clearly as if she had been physically present.

When she was very young she saw her stepbrother die in Vietnam. When her stepfather heard her crying and telling her mother about it, he beat her till she bled.

A week later, the news came. Her stepbrother had been killed in action. Her stepfather never stopped blaming her for that, or for any of the other things she knew.

Jessica knew things. She knew her stepfather was constantly cheating on his wife. She tried to kill herself after that, to stop the knowing.

As she grew older she learned to accept the visions, even the ones that horrified her. They were real. She was not crazy. She could sign herself out of the ward any time she pleased.

But she had nowhere to go. For the time being, she felt safe here.

Every morning she rode the elevator down from the third floor, walked through her favorite parts of the grounds and smoked her one cigarette for the day. Sometimes other patients or staff joined her.

This morning she was alone. She entered the elevator, pressed the button for the first floor and waited as it went down.

It seemed to be taking longer than usual today. She pressed the button again, but the elevator didn't stop or pause.

She could feel herself growing weak, the way she did when she was about to have a vision. Chills shook her body. This was not going to be pleasant.

At long last the elevator jumped and skipped to a stop. Something ripped open the outside door, the one that had to be opened manually. The putrid smell of death rushed in.

The inner door of the elevator still protected her. Through the metal grate she saw the most disturbing vision she had ever had.

Hundreds of patients lay flat on tables, with doctors in white scrubs and surgical masks bending over them. Some lay screaming in terror with the guts ripped out of them. Fully alert patients lay with their skulls sawed open and their pulsating brains exposed. Others bounced and lurched with jolt after agonizing jolt of electroshock. Dental drills shrieked and smoked as orderlies held down the screaming victims. Still others were wrapped from head to toe in sheets and thrown into tubs of ice water--unable to move or fight or even scream.

Outside of the circle of blinding light that pinned each victim, the room was dark. Each doctor, each orderly, focused on his own patient, as if there were no one else in the room. All around them was a distinct buzzing noise, the sound of countless insects swarming outside the light.

Jessica huddled in the farthest corner of the elevator, clasping her knees tightly to her chest. A shadow swooped toward her out of the deepest part of the darkness. The screams of the sufferers in the light grew immeasurably louder. They were all aimed at her, begging, pleading for help, imploring her not to leave.

"Tortured souls," Jessica whispered.

The shadow burst into the light. It wore the shape of a man, but its eyes were as white as stones. Its face was deathly pale; open wounds wiggled and writhed. It stretched out its hands, reaching for her.

As suddenly as it had opened, the elevator's outer door slammed shut. The elevator lurched and groaned and began to ascend.

Haunting Barretto

The body of Louis Barretto lay motionless, lost in catatonia, but inside his head, demons chased him down empty, wind-blown streets. Children's laughter tormented him, but no matter how he twisted and peered, he could not see them. The sky was dark but the sun would not be long. It was the time of day when darkness fought the light, just before morning twilight.

He ran down the block toward the corner, yelling for someone, anyone to help, but all he heard in response was the laughter of children running after him, barely out of sight. Sometimes he thought he could see their shadows behind him, but when he turned to face them, there was nothing.

Empty soda cans rattled and clanged past his feet, pushed along by the wind. Its cold walked through him. He wrapped his arms around himself in a futile effort to keep warm, eyes darting from side to side.

"Hello!" he called out. "Anybody home? Can anybody help?" His voice echoed in the emptiness.

The children's laughter grew louder, more sinister. Feet scampered close behind. A rock bounced past him.

He ran blindly, sobbing for breath and streaming with sweat. If only the sun would come. If the sun would just show its face, everything would be all right.

Another rock rolled past him, and another. A cloud of black flies swarmed around his face. He had not known he had any breath left to run, but somehow he found a last, desperate ounce of strength.

He lurched around the corner, and gasped as much in awe as in relief. A church steeple rose above the darkened rooftops, with a golden cross gleaming on its peak.

Now he knew where he was supposed to go. The cross blazed like a beacon, calling him home. His legs were heavy, his body taxed to its limit. Laughter echoed and reechoed around him. God, he thought. Why was the sun taking so long?

#

Panic and the horror of dark, closed spaces had taken me over. I ran through the tunnel with no more thought or sense than a child lost in the woods. My breath came hard, more with fear than with exertion.

There was someone in front of me. I slammed to a halt and dropped down into a crouch, striving desperately to get my breathing under control.

An enormous, elongated shadow stretched around the corner, growing longer and longer until it cast me completely in darkness. I made myself as small as possible, eyes wide and heart thudding in anticipation of an ambush.

The shadow resolved itself into a solidly human figure with a thick Boston accent. "Well, hello there," the man said. "Guess you're fairly new around here."

I unfolded myself warily, in case he turned into a devil with horns and a tail. But he stayed reassuringly the same: a short, thickset middle-aged man in a staff uniform. "How'd you know I was new?" I asked with a slight edge of sarcasm.

"Well," he said, "for one thing I've never seen you around before. For another, you were running like a scared puppy."

"Thanks," I said. "I think." I stuck out my hand. "Redcrow."

"Gus," he said, shaking it. "Gus Jacobs. These tunnels aren't easy to find your way around. I've been wandering them for thirty years, and even I lose my bearings once in a while."

"That's not very encouraging," I said.

"No. No, it isn't," said Gus. "Where you tryin' to get to?"

"A Ward," I answered.

He nodded. "You're not too far off. Just back the way you came, and up a couple of flights."

I must have looked a bit pathetic, because he added, "Here, I'll show you.

Come on."

It really wasn't far, though I was still so far off my bearings that it could have been ten miles and I might not have realized it. He stopped in front of a stairwell like half a dozen I'd passed since I came down in the tunnels, and said, "This is it. Just go straight up till you see daylight."

I was ready to kill for a face full of sun, but I was oddly reluctant to leave this kind man behind. "Good to meet you," I said. "I appreciate you showing me the way."

"It's entirely my pleasure," he said. I could tell he was waiting for me to get on with it so he could get on with whatever his business was down in this maze, but he was too polite to say so.

I nodded, almost a bow, and gave him a little wave as I started up the stairs.

He waved back. "Barry," he said. "Don't listen to the voices."

I almost fell up the stairs before I caught myself. That was the second time someone had given me that advice--first the crazy lady Jessica, and now Gus.

#

Steven Haskell was waiting at the front entrance of the hospital's main building when Officer Landers and Sergeant Foley pulled up. "Our friend is asking for you," Haskell said.

Of all the "friends" Haskell might have meant among the patient population of Middlesex Fells, it turned out to be Adam Sampson. Ever since Foley arrested him, for some reason known only to God and the Devil, there had been some kind of bond between them.

"All right," Foley said, resigned. "I'll go see what he wants."

"It might be a while," Haskell said. "We had to pump him full of lithium to calm him down."

"We'll see," Foley said.

#

On my way up out of the dark into the

beautiful, blessed light, I ran into Steve Haskell with the holy-man cop, Foley, and his trusty young sidekick. They looked preoccupied, and not in a pleasant way, either.

Just as we were about to part ways, the elevator doors opened. Jessica Choofane, the artist from A Ward, lay curled in the corner, weak as a kitten.

I was the first one into the elevator. "What happened?" I asked her. "You OK?"

Haskell held the doors open behind me, with the two cops peering over his shoulder. "She must have had an episode," he said. "She'll be fine. She just needs some rest."

I reached down to help Jessica to her feet. Steve Haskell gripped my shoulder. "Don't. She hates to be touched."

He was a split second too late. She looked up as my hands closed around her arms. Her eyes went wide, and her whole body tensed; her skin was pebbled with goosebumps. She pulled herself deeper into the corner, dragging against my grip.

Her skin was cold; she was shaking so hard my own teeth rattled. Then something happened. The cold melted into warmth, like an electric current flowing through both our bodies as if we were one.

She stopped trying to pull away and gripped my hand instead, staring straight into my eyes. She came to her feet as if she were weightless. "Barry," she said.

The goosebumps were gone. The small hairs on both our arms stood up straight. We must be glowing, the current between us was so strong.

We walked hand in hand out the elevator, straight past Haskell as if he had not been there. "I don't believe it," he said.

Jessica ignored him. "Walk with me," she said to me. "I need some fresh air." She still looked a bit shocked and scared, but she clung to my hand like a lifeline.

We walked together toward the main door and out into the fresh spring air. I was a little uncomfortable. I didn't know if I was allowed to hold hands with a patient, never mind an attractive one like Jessica.

At the same time I felt as if I had known her for a very long time, and that we were somehow . . . good together, for lack of a better way to put it.

"Well," Haskell said behind us. "All right then. Keep an eye on her, and bring her in when she's had enough. Don't be surprised if she conks out on you. She usually sleeps for a whole day after she's had one of those things of hers."

"Things?" I asked, but Haskell was already gone, down into the tunnels with Sergeant Foley and young Officer Landers.

It was kind of weird how he trusted me with this very attractive patient, but I'd already concluded that this whole place was weird. Must be the patients' psychoses rubbing off on the staff. Or were the staff crazy, too?

I didn't really care, when I stopped to think about it. My whole body was wrapped in a sensation of deep peacefulness. I hadn't felt like this since I was a young boy, before my parents died.

Jessica tugged gently at my hand. I

followed her toward the cemetery and the perennial garden.

She had a cigarette in her other hand, I realized, somewhat crushed and crumpled but recognizable. Once we were away from the doors, she threw it away.

"Aren't you going to smoke that?" I asked.

"Not today. It's just an excuse to get outside. You have to 'contract for safety,'" she said with a twist of sarcasm, "before they let you step outside the door."

"Do you have safety issues?"

Her eyes flashed at me. The weak and clingy kitten was gone. This was the sharp intelligence I'd met in the ward, and it wasn't giving way to anybody. "Don't patronize me," she said. "I'm just getting my head straight, until I can figure out where to go."

That's about what you'd expect an inmate of the funny farm to say. If you're crazy, you don't think you are, right? But I found myself believing her. "So what happened in the elevator?" I asked.

She hesitated. I could see her making up her mind to trust me, but struggling with it. Finally she said, "I have this ability--some would call it a gift, but not me, I never asked for it or wanted it--that picks up the energy of a place or person. And believe me, this place has energy. None of it good."

"Kind of like psychic powers?" I asked.

She shivered. Goosebumps appeared on her arms, then quickly disappeared. "You have a lot of pain and sadness in you. Death and fear have been stalking you-- have been shadowing you for a long time."

"'Ghost soldiers are only friends with the shadows of their own nightmares.'" She stared at me. "Something we used to say in Vietnam. There was a lot of darkness. A lot of killing."

"No," she said. "Not the war. You're in danger here and now. Your soul is at great risk."

She spoke so firmly, with such complete confidence, that a cold chill ran down my back. Now I was the one with goosebumps.

Her warm hand rubbed my arm, smoothing them away.

Our conversation had taken us to the hospital cemetery, which lay directly behind the church. It was overgrown with brush and briars, but I could still see the round stones set flat in the ground, just the way Haskell had described them when he gave me the tour. None of them had a name on it, just a number, and a P or a C. Protestant or Catholic.

"No names?" I said.

"State law," she answered. "Since they can't have their names, the least the hospital can do is let them keep their religion. Lost souls: that's what my mother would call them."

We walked slowly among the graves. It was peaceful and quiet, beautiful in a disheveled sort of way, and eerie, all at the same time.

I was surprised to see how many graves there were: several hundred at least. Toward the rear, the stones changed. Here were the kind of headstones you'd find in any graveyard, or boneyard as we would say in Maine.

These had names, and dates of birth and death. Some of those dates were terribly close together. "Children," I said. I felt sick.

"Yes," she said. "Back in the Twenties there was a tuberculosis epidemic. Nobody knew how to stop it or treat it. Hundreds and thousands of people fell victim to it, and not even the children were spared. They tried everything--some things you couldn't even imagine."

The way she said it, I said, "You seem to have firsthand knowledge."

She shot me such a look that I instantly regretted saying it. Of course she'd seen those things with her own eyes--through her visions.

I kept my mouth shut after that, and she was lost in thought, or memory. I wasn't stupid enough to ask what she was seeing.

After half an hour or so, she turned back toward the hospital. At the door of her room she stopped and turned to face me. Her stare was direct and clear and completely sane. "Be careful," she said. "Save your soul. The enemy is here among us."

While I stood speechless, she lay down on her bed and fell into a deep sleep, as if she had slipped into a coma.

Back on J Ward

When Adam Sampson saw Brian Foley coming through the door of his room, he was as happy as a pig in shit. He was wide awake in spite of the elephant-sized dose of psych meds he'd been hit with, and he couldn't wait to tell Foley the things that had been filling him up so full he was ready to burst.

"He's bringing a present for you, Brian. Do you like presents?"

Foley knew how to play the game. That was why Sampson was so happy to play it with him. "Who's bringing a present for me?" he asked.

"You know who," Sampson said.

"Do I? I didn't think I was on too many people's Christmas lists."

Sampson laughed and laughed. Oh, he was funny, this Brian Foley! "He's not people, Brian. He's not of this world at all. But"--He lowered his voice, so Foley had to lean in close--"you . . . are . . . on . . . his list."

That got Foley's attention. His stare was so hard it made Sampson's burned skin itch. "Don't you like presents?" Sampson teased him. "Don't you want to know what it is? You're gonna love it."

"Why don't you tell me, then," Foley said. He sounded just a little bit sharp.

Sharp was good. But it could be better. "He told me you would come. And here you are! And here you'll be tomorrow, too."

"Not if I can help it," Foley said.

"Oh, you won't be able to," Sampson said. "You'll be back. He told me so. Because he's gonna leave that very special present for you *RIGHT HERE IN MY FUCKING ROOOOM!*" He howled like a banshee and heaved as hard as he could against the restraints.

Haskell and Landers jumped back and let out a breath they were holding. That was perfect--perfect. But Foley didn't even blink.

He was supposed to blink. Why wouldn't he blink? Fucking stupid cop.

"How do you think I got the dime to get the doorknob off and bash Tomlinson's fucking head in? You'll get yours too, Foley. Oh, yeah. You'll get yours. He'll be visiting you real soon, gonna crawl right into your fucking skull. Just like you crawled into mine." Sampson filled his lungs and let it all out. "I'm done talking to you, so you can *LEAVE MY FUCKING ROOOOM NOW!*"

There was an actual echo. It bounced back and forth and back and forth, rocked Sampson halfway to sleep on a lithium tide. But there was one more thing. Just one more. "He's the cold hard truth."

"Who?" Foley said. Calmly. Damn him. Damn him. Damn him.

The drugs were taking hold, because <u>He</u> said it was time. "Who?" Sampson giggled all the way down into the sweet, sweet dark. "The Preacher. That's who."

#

Luis Barretto stood at the church doors, but they would not open for him. He stepped back onto the desolate street and looked up at the golden cross at the top of the steeple. It glowed as brightly as the sun.

This brought comfort to Barretto, but it was short-lived. The children's laughter had come back. Shadows clumped together in the street and streamed toward him. The temperature plummeted; he could see his breath. The stink of death surrounded him, and the droning of innumerable flies.

"I'm sorry, Tommy!" he cried out. "I'm sorry! Please, no more! I learned my lesson!"

The laughter rose to a howl. The flies closed in. And he saw the children. They came around the corner and stopped. Dark, ragged, angry children, armed with fistfuls of rocks.

They swarmed toward him in a cloud of flies. Rocks flew. One struck him in the head, and he went down.

The children were all around him. The flies descended, smothering him. They flew into his mouth, his eyes and ears. It was completely dark, and their buzzing drowned out every other sound.

He felt himself lifted up BY the cloud of flies. He was barely conscious now, and long past sanity.

That Night

As the darkness began to clear, I got the feeling that I was no longer alone. But then you were never really alone in the jungle.

I had just found my way out of a Viet Cong tunnel, and I waited outside its entrance, shaking with adrenaline and fear, to see if I was being followed.

How long had I been down there? Where was the team? They were supposed to be waiting for me. Were they all dead?

There were men all around me. Not Americans: they weren't tall enough. I sank as deep as I could into the elephant grass, clutching my Bowie knife in one hand and something else in the other.

I couldn't remember what my mission was, only that I held part of it in my left hand. As a hint of light peeked through the canopy and the noise of the night jungle fought the noise of the day jungle, I could see the enemy soldiers gathered around me in a circle.

They each carried an AK-47, but none of them was aimed at me. Instead they were pointing at me and laughing.

I could smell blood in the air: that stale, coppery smell that was like nothing else. I was wet all over, and so was the tall grass around me. I sank down even lower, knowing I had already been spotted, but there was no denying instinct. I did my best to make myself smaller.

Flies swarmed around me. The air grew thick with the dark stench of death. It was cold, unnaturally cold. It was never this cold in the jungle.

I looked down at my left hand. The severed head of an enemy soldier looked back up at me, blinking, its tendons and veins wriggling in my palm. Its laughter joined the rest.

I threw it down in horror and disgust, while the laughter and the finger-pointing went on and on. I leaped up and tried to run, and tripped over the body that belonged to the head. Its finger pointed, too, while yards away its head laughed and laughed.

I staggered through the circle toward the faint promise of light. My enemies parted to let me through, still laughing, still pointing, and flies swarmed after me.

As I ran through the darkness, I realized that the light I pursued was not the sun. It was nearly as bright, and it shot beams through the jungle's canopy, luring me on. I ran harder, tree branches slapping me in the face and vines tripping my feet.

I burst through the last of the jungle and fell on my face in a dark street in an empty city. The cold wind blew hard. Close by I saw a pack of dogs gnawing on a dead man's body. The air was full of the smell of death.

There were other bodies past the first one, and other dogs gnawing at the rancid meat. I could hear the tearing of flesh and the cracking of bone.

They all stopped at once and lifted their heads and looked at me. Just for a few seconds. Acknowledging me. As if to say,

"If we didn't have all this dead meat around us, we'd be gnawing on your sorry ass." Then they went back to their feast.

As the cloud of black flies caught up with me, I looked up. Off in the distance, a cross glowed brightly at the top of a church steeple. I ran toward it. Behind me, through the buzzing of flies and the whine of the wind, I heard the laughter of children.

I reached the church much sooner than I had anticipated, and slowed to a walk as I approached the doors. I was still covered in blood.

The church doors flew open with an echoing bang. A cold wind blew in my face, doing its best to drive me back. It carried the stench of death.

Inside the church was dark, but I could see well enough to recognize the two men at the end of the aisle, standing on the altar. One was Brian Foley, squinting down the aisle at me.

The other was a U.S. Army Captain whose body was badly burned and disfigured. He looked as if he had just been through an artillery barrage. Smoke still curled from the wounds of the hot, sharp shrapnel. Half his face and head had been blown off, and his uniform was drenched with blood.

He raised his burned and bleeding arm and pointed at me, looking me directly in the eyes. He was praying, I realized, though that mutilated mouth turned the words to gibberish.

Just to the right of the altar, a single parishioner huddled in a pew, head down, face hidden. Foley looked from him to me, back and forth.

I called to him, but he seemed not to hear. I quickened my pace down the aisle. Just before I entered the light from the altar, the lone parishioner raised his head.

Fear rose up and overwhelmed me. I screamed Brian Foley's name--whether to warn him or beg him for help, I could never have said.

I woke in my own bed, in a cold sweat. Once again, it was the time of day when morning met night. I had begun to hate that hour, and the last fragment of nightmare that always came with it: the NVA soldier calling me Ghost Soldier and laying the curse of truth upon me. "Your only friend is the shadow of your own nightmare."

#

Brian Foley woke startled and drenched in sweat. He had had the same recurring nightmare three times in one night. He looked down at the palms of his throbbing hands to check for blood, and wiped his forehead in search of the same.

His right side burned with intense pain, like searing pieces of shrapnel piercing his skin. He could almost taste the burning flesh, and hear his comrades from Korea all around him, screaming in agony.

He pressed his hand to his side, right where the wound should be--but there was nothing. As quickly as it had come, the pain was gone.

It got worse every time he had the dream. In it, he stood on the altar of a church, dressed in a gleaming white robe, and the Army chaplain he had served with in Korea conducted Mass in a ringing voice, as if to a great crowd of worshippers. But the church was completely dark and almost entirely empty, except for one parishioner in the front pew. He was dressed in dark clothing and slumped over in the pew, with thick black hair hanging down, concealing his face. His hands were tucked into his sleeves.

There was no one else in the church. Foley glanced at Vinny Kelley, who was still intoning the words of the Mass, and saw the wounds of the mortar attack that had killed him. He spread out his hands and raised his voice to an even stronger pitch. "St. Michael, defend us in battle; be our defense against the wickedness and the snares of the Devil. May God rebuke him, we humbly pray . . ."

A pool of blood swelled around Vinny's feet, streaming from the gaping wounds on his neck, head and face. The fatigues on the left side of his body were shredded, and the white bone shone through the torn flesh. His left eye hung partly out of its socket; the arteries pulsed like worms trying to burrow back into his body.

He was exactly the way Foley remembered him on the day he died--as he had never been able to forget in all the years since. Vinney Kelley was the reason why Brian Foley had found his way to God: his friendship and loyalty and his unshakable faith had set Foley on the path that he had followed since he came back from Korea.

The lone parishioner stirred, drawing Foley's gaze back to him. He was slowly raising his head.

"By the power of God," Vinny Kelley prayed, "cast into Hell Satan and all the other evil spirits who prowl about the world seeking the ruin of souls."

The parishioner withdrew a pale hand from his sleeve and raised it to his still hidden forehead as if to bless himself. Foley was seized with unreasoning, irrational terror.

The white hand touched the forehead. *In the Name of the Father.* The black hair slowly peeled away from the pale face, as the deathly hand made its way down to the center of the chest. *And of the Son.* The face was nearly revealed--and Brian Foley knew, with every instinct of body and soul, that that face was not meant for him to see.

Vinny Kelley continued his prayer, apparently oblivious to Foley's presence and to the terrible danger that threatened him. "Lend me, I pray, thy powerful aid in every temptation and difficulty, and above all do not forsake me in my last struggle with the powers of Evil . . ."

A strong wind roared from the front of the church. The heavy oak doors creaked open, then fell shut with an echoing boom. The wind fell abruptly silent.

Footsteps approached down the darkened aisle. Foley strained to see who they belonged to. They felt welcome somehow, and warm.

Vinny Kelley stopped praying. Foley

turned to stare at him. His eyes were fixed on Foley's face. He raised his hand and pointed toward the footsteps. Despite the terrible wounds, his face was peaceful and his expression reassuring.

The newcomer's shadow drew closer to the light. Foley could almost see--could almost tell who it was.

Just before the face came clear enough to recognize, Foley woke up. His hands and feet were aching fiercely. The pain in his side was excruciating, and his forehead burned.

#

Inside J Ward, Adam Sampson woke from a deep sleep to bitter cold and the sensation of blankets ripped from the bed. He surged against the restraints, looking around wildly, but the room was empty except for the cold and the heavy odor of death.

His ears caught the fluttering of wings-- birds, or maybe bats--and the scraping of long sharp claws. Ah, he thought, half afraid and half exultant. His new Master must be near.

"Are you there?" he called out softly.

Flies swarmed around him at the sound of his voice. He lay as flat as he could, squeezing his eyes and mouth shut.

Something punched or kicked him hard from beneath his mattress, knocking the wind out of him. Before he could move, a new blow came, worse than the first. "<u>Jee-suz Chri--</u>"

A low voice hummed and buzzed from the corner of his room. A tall dark shadow stood there, where a moment before had been nothing but air. "Jesus Christ is dead."

The swarm of flies subsided. Sampson focused on the walls, and his whole body shuddered with cold and fear. There was blood everywhere, smeared all over the white walls, half coagulated and half still wet and slowly dripping.

As he strained to make out the words that were written there and signed with a palm print, he saw a brown paper bag nailed to the wall. Something long and heavy weighed down one corner. Blood dripped from it, each droplet echoing as it struck the floor.

The Preacher took shape out of the darkness, standing over Sampson. He looked up into the white, inhuman eyes. "Let me out," he pleaded.

"Soon," the Preacher said. His voice was guttural, as if thick with anger. He gripped Sampson's face in both hands and bit down hard on the top of his scarred head.

Sampson squeezed his eyes shut and strove with all his might not to scream in pain. He wanted to be strong, to be worthy.

The Preacher's hands were surprisingly hot on Sampson's cold cheeks. In a strange, twisted way, they reminded him of his first day of school, and his mother taking his face in her warm, soft hands and kissing the top of his head before she sent him off into the world. He laughed out loud as the Preacher's teeth sank into his flesh.

Troop 394

Just before 6:30 that Saturday morning, Boy Scout Troop 394 gathered around the remains of last night's campfire and plotted out the day's exercises. This was the last merit badge required for the status of Eagle Scout, and their mission was to climb the steep slope of Pine Hill-- which in local Boy Scout lore was known simply as The Hill--and locate specific geographical features with a map, compass and binoculars.

As they bent over their map, the sound of a church bell echoed through the Middlesex Fells Reservation. That sound had not been heard in these parts in well over a decade, and the boys of Troop 394 took it for a good omen. Scoutmaster Eddie Norton had orchestrated it, they were sure, to motivate the troop for the challenge of climbing The Hill.

Scoutmaster Norton however was no more in on the secret than the boys were.

As peal after peal echoed off the hillside and reverberated in the valley below, he wondered what on earth could have got the thing going after so many years--and why on a Saturday morning? It had always rung on Sundays after noon Mass, and most of Medford, Winchester, Stoneham and Woburn had been able to hear it.

Back then, the sound had been almost comforting. People talked about the hospital where people in need went to live and where the lost souls found a home. But that was a long time ago, and the stories had grown a lot darker since. Rumors of patients raped in the endless labyrinth of the tunnels, rumors that the place was haunted, that ungodly experiments were conducted on those who had no one to remember or care for them, that the government had funded exploratory brain surgeries, shock treatments, eye transplants, dental transplants, and strange and horrible experiments on male and female genitalia--gruesome, uncivilized procedures, that had no place in the world of modern or ethical science.

He had heard about that Neveska kid, too, being beaten to death by the cops and taken up to the psych hospital during the freak storm, and now his body was missing. Everybody agreed that the kid had problems, but he hadn't deserved to die that way. That family had suffered enough, what with his poor mother, and the brother killed in action.

Now as the church bell rang and rang and the Scouts looked to him for direction, Scoutmaster Norton had a feeling in the pit of his stomach. Something was not right.

"Line up in formation," he said to the troop. "We'll go up The Hill and see what's going on."

The boys seemed not to share his sense of wrongness: they lined up with the usual amount of chatter and horseplay and started up The Hill. Brandon O'Malley took the lead, as usual. He was up for Eagle Scout, and his father had given him a new pair of binoculars just for this trip.

The morning was cool, and the sun had

not made its way to this side of the woods. Even so, the members of Troop 394 began to sweat as they raced each other up the slope.

"Stay together!" the scoutmaster called out from the rear. "Remember, we're a team!"

The trail was well groomed and smooth, but it was steep. It was a good challenge for the young and energetic troop. Brandon O'Malley pulled ahead, determined to be the first one to the top. About 100 feet down, while the rest of the troop were still a fair ways below, he stopped to catch his breath and mop the sweat from his brow.

The bell had not stopped or even paused during his whole ascent. He raised his brand-new binoculars and aimed them at the gold cross that rose out of the treetops.

The focus was blurred. He adjusted the sights and let out a long breath. "<u>Whooooa</u>! Is that real? How did he get all the way up there?"

#

Before the morning shift arrived to relieve the night staff at the Middlesex Fells Reservation State Mental Hospital, the sound of the church bell could be heard loud and clear: a deep and hollow *Bonnggggg*. Then seconds later, another *Bonnggggg*.

Gus had been standing outside the gate of the cemetery, looking up toward the cross, since the morning light fought the darkness for control of the day. "Hell's bells," he said.

Gus was not happy. He had been expecting this wickedness for quite some time. Now another battle of Good against Evil had begun, right on schedule.

As peal after haunting peal filled the Reservation, patients began looking out the windows, and staff members came out of the buildings to investigate. None of them saw Gus. Few--very few--people ever did.

All of them, however, saw what he saw.

On top of the golden cross, a man's body was impaled, pierced through the lower back.

The bell's ringing grew louder and ever louder. Blood flowed from the body down the cross, bright red against bright gold. It steamed as if it had been fresh, though Gus knew the body had been impaled hours ago, just before morning twilight.

The dead man was completely naked, and his hands seemed to be covering his ears, as if to block out the terrible clangor of the bell.

The shriek of the fire alarm filled the grounds, almost drowning out the bell. The hospital erupted as only an insane asylum can.

#

Brian Foley was already up when the call came from the Medford P.D.

"More trouble up at the Cookie Factory," the front desk clerk said. "Someone impaled themselves on top of the church up there."

Foley's heart sank, but he could not say he was surprised. "Barretto?"

"Don't know yet," the clerk said, "but he's the only patient they can't account for. Doesn't look good. Landers is on his way over to pick you up."

Of course he would be. Foley was already dressed, except for his .38. He picked it up, then put it down again. If he needed a gun, he was pretty sure Landers would have one. Rookies always did.

He kissed his sleeping wife, holding his breath when she stirred and murmured something, but she didn't wake. Good, he thought. One less explanation he didn't want to have to give.

He slipped quietly out of the house. A flock of mourning doves perched on the telephone wire and in the tree, the same as yesterday. There were a few in the woodpile, and even a couple on the ax handle again.

"Strange," he said to himself.

He walked toward them, and none of

them took flight. He almost got the impression they were welcoming him.

He reached toward the ax handle, to see how close he could get before they flew away. He just about had his hand on a bird when Landers said behind him, "Sarge? You ready?"

Every single dove erupted into flight at once--thousands of them, all in the same direction.

Landers gaped at the sight. Foley wanted to smack him for showing up just exactly then, when something was about to happen--some connection, some message. Something important.

"What was that all about?" Landers asked.

"I don't know yet," Foley answered. He had his temper back under control, though it would take him a while to be really calm again--a calm he would need, to face what was ahead of him.

"Dear Lord," he prayed. "Lead us not into temptation, and deliver us from Evil."

#

Adam Sampson had been in leather restraints since yesterday. His body ached tremendously, but he could not have cared less. He smiled at the macabre alteration in the wall of his room--or his cell, as he liked to call it. The staff would be in soon to check on him, and then they too would be privy to the Preacher's message.

He couldn't wait for fucking Foley to get here, because the Preacher had left him a most unusual present. Sampson shivered in anticipation. Oh, this was going to be bad. Very, very bad. And that was good.

#

The hospital was on complete lockdown. The Medford Fire Department had brought in a ladder truck to get the police detectives up to the crime scene. As Detective Foster got ready to climb up, Sergeant Foley said, "You mind if I take the first look?"

Detective Foster was visibly happy to hand the job over to someone else. This was no ordinary homicide, and there would be none of the black humor cops usually resorted to when they had deal with worse trauma than usual--and Barretto, asshole or not, was one of their own.

Brian Foley began his ascent. When he looked up, he could see Barretto's snow-white hair above him.

Halfway up the ladder, he stopped, seized by the sudden urge to bless himself. *Father, Son and Holy Spirit.* Thus fortified, he resumed his ascent.

As he got closer, he observed that Barretto's back must be badly broken: the back of his head was nearly touching the bottoms of his feet. The top of the cross pierced his torso, straight through the middles of his back. His hands were sutured to the sides of his head once more, covering his ears.

Foley averted his eyes and crossed himself again. As he did, he saw an old man looking up at him from below, blessing himself likewise.

"Gus Jacobs," Foley said softly. Their eyes met. Foley heard a voice in his head: *Fear not Evil. Fear not Death.*

His eyes flicked up to Barretto's body, then down. The old man was gone. Foley crossed himself a third time, in honor of the Trinity, and faced what he had to face.

Louis Barretto looked as if he had died of fright. His eyes and mouth were sewn shut. Black flies buzzed around him.

In the tall pine tree nearest the steeple, the flutter of wings caught Foley's attention. Flocks of doves filled the branches. Away up on a distant hill, a coyote sang: sad and desperate and full of pain.

Sharp and sudden pain stabbed Foley's palms and the soles of his feet. He nearly fell off the ladder before instinct took over and made him hold fast.

"Lord," he prayed, "give me strength to fight your enemies with my very life."

The blisters on his palms were getting worse, and now they were swelling on the backs of his hands as well.

He had seen everything he needed to see. He climbed back down slowly, with many pauses, and nearly dropped to his knees once his feet touched the ground.

Jimmy Landers leaped to hold him up. "Are you all right, Sarge?"

"Gus Jacobs," Foley said.

Landers frowned at him. "What? Who's Gus Jacobs?"

Foley shook his head. Steve Haskell was coming toward them, too caught up in his own problems to notice the state Foley was in. He started talking when he was still ten feet away. "At the 4:15 a.m. check, Louis Barretto was in his bed in the same catatonic state he'd been in since he was brought in. Thirty minutes later, at the next check, he was gone. Not long after that, I heard the church bell ringing--loud and angry, as if someone strong was tugging on that rope. When I went to see who it was . . ." He trailed off.

Foley finished the sentence for him. "There was nobody there."

"Yeah," Haskell said. "Exactly. I don't want to interrupt your investigation here, but if you can leave someone else in charge, there's something you need to see."

Foley leaned on Landers' strong young shoulder for a moment, completely exhausted. Then he pulled himself upright. "Sampson," he said.

Haskell nodded.

"All right," Foley said. "Foster, you got this. Landers, you're with me."

As Haskell led the two cops toward the screaming chaos of J Ward and the Extreme Caution Unit, Foley heard the doves cooing their morning song in the pine tree. Directly beneath them, a familiar old man descended through a manhole into the tunnels below and slid the cover slowly shut above his head.

Visitation

As she did every Saturday morning, Rita Foley went to the Shrine of the Holy Queen in East Boston's Orient Heights. The huge, green-patinaed copper statue of the Blessed Mother was over a hundred feet high, standing at the very top of the hill with arms spread wide, welcoming all who saw it and offering them mercy and forgiveness.

It was a federal monument and a center of pilgrimage. Rita had been going there every week since she was a little girl, to light candles at the statue's feet.

When she was small, her father used to take her and her two brothers on weekend hikes in the woods of the Middlesex Fells Reservation. From the top of Pine Hill he would point to the statue, so small and shrunken with distance that you had to know exactly where to look, and bless himself and say a prayer.

Now that she was grown and married,

she no longer hiked in the woods every weekend, but she had never missed a visit to the Blessed Mother. She always lit her candles in the same area, right up near the huge copper feet, and she always said the same prayers, but her intentions changed with her life and circumstances.

Her husband Brian had been troubled lately, and this morning she focused her prayers on him. As she knelt in front of the freshly lit candles, she felt a warm, strong breeze come up on her, and became aware of a presence behind her.

She stood and turned. A man in a U.S. Army uniform was staring at her as if he recognized her. He wore a cross on each lapel, she noticed. "Is your name Rita?" he asked.

She nodded. She wasn't afraid. Not here, in front of the Blessed Mother.

"I hope you don't mind," he said, "and I'm sorry to interrupt your prayer, but I recognized you from an old photograph. I'm a friend of your husband Brian: we served in Korea together. I'm in town to take care of some unfinished business."

Rita smiled and held out her hand. Instead of shaking it, he hugged her and kissed her lightly on the cheek. It could have been a terrible imposition, but Rita felt only warmth and peace.

"Brian is a lucky man," the officer said. "He's always been the first to praise and thank God for the good in his life-- especially you. He never stops talking about how good you are to him, and how much he loves you."

This made Rita a blush a little. "Thank you," she said. "That's terribly kind of you. Why don't you come by the house and have dinner with us tonight? I'm sure Brian would be pleased to see you."

He shook his head. His eyes were warm and a little sad. "I can't tonight, but I promise I'll be by to visit real soon. In the meantime, would you mind giving these to him?" He drew a set of rosary beads from his pocket. They were made of pearl white beads, with a sterling silver crucifix; they glowed in the morning light, radiating holiness.

"Oh, how beautiful," Rita said, "and how kind of you. Promise you'll come to dinner when you can."

"I promise," he said, smiling. He hugged her again and gave her another kiss, then turned and walked away through the rows of candles and the crowd of pilgrims.

"Wait!" Rita called after him. "I'm sorry, I forgot to ask your name."

The soldier's smile put the light and warmth of all the candles to shame. "Vincent. Vincent Kelley."

#

As I arrived at the entrance of the woods, I saw a flock of what appeared to be hundreds, if not thousands of doves, flying in unison. They were low to the ground and traveling fast, just over the top of my jeep, and continuing down Governors Avenue. It took a couple of minutes for all of them to pass by. I stopped the jeep, and Nika and I watched them until the last one fluttered by.

That was just the beginning. We found half the hospital marked off with yellow tape that warned, POLICE LINE DO NOT CROSS. A truck from the fire department was parked by the church, with its ladder angled up toward the steeple. The cross at the top glowed brightly even through the human body impaled upon it.

I knew that church. I knew that cross. I was afraid I even knew that body. I'd dreamed about them all night long.

There was a crowd of people around the truck. I saw the cop Foley and his young sidekick heading with Steve Haskell toward the main building, and the little old custodian, Gus, popping down a manhole into the tunnels.

Nika jumped from the back seat to the front, startling me, just as a good-sized red-tailed hawk flew inches over my head, letting out a long, piercing cry. It swooped up to a high peak of the administration building and perched there, while below it, Foley, Haskell, and the rookie cop disappeared into the building.

When I looked back up, I saw my grandfather standing where the hawk had been. He stood straight, perfectly balanced, staring straight at me.

Chills ran down my spine. This was heavy stuff, big-time medicine-man stuff. And I was smack in the middle of it.

Grandpa raised his hands, palm up, to the sky. I followed where they pointed, back to the gruesome scene on the steeple. A detective was climbing up the ladder with a camera; even at this distance I could tell he was not even slightly happy about his job.

I glanced back at Grandpa. He was gone again, and the hawk was back. It soared down off the height, skimming just above my head, and disappeared into the woods. A coyote wailed in the distance, and a massive flock of doves--the same I'd seen on the road, or one exactly like it--flew up all at once from a tall pine tree near the church.

"Which one of you brought me to this

place?" I asked.

I didn't expect an answer, but I got one, of sorts. Nika gave me a quick poke with her cold nose. I gave her a long pat and half a hug, and she wagged her tail.

I caught myself smiling in spite of everything--something that I hadn't done in a long, long time.

#

I rolled forward, parking my jeep away from the building and off to the side, away from the crime scene. I left Nika in the jeep with a dish of water and her favorite chew bone, tied by her leash so she wouldn't bother the cops or firemen trying to do their job, and headed over to A Ward and my new friend, Jessica Choofane. She had made an impression on me. There was something kind and, well, spiritual about her, and I had a strong feeling that I should introduce her to Nika.

The ambient noise of the hospital was even louder than usual, as if the inmates were exceptionally restless. I hardly needed to ask why. The body on the steeple was enough to drive a sane man mad.

#

Deep within the labyrinth of tunnels, the Preacher summoned snakes from every crevice and passageway. As they obeyed his call, he placed them in a bed sheet he had taken during the pre-dawn festivities.

He had already collected at least a dozen water moccasins and a few Eastern rattlers. That was good work, he thought.

He had another surprise for that fucking Indian, too, but he had to work fast. The heavy clouds could clear up at any moment, and he dared not show his head above ground without their protection. He never knew Who might be watching, and that could prove fatal to his existence.

Even with the clouds, he was taking a great risk, but he was brimming over with power after eating the eyes of that fat scumbag Barretto. "The eyes are the window to the soul," he said, and giggled. It was pitch black in the tunnels; he needed no eyes to see--not here, where his Master ruled.

Snakes were still coming from everywhere, slithering over one another to answer his call. He placed another dozen or so in the sheet, then made his way up into the open for a brief but rewarding daylight strike.

There was someone else nearby--some other presence. He could not tell if it threatened danger. Maybe it was just the Master observing his servant's wonderful work.

Maybe not. But the Preacher didn't care. He was enjoying his work 'way too much, and he had enough power in him now to destroy or enslave anything he came across.

#

The hospital was in complete turmoil as

Foley, Haskell and Landers entered the Extreme Caution Unit and the room of Adam Sampson. A few stray flies flew erratically around the room, looking for a way to escape.

All the patients were in lockup, but the noise and the smell of piss and shit turned Jimmy Landers a peculiar shade of green. Foley and Haskell had been in war and had witnessed much worse, but this kid was getting a crash course in how the other half lived.

Adam Sampson lay in his restraints, awake and aware but apparently oblivious to the deep, baseball-sized bite taken out of the front of his head. He greeted them with a lazy smile. "I told you He was going to bring you a present."

They all followed the direction of his gaze to the brown paper bag nailed to the wall, dripping blood from one corner. Suddenly the bag broke. Its contents hit the floor with a hard, wet slap.

Landers jumped back as if he'd been bitten, but the other two men stood motionless. A human heart lay on the floor, leaking the last of its blood.

Adam Sampson howled with glee. "Surprise, you fuckin' asshole! Oh, I can't believe it! Hey, Foley, have a fuckin' heart!"

Brian Foley stared at the heart. He knew, with complete and deadly certainly, that it belonged to Louis Barretto.

Sampson's eyes shifted from him to the heart, back and forth, as if they were the only two people in the room. His voice was soft and sarcastic now, needling and jabbing at him. "So, how it's fucking going, Brian? Do you like your present? He got it specifically for you. Do you like the message he left you? Do you like that, too, Brian?"

Foley made himself look up at the words written in blood--thick, clotted letters dotted with bits of flesh, as if the one who wrote them had used the heart itself as a pen.

Dear Holy Man!
Fuck You!

Underneath the words was the same symbol he had seen in the morgue: the three 6's joined at the top, and below them, *Die pig!*

Sharp, agonizing pain pierced his hands and feet and stabbed his forehead. He reached up to wipe the dripping sweat.

"Brian," Haskell said, "your forehead is bleeding."

Foley looked down at his hand. It was full of blood.

Sampson cackled. "There's plenty more where that came from, <u>Holy Man</u>!"

The pain brought Foley to his knees. He blessed himself, gasping for breath.

A great force, like an unseen hand, struck him to the floor.

#

Sergeant Foley was out cold. Blood streaked his face, running down from his forehead, and he was bleeding badly from his hands and feet.

Steve Haskell poked his head out the

door. "Get a stretcher! Stat!"

Sampson was suddenly quiet.

"Oh. My. God," Jimmy Landers said.

Haskell turned, and stopped cold.

Adam Sampson was still in restraints, but every joint and movable part of his body was twisted and distended. His neck had grown a foot longer than anatomically possible and twisted backwards on itself. His jaw was dislocated, his arms stretched so far behind him that his shoulders must have been removed from their sockets. His wrists were bent inside out and his fingers curled like corkscrews. His legs pointed in every direction of the compass. His eyes stared blankly, rolling deep in his head.

Blood sprang from the hole bitten in his skull. A wisp of smoke curled from it, as if the depths of his twisted, tortured body had caught fire.

#

Gus Jacobs stood outside the building directly below Adam Sampson's window, looking up at the metal bars. He heard the screaming, and then the silence, as if he had been in the room himself. He bent his head and continued to pray. Above him, J Ward erupted into genuine insanity.

#

I ran into Joe Burke right inside the door of A Ward. He was shaking with excitement and something else. Fear? "Bro, do you know who that is up on the steeple? It's that cop."

"What cop?" I said, though I suspected I knew.

"The cop they brought here yesterday, all banged up." Joe drew circles around his ears and eyes and mouth with a finger.

"Bad day for him," I said, the way we used to in Vietnam. Because you couldn't let it get to you. You had to push it off. Or the darkness ate you, too.

Joe knew. "Bad week, I'd say," he said.

I nodded. I could see the day room behind him, and Jessica sitting at the art table, intent on a drawing, as the Moody Blues sang "Nights in White Satin" on a transistor radio. She looked almost supernaturally young and beautiful.

I left Joe and went to see what she was doing. She was singing softly along with the radio.

It was remarkably quiet in the ward, considering what was going on outside. On my way over to Jessica, I saw Ralphie Walsh shaking dice in a cardboard cup, spilling them on the table in front of him and laughing at the game he was playing. It looked like Scrabble, combined with something else I couldn't quite figure out.

Jessica looked up. Her hand kept drawing while she spoke. "It's always nice to see you," she said.

Nobody had ever said that to me before. It kind of caught me off guard. I smiled, and maybe blushed, not knowing what to say.

She smiled back, as if she sensed my discomfort.

"You're up early," I said after a minute

or so.

"Slept till 4:30," she said, "then I just couldn't sleep any more. I had some things on my mind; I needed to put them on paper."

There were drawings all over the table, as if she hadn't stopped in the three hours or so since she got up. Each one was a portrait of a doctor operating under a surgical lamp. Outside each circle of light was utter blackness.

None of the patients was under anesthesia. The faces in the pictures were vivid with pain and horror. I could almost hear their screams.

I had seen such faces in the jungle, under fire--or under torture. In the background, Ralphie's dice rattled, spilling over and over again on the table under cover of his running commentary-- comfortable and audibly content.

"He must be winning," I said to Jessica. She laughed.

It was strange to hear her laughing and see what she had been drawing, all those images, each surrounded by a ring of fire. "I don't suppose you heard all the commotion with the fire department and the police this morning," I said.

Just like that, she shifted from laughing and animated to a near-trance. She snapped out of it just as quickly as she went in, and whispered just barely loud enough for me to hear, "Sadistic bastard." Then she said, louder, "I don't always agree with it, but sometimes people get what they deserve. I have no control over that."

"Still," I said, "whatever kind of sonofabitch he was, don't you think that punishment was pretty harsh?"

She had gone back to drawing again, intent on it, pressing the crayon so hard it broke. Without missing a beat, she picked up a new crayon and carried on. I started to think she had known about the impalement before anyone--that she'd seen it in a vision. "There's a lot of evil in this world," she said, "and apparently plenty to go around."

I could tell she was hiding something

beyond what had happened today, something she didn't want to talk about. Rather than press her about it, I looked over the other drawings on the table. Besides all the doctors and the tortured patients, there was one, right in front of her, that was different.

It was a picture of a cop in uniform. He looked a little like Sergeant Foley--the set of his shoulders, the way he stood. An angel stood on either side of him with wings spread wide, embracing him. The angels' faces were loving, peaceful and yet protective. "This is beautiful," I said.

She looked up. The shields were down again. "You like that? I do, too. I had a good feeling when I drew it. Good always accompanies evil, you know. We don't always see it, but it's there."

My grandfather used to say something like it when I was young. "There is a balance between two worlds, where good and evil meet and fight for control of our souls."

Maybe she'd seen Grandpa in one of her

visions. Maybe he had told her to say what she'd said, to encourage me to keep my faith in Good.

Jessica's finger traced the curve of an angel's wing and came to rest over the policeman's heart. "They'll make a statue of this someday," she said.

There was a pause, but not uncomfortable. Just peaceful, with the sound of Ralphie's dice spilling in the background. I finally remembered what I'd come in here to say, before Jessica's drawings distracted me. "Hey, I brought my pup with me. You want to meet her?"

Jessica's face lit up. She dropped her crayon and pushed her chair away from the table. "Oh, yes! Where is she? It's been so long since I'd seen or petted a dog."

"She's in the jeep," I answered. "Let's see if we can get you an outside pass, then we'll go see her."

But that wasn't happening. The hospital was still on lockdown, and nobody was getting in or out. Jessica's face fell so low I was about ready to sneak her out anyway, until Joe Burke said, "Just wait a while. When things cool down, I'll cover for you."

I gave Jessica a look that said, "Not to worry, my pup's not going anywhere. I'll make sure you see her before the day is over."

She answered me aloud. "Good. Because I definitely want to meet her."

Our eyes met. There was just something about her, I thought.

I tore myself away and went to work, helping Joe dispense the morning meds. I was aware inside my skin that Jessica had gone into her room and lain down for a nap while she waited to meet Nika.

Ralphie was still at it, rattling his dice, but there was something about the noise-- as if the dice were made of glass. Or maybe he was using marbles?

I brought him his medicine in its little cup, just as he dumped the Scrabble cup out on the table. A pile of teeth spilled out, mostly molars, bloody roots and all. Ralphie scooped them up, covered the can with his hand and shook, and dumped it out again.

I looked down at the Scrabble board beside him, half dreading and half expecting what I saw there. The tiles spelled out a set of linked words, positioned vertically and horizontally, just like a real game.

THE BEAST IS ALWAYS WATCHING.

DEAD PIG.

DENY YOUR MAKER.

And finally: DEATH IS COMING.

I knew where the teeth had come from. I wasn't going to ask, but Joe was either braver or more stupid than I was. "Ralphie, where you did you get these?" he asked.

"A monster gave them to me," Ralphie answered.

I stopped breathing when he said this, but Joe, the seasoned psych-ward veteran, wasn't so easily shook. "Oh, yeah? How did you know he was a monster?"

"Because I saw flies coming out of his mouth," Ralphie said, "and his nose and ears. Lots of them."

Joe blinked, but he wasn't buying it,

not yet. "Where's the monster now?" he said, obviously humoring the crazy guy.

"He went back downstairs," Ralphie answered. "<u>All</u> the way downstairs."

Joe looked at me. I don't know what finally tipped him over, but he said, low and tight, "Barry, you better get ahold of one of the cops outside. Let them know what we got here."

I glanced at the clock over the nurses' station on my way out. It felt as if we'd been there for hours, but it wasn't even 7:45 a.m.

#

Rita Foley couldn't wait to tell Brian how she had met his old Army buddy at the shrine. "Vincent Kelley," she said to herself, making sure she remembered the name.

She rolled the rosary beads he had given her back and forth from hand to hand, feeling their warmth. She got a good feeling from Vincent, that he was a good man. She was sure Brian would be pleased, and she looked forward to hearing all about his friend.

But when she turned the corner of her street, she saw a Medford Police cruiser parked in front of her house. And any wife of a police officer knew that this was a bad sign--a very bad sign.

She hit the accelerator--no fear she'd be picked up for speeding, not for this--and swerved into the driveway. The young cop was out of his car and heading toward her. She barely saw his face; just a white blur and the sound of her name. "Mrs. Foley . . ."

Rita didn't even remember getting out of the car, but she was in the driveway, facing the young policeman. She wanted to grab him and shake him, but she had too much self-control. "Where's Brian? Is he all right? What happened?"

"He's OK, Mrs. Foley," the young cop said, nearly bringing her to her knees, but then he added, "But he's at Lawrence Memorial Hospital."

"Oh my God," Rita said. "What's wrong? Tell me what happened!"

The poor kid seemed to have run out of ability to cope. "Please," he said. "I'm instructed to give you a ride. Please."

Rita was already in the cruiser. The young cop flung himself into the driver's seat and blue-lighted it to the hospital and Brian Foley.

#

Jimmy Landers, Steven Haskell and a number of superior officers, many of whom were personal friends of Sergeant Foley, waited outside the Code Room at Lawrence Memorial. Landers and Haskell were in shock from the morning's events. No one else knew what to say, so they sat or stood in tense silence.

Haskell broke it abruptly. "I took the liberty of calling Father McCarthy down at St. Joseph."

The others nodded. "Good choice," said Lieutenant Sullivan. "Good friend of

Sergeant Foley."

He might have said more, but a doctor emerged from the code room and approached the group of men. Those who had been sitting scrambled to their feet. "How is he?" Sullivan asked.

The doctor frowned. "He's still unconscious, and he's lost a lot of blood. I have to tell you, Officers, I've never seen anything quite like it. What was he doing when he was injured?"

Everyone turned to look at Landers and Haskell. "We were conducting a murder investigation," Landers began.

The doctor shook his head irritably. "No, no, don't give me the police report. Just tell me what type of weapon caused the injuries."

"There wasn't any weapon," Landers said. "There wasn't even anybody near him. He just started bleeding, just like that."

"Of course there was some type of instrument," the doctor said, and now he really did seem angry. "The wounds are quite severe. Full penetration of the extremities, with notable loss of blood."

"There wasn't anything," Landers said. "I swear to God. It just happened. One minute he was checking out a crime scene. The next, he was down."

"A crime scene?" the doctor said.

"Two, actually," said Landers. "One at the top of a steeple. The second one--somehow--in a patient's room." He glanced at his superiors, not sure how much police business he was supposed to tell this man, even if he was a doctor.

The oldest of the lot, a sergeant with a shock of white hair, shoved his crimson Irish face in the doctor's and spat out the words Landers was too chicken to say. "We had a man impaled on a cross, a hundred and fifty feet up. He wasn't going around stabbing anybody, and there wasn't anything up there that could have done it, either, except the cross--and it was already occupied. What do you say to <u>that</u>, Doctor?"

"That's enough," the Lieutenant said.

The sergeant backed down, still muttering and glaring. He looked ready to hit somebody.

"Sarge was OK when he came down," Landers said, still a little timidly, but who knew what might be important here? "Except for being kind of preoccupied. Then we went to check out the other scene, with the patient who had somehow also been--victimized--by whoever committed the first crime. There really wasn't anything there: patient's room, you know. They can't even have forks to eat with. Just spoons." He was babbling, he realized. He made himself stop. "Sarge said something when he came down off the ladder. A name. Gus Jacobs. I don't know why, but it stuck with me."

"Yes," Haskell said. He sounded odd-- tight. "Yes, that's what he said."

The police officers looked at one another. Sullivan, whose proper title was Supervisor of the Investigation Section, had an odd expression on his face. "Gus Jacobs was one of six victims of a shooting at the psych hospital in '69. One of the patients got a cop's gun away from him and turned it on the staff. Jacobs was a maintenance man; he happened to be working in the ward that day. He was one of the first to go down. There was only one survivor." Sullivan leveled his stare at Steve Haskell.

The younger cops regarded him in something like awe.

"Gus Jacobs was a good man and a friend," Haskell said with none of his usual good humor. He turned abruptly and walked away, straight out the door.

"Will someone please tell me what is going on here?" the doctor demanded, clearly and thoroughly out of patience.

There was a deathly silence. A new voice broke it, speaking from behind them. "Stigmata." It was Father McCarthy.

#

As Jessica went into her room to rest, the darkness gathered around her. Her legs grew heavy, and her head began to pound with pulsating pain. A vision was coming--a bad one.

As the dark closed in, she heard Barry and Joe talking to Ralphie. She could not make out the words, only the sound of the voices.

She just needed to make it to her bed. Her feet were like lead, dragging across the floor. Finally, after what seemed like a lifetime, she fell onto her mattress. The lights went out.

#

Jessica passed through the darkness of the tunnel just behind a hulking dark figure that carried a large, wet, wriggling sheet slung over his shoulder. There were snakes inside: she had seen the figure talking to them as he gathered them.

She could not make out his face, but she sensed he could feel her presence: every couple of seconds he stopped and cocked his shadowy head as if listening. It was cold in the vision, so very cold, and she could not shut her eyes or will herself out. She was trapped, following him up the first level of the tunnel.

He moved easily under his heavy burden. She shivered with cold and impending evil and fear, but she stayed close behind him. Somehow it was very important that she do that.

He came to a ladder that led up to one of the manholes. She was right behind him as he popped the cover easily. Light poured into the tunnel.

It was gray, dim light from a heavily overcast sky, but the dark man shrank down as if even that small bit of light pained him. He heaved the writhing bag through the opening.

#

The sky was not going to clear any time soon. That was going according to plan. The wet sheet full of venomous snakes wriggled and squirmed as the Preacher carried it over his shoulder like an evil Santa Claus.

That thought made him laugh. So did the ease with which he carried the heavy bag. He was stronger than any man alive.

He popped the manhole cover as easily as flipping a coin, and shoved the bag up through the manhole. Then he paused. He could not shake the sensation of being watched, but there was no way anyone could be lurking behind him. The tunnels were deserted.

He could hear the water through running channels below. He couldn't wait to get back there, but first there was something he had to do. He would have to do it quickly, because it was dangerous to show even this much of himself above the surface.

He knew exactly where to go to send a message to that fucking Indian. His dead-white eyes glowed with anticipation; he grinned at his own cleverness.

The manhole was just inside the trees near the hospital, where he could take shelter if he needed to. There was the jeep, just where he had known it would be. The dog inside growled menacingly, though the Preacher knew it was scared shitless.

The Preacher threw the sheet full of snakes at the dog and yanked it back the way a magician pulls a sheet off a laden table. The snakes writhed and wriggled and coiled on top of one another in the jeep. Even before he ducked down into the manhole again, the snakes had swarmed over the dog.

#

Gus Jacobs cut the leash that bound Nika to the jeep, even as the snakes sank their fangs into her legs and belly. The rest of her body was thickly enough furred to keep the venom from penetrating to the skin, but those parts of her were all too vulnerable.

A huge red-tailed hawk screeched and swooped down from high above like a dive-bomber in a World War II movie. It crashed into the jeep with beak and talons wide and tore into the snakes, snipping off their heads.

Nika cried in pain as she snapped and bit at her attackers. The snakes held on without mercy. Bright red blood glowed against the white fur on her belly.

Nearby in the woods, the coyote sang her lonely song. She could do no more, not yet. Her orders were specific. She was not to interfere.

#

About two hours after what the cops were calling the "Scrabble Teeth" incident, after we'd come off lockdown but before I had a chance to keep my promise to her, Jessica Choofane ran out of her room, half sobbing, half screaming my name. "Barry! Barry! They're hurting Nika!"

She collapsed by the outer door of the ward, as if her legs had lost the power to hold her up. I caught up with her there, just a little too late to break her fall. "Nika?

My dog? How did you know her name?"

She shook her head, squeezing her eyes shut. "Hurry! They're hurting her!"

Part of me said she was crazy, and so was I for listening to her. The rest was running full speed out of the ward while Joe Burke called out behind me, "Barry! Hey! Redcrow! Where you goin', man? You have to--"

I didn't care what I had to do. I sprinted down to the main entrance and out into the gray, heavy air, just as a big red-tailed hawk plummeted down out of the sky and disappeared into the jeep.

Grandpa stood in the back where the bird had been, sweeping up snakes with his bare hands and hacking them in half with a knife. He moved with amazing speed, and snakes literally jumped from the jeep in an effort to escape.

Then I forgot that astonishing sight, because Gus Jacobs walked toward me with Nika lying limply in his arms. She was hurt, and hurt bad.

She whimpered softly as Gus laid her in

my arms. "Nika," I said. "Nika, girl, are you all right?"

Of course she wasn't all right. I was stupid. She was all I had, and I could feel her body grow heavy in my arms, slipping away. "I have to get her to a vet," I said to Gus.

But he was nowhere to be seen. Neither was Grandpa, though the ground was littered with dead and dying snakes. I screamed at the empty air. "Where the hell did you go? She needs help!"

Steve Haskell pulled up in a blue Ford Crown Victoria with a sticker on the door that read, *Massachusetts Department of Mental Health.* I saw that very distinctly, with the clarity that comes when you're right on the edge, just before you snap.

"What happened?" he asked. His voice pulled me back from the brink.

"This is Nika," I said. I was proud of how steady I sounded. "She needs a vet. Will you take us to a vet?"

Steve Haskell got a good look at us-- limp dog, blood all over my white uniform, carved-up snakes everywhere--and reached back and shoved the door open. I crawled in, trying to jar Nika as little as possible. She was so limp, and so heavy.

"There's a vet in Winchester," he said as he peeled rubber off the hospital grounds. "I'll get you there. Don't you worry."

#

Cops and firefighters slowly slid the body of Louis Barretto down the ladder of the fire truck. Mist and fog rolled across the green grass and the red brick buildings, creeping up toward the church and the macabre scene that unfolded there, like something out of a horror movie. It was deathly quiet; not even a bird sang.

The air was damp and cold. The sounds of their breathing, the slide of the canvas stretcher, the occasional, laconic order, were muffled.

Suddenly a coyote began to sing, high and penetrating, echoing through the grounds.

Brian Foley lay unconscious in the hospital, caught up once more in the same nightmare: he stood on the altar of a darkened church wearing a shining white priest's cassock, while Captain Vincent Kelley conducted mass in a loud voice as if to a huge congregation. But as always before, the church was empty except for a lone parishioner slumped over in a front pew. The black hair was the same, the hidden face, the hands tucked into the sleeves of the dark coat. And as always before, when Foley looked at Vinny Kelley, he saw the same terrible wounds that had killed him in Korea, and heard the same prayer, over and over and over:

St. Michael, defend us in battle; be our defense against the wickedness and the snares of the Devil. May God rebuke him, we humbly pray . . .

And as always before, the man in the

pew raised his head but never quite revealed his face, and the church door flew open and a new arrival walked audibly down the aisle--and just as he was about to reveal himself in the light, Brian Foley woke.

His wife Rita clung to his hand and cried. He realized that he was in the hospital, and he was in great pain. It was morning twilight, and he began to mourn its arrival. Because this time, he knew, it was all coming to pass. The end was near.

#

The day after the body of Louis Barretto was retrieved from the top of the steeple and Sergeant Brian Foley was admitted to the hospital, Lieutenant Detective Robert Sullivan and Detective Stevie Foster began going through the evidence that had been gathered at the hospital. Something strange was going down here, and they wanted to keep it within the confines of the

Medford Police Department.

They gathered everything they had: the death of the Neveska kid and the disappearance of his body from the locked morgue, Barretto's body impaled at the top of a church steeple, a loony named Ralphie playing Scrabble with a boxful of freshly pulled teeth, the still bleeding heart apparently thrown into a paper bag and nailed to the wall in Adam Sampson's room, the bite mark on Sampson's head, and the two similar sets of macabre graffiti written in blood in the morgue and in Sampson's locked room. All captured on film. All of it--and it was ugly.

They were trying to compare the photos Foley had taken of the fingerprints at the morgue to some partial prints found on top of the church's cross and other prints that were apparently deliberately left in Sampson's room. Lieutenant Sullivan was confident that science would do a lot of the explaining, because after thirty years on the job, he had never known science to lie. It was just a matter of elementary evidence--piecing it all together--and he had witnessed some pretty gruesome crime scenes in his day.

The Medical Examiner's report stated that Louis Barretto's body was missing its heart and many of its teeth. Foster and Sullivan could reasonably speculate that the heart in Sampson's room and the "Scrabble teeth" were the answer to that mystery. Barretto's eyes, however, according to the M.E., were still missing in action.

"You ever see anything like this, Lieu?" Foster asked.

Lieutenant Sullivan grunted negatively, not looking up from the magnifying glass and the photograph of fingerprints that he had poring over for the past fifteen minutes. "Get me those pictures that were retrieved from Neveska's place out at the cemetery," he said.

Before he collapsed and had to be taken to the hospital, Sergeant Foley had been headed over there to crime-scene Neveska's room for matching fingerprints.

Sullivan and Foster had taken over the job, and the Crime Scene Unit had found just one set of prints in the whole room. They all matched, and one set in particular was crystal clear. That one had been found on a Black Sabbath 8-track tape.

Lieutenant Sullivan went back and forth with the magnifying glass, from the pictures of the prints at the morgue to the picture of the prints on the 8-track to the picture of the prints on the Crucifix where Barretto's body was impaled and back to the pictures on the 8-track. He did this for the next half-hour, marking the photographs with a pinpoint marker. Then finally he sat back and rubbed his aching eyes. "Dear Lord," he said.

#

At 2:00 p.m. the following day, the telephone rang in my apartment. The room was in total darkness: I had every shade pulled and every light out. I didn't want to speak with anyone.

The phone rang on and on and on until I lunged at it and screamed into the receiver. *"Who the hell is this!"*

There was a silence. I was just about to slam the thing back into its cradle when a soft female voice said, "Barry? It's me. Jessica."

The only way she could be calling me was through the pay phone in the main building. She must have faked one of her cigarette breaks just to make the call.

I felt like an asshole. I hadn't seen her since yesterday morning: I'd been knocked flat by what happened to Nika, and Haskell had given me the rest of the day off. I hadn't even gone back inside to punch out.

"I'm sorry," I said. "I didn't mean to yell--not at you."

"I know," she said. Then, hesitantly, "Is Nika all right?"

"She died early this morning," I said. Right around the time darkness met light. My throat was tight. I could hear her start to cry on the other end of the line. "I buried her in the yard. Vet said she got bit too many times, and they couldn't stop the venom from going into her bloodstream. Even if she'd got bit that many times right outside his office, he said, he still couldn't have saved her."

"I'm so sorry," Jessica said with her voice full of tears. "If I hadn't--if you hadn't--I wish I could have helped!"

She was blaming herself, which made me feel even worse than I already did. Not that I accepted any of this. Not even slightly. But I was trying to make her feel better.

"I'm all too familiar with that," she said and hung up.

It figured, the one person I did want to talk to, and now she hung up on me. I stayed by the phone in case she got hold of another dime and managed to call back.

About fifteen minutes later, the phone rang again. I picked it up eagerly. "Jessica?"

"Sorry to disappoint you," said the light male voice, "but it's Steve Haskell. How's Nika?"

"Dead," I said flatly.

"I'm sorry to hear that," he said. "I'm also sorry I didn't get to stay with you at the vet's office, with all the trouble we had going on out here. I just wanted you to know, you'll be paid for the entire shift yesterday."

"Thanks," I said. I didn't really care, but the practical part of me knew I could use the cash.

"Look," said Haskell. "I got to ask. What the hell happened with the dog? We had so much other weird shit going on, it kind of got lost in the craziness."

"You think it's related?" I asked.

"I don't know, is it?"

I paused. I couldn't tell him about Jessica's vision, or about my dead grandfather shape-shifting into a hawk and killing snakes. I gave him the one part that did make any sense. "I was coming out to check on my dog. Usually I just let her run around, but with all the cops and firemen and the crime scene and all, I tied her to the jeep. I was coming out the front

367

door when I saw Gus carrying--"

"Gus?" Haskell interrupted me. He sounded strange--surprised, kind of shocked.

"Yeah," I said. "Gus Jacobs--from maintenance. Is there any other Gus on staff?"

"Barry," Haskell said. "Gus Jacobs has been dead since 1969."

#

Brian Foley had little strength, but what he did have he used to insist on being taken home. With his wife Rita beside him, supporting him, he argued with the doctor in a weak voice. "Doc! This is not something that can be cured by medicine. I'm going home whether you like it or not." He glared the doctor down, and all the nurses, too. "What are you gonna do? Call the cops?"

The doctor had to laugh at that. "All right," he said. "I'm putting it on the record that you checked yourself out against my

368

strongest recommendations. Honestly--
between you and me and that bedpost--
there's not much I can do for you, anyway.
But--"

"No buts," said Foley as Rita helped him
into a pair of sweat pants and a sweatshirt
she had brought. His breathing was
shallow, and kept catching with pain.

He was a man of great pain tolerance,
but this pushed it to the limits. Rita tried
to go slow and be gentle. It didn't help
much.

Halfway through the ordeal, Lieutenant
Sullivan, Detective Foster and Officer
Landers provided a sort of reprieve.
Sullivan had a thick folder with him,
bulging with photographs.

Foley lay down gratefully, though he
tried not to be too obvious about it. "So?"
he said.

"So," said Lieutenant Sullivan.

His expression told Foley what he had
been expecting. He stopped to breathe, and
for a few seconds the pain was almost
insignificant. "The fingerprints match."

Sullivan nodded. "There's something else, too," he said. He pulled out a set of photographs that had been banded together, pulled the bedside table over and spread them on it for Foley to see. "We took these in Neveska's room at the cemetery."

They showed intricately detailed carvings on the wooden floor under the bed--signs of Satanic ritual. The number 666, arrows pointing in different directions, a beast with horns and tail. "Same as in the morgue," Foley said.

Sullivan spread out a second set--same thing. Same handiwork, same symbols, but this time carved into a wooden baseboard under a bed and a cheap, battered bureau. "We took these at the foster home Neveska grew up in."

And finally, he showed Foley shots of a tree carved with the same images all over the base of the trunk. "These come from a hilltop across from a grave, where witnesses say Neveska spent a lot of time reading."

"And the grave?" Foley asked.

Sullivan dropped a photo in front of him. It was a closeup of a headstone. Foley read the inscription aloud. "<u>Mary Neveska. Beloved Mother of Paul and Tommy</u>." The line below had been chipped out, but Foley could piece together enough letters to decipher it. "<u>Beloved Wife of Tony Neveska</u>."

The photographs were in black and white, as evidence photographs tended to be, but there was something strange about them--creepy. Not just the carvings, either. The whole thing, what they told him and what they meant. It was like something out of a horror movie, not a crime scene in a suburb of Boston.

Foley sorted through the photos, his heavily bandaged hands shaking with weakness. After a while he said, "Take this stuff to my house so I can go over it thoroughly. I need to get out of here."

With the help of his wife and his colleagues from the Medford Police Department, Brian Foley made his way out of the hospital to die in the comfort of his own bed, in his own home.

#

Even after Steve Haskell told me the whole story about Gus Jacobs, I didn't believe him. I was no stranger to talking to the dead--I talked to my grandfather often enough, and I knew for a fact he had died-- but this was different. I felt like I knew Gus, and I told myself there had to be some explanation.

Besides filling me in on one of the hospital's darker moments, Haskell asked me if I wanted to switch to the night shift. "We're short-staffed," he said, "and we could really use you. But if it's too much for you, after the introduction you've had, I'll understand."

"No," I said. "That's better for me actually." Less time in my darkened apartment, all alone without Nika. More time, maybe, to talk to Jessica. I felt drawn to her, and to the hospital.

I went home halfway through the day shift, since I'd been transferred over to nights, and slept as much as my body would allow before I had to get up and go back for my new shift.

On my way out to the jeep, I had to pass the part of the yard where I'd laid Nika to rest. I paused by her grave, too fucking pissed to shed any tears. What the hell had happened to her yesterday?

I pulled myself away and inspected the jeep before I got in. It was clean. I'd made absolutely sure of that yesterday, and again this morning, and a third time when I came back from the hospital at noon. I'd be doing it for days to come, I knew. Until I convinced myself that there was no sign anywhere near it of anything resembling a venomous snake.

Those That Whisper

The ward looked different on the 11:00 p.m. to 7:00 a.m. shift. A lot different. Quieter, darker, and the staff was limited to two people per ward.

Some of the wards were so understaffed that they only had one person on duty. This was against state policy and procedure, but there were simply not enough people to go around.

Tonight I was teamed up with Joe Burke again--he'd changed shifts, too. There were two of us, because we were staffing J Ward.

I'd been hoping, and unrealistically assumed, that I would be working A Ward and I would get to see Jessica, but that wasn't my kind of luck. Instead I had every fucking violent maniac in the state sleeping down the hallway from me.

Joe was snacking on Slim Jims with his feet up on the desk in the nurses' station. The station was secured with glass-encased crisscross metal, and the heavy doors were locked from the inside. All this was supposed to make everyone safer if the shit hit the fan, but we were in a locked unit for the criminally insane. How secure could it possibly be?

Joe was a good-sized man, and I felt a lot more comfortable working with him than I would with anybody else around here. I was a FNG, "fucking new guy," but I could recognize a good man when I saw one.

Joe must have been reading my mind, because he gave me a shit-eating grin and a wise-guy wink. He was wearing t-shirt with a picture of a green frog holding up its middle finger. The caption above it said, "I'm so happy I could shit!"

Things were a lot more casual at night. You didn't need to wear the ice-cream suit unless you left the ward.

The hallways seemed even darker than they had just a few hours ago. I remembered an old saying. *It's always darkest just before dawn.*

I said it aloud to break the monotony of silence. My voice echoed down the empty corridor. The ceiling lights didn't brighten it up much--just enough to read a name or room number off a patient's door. Which was totally ironic because if someone was having a conniption, you knew exactly where to go. You didn't need names or numbers.

There were no patients here anyway, in the sense of people who could be cured and eventually discharged from a hospital. This was the Extreme Caution Unit. Everyone here was completely off his rocker. If he was ever allowed to leave his room, it was only for showers and break-room activities.

My eyelids were getting heavy. I opened and closed my eyes. The corridor was like a stretch of desolate highway, narrowing as it stretched away in front of me until it disappeared into the darkness.

I shifted to get more comfortable in my chair. A shadow caught my eye, off to the left. It looked like a bunch of bed sheets rolled up into a ball and glued halfway up the wall.

I sat perfectly still. For a few seconds I was in the jungle again, remembering my training. Anything dark, any shape in the distance could be death itself. I'd learned to look for silhouettes, to wait and see what the thing did: if it moved, if it betrayed itself. If I waited long enough, the morning light would expose it.

More often than not, the shadow would be a piece of vegetation or some exotic bird. Neither of which was at all likely to show up here in this brick wasteland. My eyelids got heavier. My eyes slipped out of focus.

As if the loss of sight had made my other senses keener, I heard a soft whispering, like a group of people trying not to be heard. That woke me up.

I looked for Joe. The chair he'd been in was empty. I couldn't see him anywhere. He must have gone off to the can.

I pushed myself to my feet. The whispering went on uninterrupted. It was muffled with distance, but it was obviously there. I wasn't dreaming.

At first I thought it was coming from the ward, but it wasn't. It continued softly, like the steady hum of a fluorescent light: low, vibrating, consistent. I left the nurses' station and headed toward the corridor that led to the next building.

I stopped by the door. Warning signs screamed at me: WARNING! EXITING EXTREME CAUTION WARD!

No shit, I thought. I listened for the noise again. It was coming from below: like a group of adults and children whispering, some crying softly, as if in grief or pain. People in misery, with a rhythm almost like a chant, the same indecipherable phrases over and over.

"Friggin' hell," I said. "Joe, where the fuck are you?"

The whispering stopped. I started back toward the nurses' station--and stopped in my tracks. From down below, where the whispering had been, came the sharp and unmistakable cry of a newborn baby.

My whole body shuddered with cold and fear. If this was some kind of initiation rite, it was one hell of a good one.

I quick-marched back to the nurses' station, heading for the phone. I'd call the nursing supervisor, tell her what I was hearing, get her to explain it to me. And where the hell was Joe?

My footsteps echoed down the hallway. I tried to step lighter. The nursing supervisor would be pissed when I woke her up, but I didn't know what else to do.

The phone rang several times before it got picked up. A terrible scream rang in my ear. I hadn't heard anything remotely like it since Vietnam, and I'd never got used to it there. I looked around wildly, searching for the gun I didn't have.

The scream cut off. I heard slapping, the pounding of flesh, like punching a side of beef with bare knuckles, over and over. A new scream rang out, and then a second one--a different voice. They echoed and re-echoed inside the receiver.

Far in the background, I heard the

same mournful whispers, as if whoever it was witnessed the horrible beating. Then came the sound of a brief struggle, followed by sudden silence, except for the steady drone of the whisperers.

A baby began to wail--loud, angry, screaming in fury. I could feel that anger inside my own head, fighting to get out.

I slammed down the phone and bellowed into the darkness of the ward. "<u>JOE!</u> Where the fuck are you? Joe!"

I was completely, totally spooked. Just this side of panic. I had no fucking clue what to do. Couldn't leave the ward. Couldn't save the women. Couldn't find Joe.

The shadow on the wall caught my eye again. I could have sworn it had moved closer. It was a black ball of cloth, sticking to the wall--suspended there.

Part of me had absolutely no desire to leave the secure cage of the nurses' station. The rest, the part that was just about crazy enough to get me admitted to this hospital, got me up out of the station and down the hall toward the thing on the wall--wishing to God I had my piece with me.

The thing was moving, arching the way a cat does when it pounces on its prey. It had a head, and jet-black hair falling away from a dead-white face, and dead-white eyes sunk deep in a tracery of purple scars.

The scars were pulsing. I stopped, frozen. My breath puffed in front of me. The smell of death filled the corridor.

This was my vision, the horror I'd seen on the reservation when my grandfather was still alive: the day my parents died. I wished Grandpa was here for me now. I didn't know whether to run, cry or just let it take me once and for all.

I stood petrified, unable to move, my eyes locked with the eyes of a demon.

I remembered Ralphie Chen playing with Barretto's teeth, and the answer he gave when Joe asked him where he got them: "A monster gave them to me."

This is my destiny, I thought. Whatever

will happen will happen.

But oh God I'm so friggin' scared!

The demon arched its back like a cat, its shoulder blades almost touching each other, like a freak in a carnival. It was stuck to the wall as if its hands and knees had been nailed to it. Its head hung low, its eyes never blinking, staring straight at me, acknowledging me--recognizing me.

It moved ever so slowly in perfect balance, crawling sideways along the wall like a giant insect. Flies swarmed around me. Their buzzing was the only sound in the ward.

As I held eye contact with the demon, or whatever it was, I felt something slithering under the sole of my foot. I jumped back in horror and looked down.

There was no snake, and I still had my sneakers on. I glanced back toward the demon. Its malevolent smile told me who was responsible for what I'd felt.

The smile widened and the demon leaned forward as if to lunge at me and end my suffering. I braced for the attack--

and the demon scuttled backward into the darkness of the corridor, disappearing with inhuman speed, like a spider into its hole. Its eyes never left me, until the vanished into the shadows.

I was literally petrified. The humming of flies was gone; the ward was deathly quiet. I strained to see if the demon would come back for me, or if I could see any sign of the snake.

I heard Jennifer Choofane's voice in my head. Don't listen to the voices.

The hospital's alarm went off, whooping like an air-raid siren. That only happened, I'd been told, if something had gone dreadfully wrong.

No one had to tell me that. I was in a universe of shit, and its source was not of this world.

The rolling of distant thunder snapped me out of my shock. I ran like hell back to the nurses' station and locked myself in.

I looked out through the caged windows, hoping to see sunlight, but all I could see was the flicker of lightning through the pines, high above the hills of this lonesome valley. Dawn would soon be upon me, but the thick, bruised clouds would most certainly delay its arrival.

Directly outside the building, the howl of a coyote filled the gap between the warning siren and the soft patter of the first drops of rain. I was sure at that moment that I would not live to see another twilight--and that would be a good thing, because I was not sure if I wanted to.

The ward exploded into life. One voice rose above them all in a dreadful solo.

#

Nursing Supervisor Fletcher was the first to discover the bodies.

Joe Burke and the nurse escort were long overdue at the medical building with a patient who had developed a medical emergency. She decided to follow the path they should have taken, to see if she could intercept them--and hopefully find out what had caused the delay.

As she descended the tunnel stairs, she felt a chill in the air that she had not felt before: cold, damp, with a smell almost like that of a burst sewer pipe in the winter. She walked briskly, pulling her sweater up over her shoulders. She kept feeling as if she was not alone--as if someone was just ahead of her, or perhaps just behind her.

As usual, the tunnel was dimly lit. Her eyes flicked back and forth. She wished she had stayed where she was and waited.

She walked faster. Waves of black flies flew past her, bringing with them a strong smell of death and decay. Some kind of animal, a raccoon maybe, must have drowned in the drainage system during the storm.

She turned a corner and saw what looked like a giant bag of trash on the floor of the tunnel--but the trash was rocking back and forth. She paused, peering into the dimness. Whatever or whoever it was was crying softly, and there was blood everywhere, trickling slowly and steadily down the tunnel toward her.

The movement snapped into focus. A woman knelt in a pool of blood, rocking and weeping over the motionless body of Joe Burke. His torso lay parallel to his long legs, as if cut in half by a gigantic razor. His entrails spread beside him. The woman patient lay beside him, completely covered in dark red blood. Even at that distance, Supervisor Fletcher could see the hollow sockets where her eyes used to be.

A swarm of black flies feasted on the bodies. The air in the tunnel had grown desperately cold. The woman rocked back and forth, sobbing steadily but softly, as if she dared not raise her voice too loud and bring back whatever had destroyed the others.

She raised her head, and with a shock, Supervisor Fletcher recognized her. It was the escorting nurse, Sharon Corcoran.

Fletcher called to her across the river of blood. "Sharon? Sharon, come. I'm here. Come to me."

Sharon shook her head, rocking and sobbing, sobbing and rocking. Supervisor Fletcher took a deep breath and gathered all her courage to splash through the blood. It seemed to take forever before she reached Sharon.

She held out her hand and said in her firmest and most authoritative voice, "Come, Sharon. We have to go."

Sharon's stare was blank, looking right through her, but she did not resist as Fletcher pulled her to her feet. They were covered in blood, like the rest of her--like Fletcher's own feet in their white shoes and stockings.

Fletcher got a solid grip on Sharon's wrist, turned and strode back down the tunnel. To her relief, Sharon stayed with her. So did the flies, swirling around their ankles, all the way up to the next level, where the panic alarm was.

#

Brian Foley lay unconscious in his

hospital bed. Deep within his mind, over and over again, he endured the same, endless recurring nightmare: the dark and deserted church, Vinny Kelley as he had been when he died, all blood and bone and shredded fatigues, and the faceless parishioner in the front pew.

This time, he swore to himself, he would see it through. He would hold on to the end.

Just as always before, Vinny Kelley prayed in his strong and steady voice, and the parishioner slowly, slowly threatened to reveal his face. And yet again, the great wind roared through the church and the outer doors slammed open, and footsteps approached through the darkness. Vinny Kelley's mangled arm rose, pointing toward the one who approached. And that also was as before.

But this time Brian Foley made himself break the pattern. He looked at the parishioner.

The parishioner looked back, and with two fingers, made a motion as if to slash himself across the throat. Tommy Neveska laughed in Brian Foley's face.

Brian Foley turned away, toward the shadow that advanced into the light of the altar candles. Little by little the figure took shape.

Barry Redcrow stood in the flickering glow. He held out a hand, reaching out to Foley: peaceful, comforting.

Vinny Kelley stopped praying. He was no longer disfigured; he was whole again, and he shone as bright as the sun. His face was full of peace.

Tommy Neveska let out a roar of purest, most unnatural rage and sprang backward onto the back of the pew. He perched there on all fours like a beast ready to spring. His scream went on and on.

#

Brian Foley leaped out of bed. His forehead was covered with tiny drops of blood; his hands and feet bled profusely.

#

Jessica woke to the whoop of an air-raid siren, accompanied by the roll of thunder and the flash of lightning right in her face like Mother Nature's own alarm clock.

Something was dreadfully wrong. The siren wailed like a living creature: soft to loud, loud to soft, stopping only to take another breath before exhaling its mournful song. She had never heard it before. If she lived through this, she hoped never to hear it again.

#

"HE'S COMING FOR YOU, REDCROW! HE IS! THE COLD HARD TRUTH! HE'S COMING FOR YOU! AND HE'S BRING HELL WITH HIM!"

I heard Sampson's voice over all the other screaming lunatics.

"HE'S HERE FOR YOU! BECAUSE OF YOU! HE'S GONNA TEAR YOUR SOUL TO

TINY FUCKING PIECES! AND HE'S GONNA LET ME BURN IT!" Suddenly, shockingly, his voice dropped. It was soft, calm. "That's the cold hard truth."

I shouldn't have been able to hear that at all, but it came through perfectly clear. I could picture his horribly burned face smiling at me the way the demon had just a moment ago.

Sampson knew the demon. Oh, yes. He knew all about him.

My mind went blank. I bolted out of the nurses' station and ran down the steep stair. The only thing in my head was my dream of Brian Foley in the tunnel, wearing a priest's cassock.

The door slammed behind me. I heard the tiny extra click that told me it had locked.

I'd left the keys in the nurses' station. There was no way out for me except through the tunnel.

I was sick to my stomach and near blind with horror, but I kept on running. What choice did I have? I just wanted to get out of here. And never, ever come back.

I balanced myself on the railing, taking the stairs by twos and threes. Down into the belly of the snake, I thought.

The bottom came up surprisingly fast. I veered right, looking for any sign of a ladder that would lead me to a manhole and eventually topside, but I found none.

The air was suddenly much colder, and I heard the buzzing of flies. Around here that was never a good sign. I slowed to a fast walk, hunching down to make myself a smaller target.

Up ahead, dark shadows lay on the ground in a way I'd learned long ago to recognize. They were dead bodies.

I didn't want to go that way, but I couldn't go back the way I had come. I edged closer. Blood and feces--lots of both, stinking in air so cold I could see my breath in front of me.

One of the bodies was Joe. His eyes were plucked out of his head; his face was set in a rictus of pure horror. His chest was cracked wide open. His legs and his torso lay side by side, still dressed in the white ice-cream suit, now saturated with blood. His entrails spilled out of his stomach and stretched across the floor.

A patient in a hospital nightgown lay beside him, her eyes also gouged out, her face deeply bruised, her body butchered. The VC had left presents like this in 'Nam, to scare the living shit out of us and kill morale.

While I stood staring at a scene of butchery that I'd hoped never to have to see again, I realized that the blood was moving. It was creeping toward me, slowly but unmistakably, as if it sensed my presence.

It was dark and thick, with that distinctive coppery smell. It covered the entire width of the tunnel. There was no way to get past except by walking through it. On the other side, just visible in the dimness of the tunnel, I saw footprints leading away.

I was stuck on this side, and the pool of blood was creeping toward me. Coming after me. Stretching out thick, glistening tendrils, reaching for my feet.

I couldn't move. I could barely breathe. The blood was almost lapping my toes.

A hand fell on my shoulder.

FIRE STORM

Adam Sampson lay in his bed, beside himself with joy, though he'd been bound with leather restraints for the past twenty-four hours. It had begun, and the Master had promised to make him a part of it.

As he cherished the thought, the restraints at his wrists and ankles began to shift and slither. He looked down. The leather straps were gone. In their place were snakes, unwinding themselves and sliding off his body onto the floor.

He heard the heavy clank of the door's lock releasing, setting him free. He sat up and stretched, then hobbled out into the hallway. His body was stiff and sore. He rubbed his wrists as he looked around.

There was no staff anywhere in the ward. The nurses' station was empty. He laughed out loud, got hold of a wheelchair and threw it at the glass.

It took a couple of tries, but the weight of the chair finally won the battle. He climbed through the jagged opening.

The master keys lay on the desk. He pounced on them with glee and headed for the medicine closet where the staff kept the cigarettes and the leather restraints as well as the patients' medication.

He picked out a cigarette and relaxed with it at the supervisor's desk, feet up, not a care in the world. While the smoke filled his lungs and wreathed around his head, he contemplated the open closet and plotted his next move.

There were plenty of meds he could and would take with him, along with some restraints, but he was looking for something more powerful. He took one last, long drag on the cigarette and stubbed it out, then searched until he found what he was looking for.

There it was. He leaped on it with a cry of glee.

He walked down the hallway swinging the ring of master keys around his index finger, humming a song that was stuck in his head. He stopped by the door of one of the psychos he knew to be in four-point restraints. Larry Enfield, his name was. Sampson opened the door.

Light seeped in from the dimly lit hallway. Compared to the dark in Enfield's room it was dazzling. Enfield squinted at Sampson. "Who the fuck--" He stopped and did a double take. "You? Hey! Let me out of these fucking restraints!"

Sampson laughed. "Let yourself out," he said.

Enfield howled at him. Sampson howled back, practically rolling on the floor at the joke.

Enfield had bit his own fingers off and eaten them a long time ago. That little habit of his was what had got him committed to Middlesex Fells in the first place. He liked to break into people's homes and strangle them, then chew off some of their fingers and eat them. He got a life sentence in prison for the strangling part, but in prison he'd skipped the strangling and gone straight to chewing off his fellow inmates' fingers--usually with an audience cheering him on.

For that he got sent to protective custody in the prison's psychiatric ward, where he branched out to his own fingers-- one at a time, until there was nothing left to eat. Some of his buddies encouraged him to start on his toes, but he didn't like toes. Too short. Gristly.

And that got him a one-way ticket to the Middlesex Fells Reservation Insane Asylum.

Sampson fished in his pocket for a fresh cigarette and lit it. Enfield was still screaming at him. He poured rubbing alcohol down the length of Enfield's body.

Enfield was batshit but he wasn't stupid. His screaming changed from rage to panicky pleading. "No! Noooo! Sampson! Don't do it!"

Sampson finished his cigarette and flipped the Zippo lighter, smiling lovingly at the pretty blue flame. Equally lovingly, he lit the puddle of alcohol over Enfield's belly button. The whole thing burst into flame, a beautiful rush of light and heat and the rich smell of burning flesh filling his nose and lungs.

Enfield's screams washed over him. He teased the flames with a new dousing of alcohol.

Nice, he thought, but not flammable enough. Around him the ward was like a mob of chimpanzees in a feeding frenzy: screaming, pounding, slamming into walls. Sampson ignored them, feeding the flames with a steady stream of alcohol. "I'm back," he said, and giggled.

Enfield fought like the mad thing he was. His shoulders cracked, breaking out of the sockets. He went still, as if the sound or the pain or both had stopped him short. His mouth gaped as he sucked in air.

Sampson poured the last of the alcohol into the opening Enfield so kindly offered. With his last breath, Enfield breathed fire and spit forth flames.

Adam Sampson laughed and applauded. "Larry Enfield, the human dragon!"

He left the body to burn itself out, went back to the medicine closet and pulled out a handful of restraints, a syringe and a bottle of Phenobarbital. He was about to have some fun.

#

The Preacher lay in the deepest of the tunnels, drunk on his own power, plotting his next grand move. He had only dreamed of power like this; now he was living it.

Killing had never been so easy. Before, when he killed, he had to be careful. He had to work in secret, and hide. He had to learn as he went.

Now, who could stop him? With each new killing, his power grew. Eating the heart of the big man in the tunnel--it was like a drug. All that strength, all that life and vigor, had poured into him with each rapturous bite.

And the eyes--as he swallowed them, he saw even more clearly in the dark. It was right. It was meant. This was what he had been born to do.

Swollen and near to blowing wide open with beautiful, intoxicating power, he howled to the unseen heavens. Before the last of the echoes died, he lay on his belly and slithered through the storm pipes toward the Mystic River.

#

The hand on my shoulder sent a jolt of sheer terror through me. I whipped around--and came face to face with Gus Jacobs.

"Come with me," he said softly but firmly.

Whatever he was, alive or dead, he took the edge off my fear. I could trust him. That was completely not rational, and purely instinctive.

I went with my instincts. I followed him. He navigated the dark and lonesome tunnel with speed that should not have been possible for a man of his age. I struggled to keep him in sight, sucking wind, scared shitless.

Left, right, right again, left, then straight. Suddenly he stopped and raised his hand in a signal I remembered well from the jungle: *Stop. Wait.*

Gus stared straight ahead without blinking. I peered into the darkness. The tunnel was full of people, or shadows of people.

"Stay close behind me," Gus said. "Do exactly as I say, and you'll be all right."

My heart was beating so hard that the demon would surely hear it and track me down. "Who are they?" I whispered.

"They're victims of this wretched corner of hell known as the Middlesex Fells Lunatic Hospital," he answered, "destined for fear and suffering long before the place was ever built."

We approached them cautiously. There were a large number of adults, but even larger number of children: horribly disfigured, missing limbs or eyes or with the blank faces and empty eyes of lobotomy patients. Their skin was pale and sagging; some were clothed, some not. And it was cold, so very cold. I saw my breath in front of me, but not Gus's.

Some of the children looked as if one side of their ribcages had been removed. Their spines were twisted, their bodies out of balance: one side curving outward, the other collapsed on itself. Their faces were angry. They had no welcome for us, and no desire to let us by.

"Those had tuberculosis," Gus said. "Doctors experimented blindly, trying anything that might possibly work--or not. Mostly not. Trial and error. Cruel, un-Christian . . . Removing ribs and lungs. Swaddling them in bed sheets and immersing them in ice water for hours. Chemicals inhaled into the lungs, scorching the sensitive tissues." His face twisted in disgust and grief. "The same went for mental illness. Blind, heartless experiments: lobotomies, amputations, castrations, surgeries without anesthesia, electroshock therapy. Things worse than your mind can imagine."

He spoke so softly, so steadily, that his voice held me rooted. But if I did run away from all this, where would I go?

"They have witnessed firsthand the horror of this evil place. The evil itself feeds on their fear. All this was destined from the very beginning, just as you were destined to come here."

"But why?" I cried, forgetting to be quiet.

"Some things are not meant to be understood," he said. "Not in this life. It's God's way. Just know that you are exactly where you are supposed to be--for better or for worse." He hesitated; then added, "And so is He."

The demon, Gus meant. I could tell by the shudder in his voice. The dark spirit. I had a feeling Gus knew all about it. I also knew, deep down, that Gus too was exactly where he was supposed to be.

He nodded as if he could read my mind. "Now you begin to understand and accept your destiny."

I wasn't so sure about that, but I wasn't

sure enough to argue, either.

He nodded toward the shadows ahead of us. "These are lost souls, suffering from unresolved anger at what happened to them in life and in death, waiting for their deliverance." He drew a set of rosary beads from his pocket and hung it around his neck where the shadows could see. The beads glowed softly in the darkness. "He has not forgotten you."

The lost ones gazed in awe at the shining beads. As he reached the first of them, they drew aside, parting like the Red Sea. Rocks fell from the children's hands, dropping to the floor with an echoing thud.

My breath came shallow; my whole body shuddered with cold. "What--what are they doing here?" I said through chattering teeth.

Gus paused. He turned and looked me in the eye. "They are here to bear witness to the evil that long ago descended upon this place, sentenced to walk here until their souls can be saved." An expression of great sadness crossed his face. "They have suffered terribly."

Looking into those deep and mournful eyes, I knew that what Haskell had told me was true. Gus too was dead.

I wasn't, was I? I was still alive. I wasn't a ghost.

As before, Gus heard me, though I hadn't said the words aloud. "Not yet. This is why you are here. You can never outrun your destiny. Pray that God has mercy on your soul, and ask for His power to assist you in this fight against evil. Do not let yourself forsake Him."

He stopped abruptly. In front of him was a narrow metal ladder.

I looked back toward the horde of lost souls and found the tunnel empty. The cold was gone. But I could see the shapes of rocks on the floor, where the children had dropped them.

I turned to Gus again. "Who are you?"

"A mere servant of God," he answered. "May He bless you and always be with you."

I set hands and feet to the ladder and

began the ascent. When I looked down, Gus was gone, all but the whisper of his voice echoing in the tunnel below: "Find your faith. Save your soul."

The last words faded into shrieks and wailing, the chorus of the damned and the hopeless and the forgotten. It was the saddest sound I had ever heard. It echoed around me, reverberating through the tunnel.

Another sound rose to overwhelm it: the howl of something far more malevolent. Evil, unnatural--demonic. It pierced through my body.

I was almost to the top of the ladder. The siren whooped beyond, interspersed with what sounded like a pack of coyotes in full cry. With a surge of pure adrenaline, I thrust open the manhole cover.

The demon shrieked like a banshee, mocking me. *There is no escape,* its howl said to me. *This is your destiny. You know it, and I know it. I'm coming for you, you worthless scrap of humanity. I'm coming for* you, *because of you, and I will tear your soul to pieces.*

I gulped in air as if I'd been drowning. A low fog spread across the ground. I'd seen mornings like this in Vietnam: coming up out of cold, damp, stale-smelling tunnels into the cool freshness of night just turning into dawn.

Cool air meeting warm ground, low fog. . . snakes creeping through the tunnels and hiding in the fog. Snakes in the jeep. The demon in the ward, and the snake turning, invisible, under my foot . . .

Must . . . not . . . panic. Panic was death.

I looked up. There was the church, and there was the golden cross that shone in my dreams. Behind it was the cemetery where Jessica spent her days, among the sad and lonely graves marked only by a number and a letter. No names, no dates. No memories to pass on to later generations.

A great sadness overwhelmed me. Lightning slashed the sky. It began to rain.

I ran out of that hellhole as fast as my

body would go. In my head was the image from Jessica's painting of people climbing a rainbow out of a dark tunnel, while others fell into a blood-red abyss.

Was I one of the ones who would make it out? I was leaving, that was for sure, but I didn't feel safe.

My jeep was almost alone in the parking lot, with no other vehicles around it. I balanced on the side bumper to get my feet out of the crawling fog, peering under the seat for signs of snakes.

Nothing there. I jammed the key in the ignition and ground the engine into gear. I peeled out of there so fast I almost snapped my own neck.

All hell broke loose around me: coyotes wailing, air-raid siren whooping, lightning cracking and thunder rolling, and demon howling to drown out all the rest. All of them fought for control of the air--and my soul.

The jeep's radio came on by itself. <u>Delta Bravo Six! Delta Bravo Six! We are in contact! Repeat! We are in contact!</u>

<u>Receiving heavy enemy fire!</u>

That wasn't any radio show I'd ever heard in this part of the world. It was an Army broadcast--and it was blaring out my old unit's call sign. Machine guns and grenades went off in the background while the voice screamed for air support. *Coordinates: 9-er 5 . . .*

I punched the off button, but the radio kept on broadcasting. A loud explosion, a spray of machine-gun fire. Men screaming. Men dying. Voices calling out in Vietnamese.

The radio cut off. I floored the accelerator and aimed the jeep toward home.

"The eyes of the Lord are on the righteous, and His ears are open to their cry."

Psalm 34:15

Brian Foley walked in a white priest's robe through the bloody fields of Korea. Captain Vincent Kelley held his hand as they made their way through the hot, dark summer night. Men on all sides screamed in agony.

The darkness was no barrier to Foley's sight. Vinny Kelley was just as he had been on that night, and in many nightmares since: badly wounded, bleeding, flesh burned away, white bone shining through, one eye hanging from its socket.

Soldiers ran past them, firing their weapons, as artillery rounds exploded on all sides. No one seemed to see Foley or Vinny. They were invisible: ghosts walking through a landscape of death.

"Everything happens for a reason,

Brian," Vinny said. "You're exactly where you're supposed to be. Don't ever question it. Some things are just not meant to be understood."

Vinny paused by a young soldier screaming in pain and fear--crying for his mother, though the language he spoke was not English. His eyes darted blindly. He knew he was dying, and it terrified him.

Vinny wiped blood from his own wounds and drew a cross on the young man's forehead. It glowed bright in the dark night.

The young man stopped screaming. His eyes steadied; he looked into their faces. He could see them.

Foley took the young man's hand. Beside him Vinny said, "Go in peace, child."

The young man closed his eyes. Foley felt the life drain out of him.

Foley's white robe was all stained with red. His hands bled. He wiped his forehead; blood streamed from it. His feet were bleeding: he left a trail of bloody footprints as he walked away from the dead soldier.

He looked up toward the horizon. Night battled the day for control--but of what?

Vinny was still beside him, but all his wounds were healed. He was in full battle uniform, meticulously clean, and not a scratch on him, just as Brian had always wanted to remember him. He glowed in the darkness, radiating peace.

He took Foley's hands in his. At his touch, the wounds were healed; the blood was gone. "The eyes of the Lord are on the righteous," he said, "and His ears are open to their cry."

Then he turned and ran to the next wounded soldier and the next and the next, leaving Brian Foley alone and crying his name.

Foley woke still calling for Vinny, with Rita clutching his bandaged right hand and sobbing.

#

It had been so long since my parents

died, and my world had changed so much, that I'd stopped believing in what happened to me that day in the lake. Now I knew that it was all real, waiting for me for to come to it, just like Grandpa said. I thought I had escaped my destiny, but I'd been completely and totally wrong. There was no escaping fate.

That was the cold hard truth, just like that fucking psycho Sampson had said. I had fought so hard to bury it and run away from it and wish it away. But I'd always known it was there, just below the surface, waiting patiently, biding its time.

Grandpa's voice echoed in my skull. I was exactly where I was supposed to be-- and it was time for the dark spirit to show itself once again.

I shifted the jeep into third gear, roaring down the dark road, trying to get home as fast as I could--to end it all. A rush to death.

The woods flashed by me. The demon's sick smile gleamed in the shadows, tormenting me from behind every tree.

Ghost soldiers are only friends with the shadows of their own nightmares. My war with myself was over. I'd known that as soon as I recognized what I was seeing, perched like a huge spider on the wall of the ward. It wanted me, and it wanted me dead.

This time I wouldn't fight. I'd seen so many dead bodies, and created so many. The smell of burning flesh, the screams of the dying, the unmistakable smell of spilled blood. The suffering of soldiers so far away from home, calling for their mothers. The tears and anguish of war.

It wasn't over. It was still happening, following me wherever I went. Joe's blood, so red against his bleached white uniform.

I kept seeing the pool of deep red blood creeping toward me as if it had a mind of its own, clutching at me with soft, searching fingers. I saw the cop with his hands sewn to his ears, impaled on a cross a hundred and fifty feet up in the air, and Nika bitten by that swarm of snakes.

Jessica had warned me. She'd predicted

almost of all of it. "Sometimes people get what they deserve," she'd said.

Maybe that was true. I was getting what I deserved. I was alone, and I was cursed. The cold hard truth: just like Sampson said.

#

Jessica looked out the window of the hospital. The siren sang its mournful song. Low fog shrouded the ground, and in the distance she saw the flicker of approaching lightning. The rain began to drizzle down.

The entire hospital was awake and in frenzy. Outside her circle of conscious quiet, normally peaceful patients were out of their rooms, rampaging through the day room, tearing apart books, throwing crayons, destroying board games.

In all this commotion, she could not stop thinking about Barry--worrying about him. Something was not right there.

Suddenly she felt cold and weak. She tried to get up, to make it back to her room

416

before she had another one of her episodes.

She stumbled and fell. None of the staff saw her: they were struggling to get the ward under control. She fought to stay conscious, but the darkness crept in around her. Oh, this was not good. Not good at all.

#

I made it back to my apartment. The sanctity of the home, isn't that what they say? But I didn't feel any safer.

I ripped through the clothes in my drawer. It was in there somewhere--the means to end all this. To take my life.

It was still dark. Twilight was overdue, and I wanted this to be over before the sun came up.

Lightning split the sky. Thunder rumbled in the distance.

My fingers found the gun. I didn't look down--couldn't look it in the eye. I carried it to the chair in the living room.

I held it between my knees. It was loaded. All I had to do was find the balls to put it to my head. Careful not to look it in the eye, the steel eye, staring back at me, the eye of death, daring, taunting, wanting . . .

I was so alone.

Never look at that smiling eye. Just pull the trigger. Pull the fucking trigger.

I closed my eyes and raised the gun to my head, pulling ever so slightly on the trigger, closing, closing . . . almost there . . . waiting for it . . .

A flicker of lightning through my closed eyelids. A rumble of thunder, closer this time.

Pressure on the trigger . . . pressure . . . almost there . . .

My Grandpa spoke from the corner of the room. His voice was soft but confident.

I turned. I could barely make out the shape of him in the darkness. Then a small flame appeared in his palm, illuminating his face. "A daughter of the earth will guide you and release you from the depths of your pain. It is not your destiny to end your life by your own hand. To do so would rouse the wrath of the Great Spirit and condemn your soul to the world of the dead, never to see your ancestors again. You will breathe your last breath this hour, but you must find your faith."

Lightning flashed again and again. Thunder rolled louder. The storm was closing in, moving fast now.

"Follow the path that has been ordained for you by your people."

I threw the .45 on the floor and lunged toward Grandpa, but he was gone. In between the lightning and the thunder, I heard a hissing voice calling my name. It seemed to be coming from the river.

I left the gun where it lay and ran outside into the yard, heading toward the river. It was raining a little heavier now, but the worst of it was still to come.

I turned toward Nika's grave. The voice on the wind hissed my name again, louder. It was coming from the water.

I waded through the fog, expecting at

any second to feel the sharp pain of a snake's fangs in my leg, but I made it free and clear to the dock. No fog hovered there. I could see the worn planks under my feet.

I opened my mouth to yell, "Come and get me, motherfuckers!"

The words never came out. The Messenger landed in a tree almost next to me. His eyes glowed through the darkness.

Grandpa had warned me when I was a child: "When an owl looks you in the eye . . ."

A cold hand reached up through the dock and gripped my ankle like a vise, spilling me sideways into the dark water.

The water was cold, and black. Black as midnight, cold as ice. It should have been only two or three feet deep at that particular spot, but I was sinking down and down, deeper and deeper.

I saw the lightning far above me and heard the fading roar of thunder, while I fell farther and farther away, dragged down into a bottomless pit. I reached up toward it, but cold dead hands dragged me down--

one at first, then many. So many. The chill of their touch spread through my body.

It felt as if I'd been sinking for an hour, but I hadn't lost my breath yet. The cold deepened. I thrashed in panic, clutching at something, anything that could help. But there was nothing.

I closed my eyes and went limp. More and more hands came at me from below, not just grabbing or dragging now, but pulling and scratching, tearing at my skin.

Were these the tortured souls I'd seen in the tunnel with Gus? Was that where I was?

I tried to scream, but the water silenced me. My heart pounded inside my chest.

I heard my name once more, in the same hissing voice as before. It was crystal clear, as if someone was whispering directly into my ear.

I opened my eyes. I was still underwater, but I was not alone.

The demon floated in front of me. Its black hair streamed in the current. Its white, dead eyes were fixed on me, and its blue and bloated face with its livid, writhing scars was smiling at me, mocking me.

It grabbed me by the throat with both hands and began strangling me, pushing me straight down. Its fingers were like ice. Its grip was unforgiving. And all the while it stared and stared and smiled and smiled--that sick, evil smile that haunted my nightmares.

Everything went black. I whispered one last word before I gave myself up to it: "Momma . . ."

#

Sampson had three desperados from his floor heavily medicated on Phenobarbital. He had juiced them up pretty good while they were still in restraints. After all, he was in a hospital for the criminally insane, and these men were a danger to everyone.

He tied their hands behind them with leather restraints and led them like dogs, each with a restraint around his neck, connected by a long series of leather belt restraints. He made them walk in single file, just like captured gooks in Vietnam-- when they captured some alive.

He still dreamed about burning them all. He wished he could have experimented more back then: made them swallow gasoline and stuck a grenade in their mouths, or shot 'em in the belly and tried to get the gasoline to explode.

Maybe he'd get to do some of that after this was over. But he had other things to do first. His captives walked like zombies, eyes heavy, mouths hanging open with dried spit in the corners, feet dragging, as if they were dead already and didn't know it.

He walked his dogs through the steel door and into the stairwell. There he found a sign from the Master, which looked as if it was written in blood: two parallel lines, with an arrow pointing down.

Sampson had to be careful with the dogs on the stairs. If one of them fell, he would drag the others with him, and it was not time for that yet.

He guided them slowly down the stairs and into the tunnel. The Master's sign peeled off the wall, turned into a swarm of flies and disappeared down the tunnel, leaving no indication that it had ever been there.

Sampson had a powerful urge to run after them, but that would be the end of his dogs. He concentrated on leading them slowly down through the belly of the snake instead, and that gave him a little bit of happiness. Not as much as burning Enfield, but enough to keep him going.

At the bottom he found a tremendous, a wonderful surprise. It was like being a child again and waking up on Christmas morning. There, in front of the very last step, as big and proud as Sampson had ever seen, was a five-gallon can of gasoline.

Just like always. He checked his crotch for the lighter, knowing full well it was there, but he had to check anyway. This was just too good to be true.

On the floor next to the can was another arrow painted in blood. He picked up the can and led his dogs where it pointed--and as before, it rose up into a swarm of black flies and flew ahead of him, leading the way.

Sampson was very pleased. The Master had included him in His plans--and He had thought of everything.

#

Through the darkness leaked the barely audible hint of a whimper, as if a small animal was caught in a trap and unable to free itself. I strained to hear it again in this wretched place, but only felt the last of my pulse leave my body through the tips of my fingers.

Countless ice-cold hands gripped me. Their sharp nails pierced my skin to the bone, pulling me down with irresistible force. I felt the hands' owners watching me with terrible malice and hatred. Their bitter cold presence pierced me through.

There was no escaping them, not now and not ever.

They laughed at me as the last of my life seeped from me. They were ruthless; they had no mercy.

They were soldiers of the dark spirit, and they had been with me all my life. Somehow I had always escaped them.

My grandfather had made that possible. The ceremony he had conducted on the reservation after my parents' death had protected me.

That protection was gone. This was where I was meant to die. There was nothing but dismal cold and the feeling of deep sadness all around me. I was all alone, as I had been for a long time, and I prayed that my life would end soon.

Then I heard it again: the whimper, but this time a little louder and longer. It bounced off my body like a radar ping.

It came from directly above me--far above, aimed deep into whatever level of Hell I was in. But it didn't matter. I just wanted it all to end.

I had suffered enough. I wanted to see my parents and my grandfather. I had had enough of this world.

The whimper turned into an elongated howl. It drew me out of myself and gave me the last tiny bits of strength to see through the abyss.

My life played out before me. My eyes were locked on it. I couldn't close them or turn away. All the fears and the horrors: Vietnam, my parents' death, my grandfather, my vision in the lake--they had all finally caught up with me.

It was time to face what my grandfather had protected me from for so long. It was time to finish it.

I was deathly afraid. Although I desperately wanted to die, I did not want to be alone. I prayed for Grandpa to be with me now.

The sound from far above me was louder than before, as if it sensed that I could hear it. A dog barked in answer.

I knew that bark. That was my dog. My Nika.

My heart exploded with a last burst of life. I stretched my arm as far above my head as I could, despite the unseen force that dragged me down.

Nika's bark grew louder and more ferocious. The sharp nails sunk in my arm peeled the skin from it like an orange.

The pain was excruciating. Teeth tore at my flesh, gnawing and worrying at it. There was something desperate about them, something like panic.

They were afraid. Of me. That fear gave me strength. It gave me the will, after all, to survive.

Nika howled just above me. I screamed her name.

The dark spirits screamed back. If they failed, if I escaped, the evil that ruled them was afraid of what would happen to it--and then it would be back with vengeful anger.

I fought with all the strength that was left to me. A sharp burning pain pierced my arm, and a tremendous force wrenched me upward.

The last of the claws and teeth dropped

away. Jubilation filled me. Grandpa had heard me. My whole body down to my toes was one stinging, throbbing wound rubbed in salt--and I didn't care. I wanted <u>out</u>.

Nika's barking reverberated around me. Through what seemed like miles of water I saw a pinpoint of bright light directly above me. The white-hot grip on my arm dragged me closer and closer to it.

It seemed to be struggling against the weight of my dead body. Yes, I was dead. I'd been granted my wish. The pain had slipped away. The unforgiving evil had ceased to exist--for now. For evil never truly goes away.

Now more than ever, I was at peace with myself. The pinpoint of light grew larger, and many other tiny particles of light joined it.

After what seemed like hours, I could feel the cool air on the tips of my fingers as my hand broke the surface. The rest of my body would follow, I thought, and float to the heavens where my ancestors would greet me. I looked for my grandfather, but instead saw the most beautiful and loyal sight that I had ever seen.

Nika had me by my arm, pulling me up. As my head broke the surface, cool air brushed my face. Crickets and peepers chirped, and the trees swayed and rustled in the light spring breeze.

The earth was dark around me, but when I looked up, the moon shone brightly, still lighting the path of my escape. The storm was gone. The sky was full of stars, a dome of light stretching from horizon to horizon. I stood with my head back, gaping in awe.

Nika let go of my arm. Water lapped my knees. I lowered my eyes from the panorama of the heavens and saw my dog sitting on the shore, panting slightly. Her tail wagged. She was happy to see me.

Not near as happy as I was to see her.

Off in the distance, an owl hooted. It was the Messenger, and it was speaking to me. I moved closer to it, wading out of the river and onto the bank.

I was surprisingly calm; my spirit was

at peace. As I passed under the trees, the breeze whispered around me. Its touch relieved the pain of the deep cuts and scratches all over my body.

The owl perched on a branch twenty feet from me. Someone had died, its presence said.

My grandfather's voice spoke through the rustling of wind in the leaves. "You must hurry. It is coming, and there isn't much time."

#

Lieutenant Detective Sullivan and Detective Foster made their way to the Nurse Supervisor's office in the medical building at the Middlesex Fells Reservation Psychiatric Hospital. The hospital was on complete lockdown, and the Medford Police Department had called in the Massachusetts State Police to help with the investigation. All these homicides were more than the Medford P.D. could handle; it needed all the help it could get.

Supervisor Fletcher was in much the same condition. She was bending over one of the nurses, Sharon Corcoran, who looked as if she had literally bathed in blood. Her eyes were completely wild, and she was talking in a rapid monotone, never once stopping for breath. "I've seen death before, of course I have, I'm a nurse, we see it all the time, but never like this-- usually they just come in an ambulance, but this--right here, Officers, right *here*, and beaten to a pulp, I can't--I never--I don't--"

Lieutenant Sullivan tried to slow down the stream with a question pitched in a level voice, low and intended to calm both women. "Where in the tunnel did you first observe--"

The nurse passed out in mid-babble, folded up and fainted dead away.

#

The darkness dissipated. Sharon woke in a wheelchair. Someone was pushing it,

432

but she could not see who it was: she could not turn or in fact move at all.

She was in the tunnel. The walls were in fire, but she could feel no heat, only a deep and penetrating cold.

She tried to get up, to run, but she was trapped, immobilized, by leather restraints at wrists and ankles. There was a watch on her wrist, but it had no hands to tell the time.

The chair rolled forward slowly but inexorably toward a looming dark figure, like a carnival ride in Hell. The figure's head was down, its jet-black hair falling around its face.

The flames on the walls grew brighter as she approached. She struggled frantically to escape, but she could not even scream. She pressed herself as far back in the chair as she could, as if those few inches could protect her from the dark thing.

She was almost upon it. It lifted its head, baring its corpse-white face and its writhing wounds, fixing her with its dead eyes.

It lifted its hand. A living heart pulsed in it, pumping blood with every beat.

The dead thing raised its hands, scraping the walls. Flames danced all around it, transfixing it in their bright glow.

It threw back its head and swallowed the heart whole. Blood rolled down its pallid chin.

It spoke with its head still flung back, staring blankly at the vault above its head. "Sharon," it said in a guttural voice, raw and demonic, with a timbre that was not of this earth. "You shall bear witness."

The unholy fire reached toward her and surrounded her. She burst into flames.

#

Sharon Corcoran screamed at the top of her lungs, startling the living piss out of the two detectives and Supervisor Fletcher. She threw herself to the floor and rolled frantically. Smoke was coming off her, as if her body had begun to smolder.

The officers got hold of her hands and feet and held her down. Her screaming went on uncontrollably, but neither of them could spare a hand to clamp it over her mouth.

Her skin was almost too hot to touch. It was all they could do to hold on while Nurse Fletcher ran to get a doctor and a syringe. After several tries, he shot it into her buttocks.

Whatever was in the syringe, it did the trick. She gave one last massive heave that flung Detective Foster clean away, then passed out cold.

#

Jessica Choofane pushed a patient in a wheelchair through the darkest and deepest of the tunnels. Flames climbed the walls and licked the ceiling.

She strained to see the face, but it was completely concealed in the mass of hair. No eyes, no nose, no mouth--nothing.

The flames around her generated no heat at all. She was cold to the bone, and colder still when she saw what waited ahead: the dark figure, the hideous face, the heart gushing blood.

Could it see her? She wasn't sure. It was focused on the woman in the chair, and its words were aimed at her, tormenting her.

The woman burst into flames. Jessica woke on the floor of the corridor in A Ward with the woman's screams still echoing inside her skull. She crawled toward the safety of her room.

#

Just ahead of me in the woods, a campfire flared up out of nothing, as if someone had thrown gasoline onto a smoldering log. Off to the left of it I saw my grandfather leaning over a figure on the ground, drawing on its face.

I had seem him do this many times when I was younger. He gathered herbs and plants from the forest and extracted their colors, and used them to perform our ancestral rituals.

The figure Grandpa was working on was male, and pale--deathly pale. His eyes were wide and staring blankly into the sky.

It was a funeral ritual, like the one he had celebrated over the bodies of my mother and father. Grandpa moved from the face to the body, still drawing the symbols that I could just barely remember. He was praying, but his lips never moved. I heard the words inside my head.

The world beyond the firelight was pitch black. Crickets sang in staccato, and the breeze whispered gently through the trees.

I was on the reservation, reliving my vision, but some things were different. The wind kicked up behind me, and I could hear water splashing--not on the Mystic River in Medford, but on the lake, Lake Abenaki, back home where I was born. It sounded like an enormous fish thrashing in a tank much too small for it.

I felt extremely light on my feet. I ran,

almost floating, toward my Grandpa and the body. I couldn't make out who it was, but something told me it was someone I knew very well.

Grandpa had drawn a circle in the dirt, twelve feet or so across, and placed the body in the center. It was surrounded by wooden bowls, each filled with a different color. Those colors were drawn all over the body, mixed with the bright red of blood that streamed from numerous cuts in the flesh.

The lake behind was boiling with rage. I darted forward in sudden terror. I didn't know what was going to happen or what I was supposed to do. All I could think of was to go into the circle and hope Grandpa could help me.

A small shock wave passed through me as I stepped over the line. It was just like the warm blast of air and percussion passing through our perimeter in Vietnam when the jets dropped their bombs close by. We used to say it was the souls of the dead rushing past us on their way to

Heaven or Hell.

It knocked me to my knees beside the body. Then finally I saw who it was, and I nearly passed out in shock and despair.

Nika pressed against me. She'd followed; she was here, in the circle, warm and steady, telling me not to be afraid.

"Listen to Nika," Grandpa's voice said in my head. "She has traveled a great distance to be with you. It was not by chance that you found her. She is a good dog. She knows where she is supposed to be."

I shook the words out of my head. I was glad Nika was here, yes I was, but that was nothing compared to the shock of seeing my own dead body in front of me, painted all over with sacred symbols. I hadn't realized how thin I had become--I barely recognized myself.

The symbols did nothing to hide the deep wounds all over. They were open, purple as if they had been submerged in water for hours. My face was blue, my lips swollen, set in a rictus of terror.

I looked down. I felt solid. I looked solid--and I was exactly as bruised and battered as the body on the ground.

I wanted to get up and bolt, but I knew better. Grandpa held out his hand. There was something in it.

Peyote. I took it without a word and raised it to my lips.

He did the same, chewing and swallowing with ceremonial deliberation. Then he stood up and stretched out his arms and lifted his face to the sky.

He spoke in our native language, slow and sonorous while the fire blazed and crackled behind him. "Life has not been easy for you. You have been given a difficult path to walk, and the challenges you have conquered have been far from simple. I fear that you have lost your way, and no longer have the faith that has sustained our people. You have been alone for a very long time and have believed yourself forsaken.

"And yet that faith endures. From beyond the regions of thunder, in a land of great peacefulness and beauty, the Great Spirit has guided your journey on Mother Earth. I myself have walked with you for many years."

That, I knew. I looked into his eyes and nodded, agreeing and thanking him.

He nodded in return. His face was somber. "For all that you have suffered, your journey is not yet over. For generations our ancestors have fought the dark spirits. We are constantly in battle, Good against Darkness. It has no end.

"Yet we are not alone in our fight. Other spirits join us in the struggle, and it is your task to discover where they are and how they can guide you." His voice softened. "You must be very weary. Your vision as a child, the death of your parents and your arrival at the place of darkness has all been part of your destiny. You believe you are ready to rest. But as dangerous as your past has been, your future is even more difficult." He paused and drew a breath.

Here it comes, I thought. I wasn't sure

what I felt. Tired, yes, he'd been right about that. Scared--shitless. But somehow I managed to stay there and hold on and listen.

"Now, on behalf of the Great Spirit, I must ask you to make a decision. You may end your journey and come join your ancestors in the spirit world . . . or you can fulfill your destiny and attempt to triumph over the darkness that our ancestors have fought for generations."

It didn't sound like much of choice to me. Go back among the living and fight and suffer and die anyway. Die now, join the ancestors. How crazy did he think I was?

"My mother's father before me," he said, "their mother and father before them, all fought the ancient battle. You are not the first to walk this difficult path. But the decision is yours and only yours to make."

I lifted my eyes to the sky. Shooting stars blazed across it, but there were always more stars, millions of them, billions, all wheeling overhead.

"My mother," I said. "Your daughter. Why hasn't she ever come, the way you have? Why did she abandon me?"

"Your mother is with you," Grandpa answered, "and always has been. Just because you cannot see her does not mean she is not there."

As if his words had conjured her presence, I felt it near me, surrounding me like warm and nurturing arms. The stars above me wore the faces of my ancestors, looking down on me and giving me their blessing. I heard them singing in the breeze as it whispered through the branches.

The peyote kicked in. My body felt warm and fuzzy.

A sudden blast of wind smote the circle. It was warm; for all its force, it brought a powerful surge of welcome, and the prayers of my people.

They knew what choice I had made.

So did Grandpa. "Your mind was made up the day you took your first breath. The

Great Spirit has known and loved you since long before you were born."

I felt the rightness of his words deep within me. For the first time in a very long while, I no longer felt despair. I was no longer alone.

The homes of my people were all around me, scattered through the woods in which I had been born and raised. It was peaceful and calming and yet very powerful.

They were with me, watching me. Below, the lake thrashed in a frenzy of rage. A putrid smell emanated from the water; the air was suddenly very cold.

Grandpa frowned. "We will be safe here," he said. "The spirits will not allow any forces of evil to enter our circle."

As if to show her agreement, Nika left my side and lay down next to Grandpa, relaxed and panting slightly. She looked as if she was smiling.

The wind swelled to a gale and began to swirl like the start of a tornado. The trees shook and tossed. Branches snapped, flying through the air. The water of the lake was boiling.

None of it could penetrate the line my grandfather had drawn. The campfire blazed, dancing brightly as shadows rose up out of the lake and oozed toward us. I gagged on the stink that came with them.

The ancestors' song continued unabated. On impulse I added my voice to theirs.

Grandpa's own voice ran beneath the singing, slow and sonorous. "The dark spirit was once a man. He was angry in life and is angry in death. He has surrendered his soul to damnation, and has become a terrible power because of it."

The wind howled around our protective circle, battering it with branches and dirt, leaves and rocks.

Grandpa never flinched. "He knows of your presence, but does not know why you trouble him so deeply. You must use this to your advantage."

"But how?" I asked.

"That is not for me to tell you. You must find your own path, and see your own way through the darkness."

The stink was so bad now that it was all I could do not to hurl all over the circle. A faint vibration thrummed in the air, like the hum of an electric power line.

I knew that sound. I had heard it in the hospital. But what--

Grandpa took a flaming stick from the fire. The shadows were almost upon us. I couldn't make out their faces, though they were only a few feet away.

Grandpa traced the circle's perimeter with the stick. A wall of fire sprang up.

A shrill, inhuman moan drowned out the ancestors' song. Just as suddenly as it had begun, it cut off.

It was a cry of pain. The shadows collapsed to the ground. A swarm of black flies rose up where they had been, millions and millions of them, buzzing around the wall of fire, striving in vain to force their way in. The ground itself vibrated with the force of their fury.

The circle of protection held. The ancestors' song, combined with Grandpa's and mine, gradually overwhelmed the droning of the flies. Slowly but surely they began to drop dead.

A horrible smell rose from their carcasses. A perfect circle of them surrounded us, piled on the ground like a drift of coal-black snow.

The earth went still. Grandpa stretched out his hand. "It is time for your resurrection."

I bent my head. The peyote held me firmly in its grip.

I stood in front of my own dead body, with the back of my heels pressed against the soles of its feet. I stretched out my arms and turned my face toward the stars.

Grandpa's warm hand lay on my forehead. My whole body was warm, and it tingled. It was a comfortable feeling, but the pit of my stomach fluttered with apprehension.

The cuts all over my body were wriggling and squirming, turning into tiny black snakes that slithered across my skin--traveling downward to the ground and then into the campfire. Each of them hissed as it entered the flames and disappeared in a puff of smoke.

Grandpa eased my head backwards ever so slowly, lowering my soul into the body that lay beneath me. Dawn was coming: I saw the first pale hint of it through the trees.

A hot, almost electric current ran from my head down to my toes. The last thing I remembered was a bright flash of light and Grandpa's words: "When the morning twilight battles the darkness, then the chosen spirits of the dead will rise and fight for the forces of Good. Listen to your spirit guides. They will help you find your way."

"Seek the Lord and His strength; seek
His face continually."

Psalm 105:4

Even though it was early morning,
blessed candles burned brightly all over the
room. Brian Foley lay quietly in his bed as
members of the Boston Archdiocese
examined the Christlike wounds on his
body.

There were three of them, all dressed in
the garb of Catholic priests, but only the
oldest priest inspected the wounds. The
other two were simply observers, sent by the
Church to learn from the older priest.

It was obvious that they had not seen
apparent stigmata before. They looked to the
older priest the way a Little Leaguer looks to
a coach.

The older priest, Father Antonelli, looked
like a man who had aged long before his
time. His face was smooth except for the fine
laugh lines around his eyes and mouth, but
his hair was snow white. His bright blue

eyes were wise and deep but gently humorous as he peered through a magnifying glass at the tiny sweat-like droplets of blood slowly forming on Brian Foley's forehead.

Foley seemed oblivious to the priests' presence. He must have been exhausted; he was clearly in pain.

Father Antonelli motioned to one of the younger priests, who stood by with a 35mm camera to record and document the wounds. He started to raise it, but Father Antonelli shot him a look that made him hand the camera to his superior and step back smartly.

Father Antonelli photographed the wounds from all angles, even turning the man's head ever so gently to capture a new direction. Every so often he wiped the sweat and blood from Foley's forehead.

Father McCarthy, the parish priest, was a personal friend of Brian Foley. He sat quietly in the corner, though he could not stop wringing his hands and wondering if he had done the right thing in calling in these men.

He knew that the investigator was watching him even while he recorded the evidence for the Archbishop. Father McCarthy deliberately avoided that keen stare, keeping his eyes on his old friend's face.

Brian Foley was a deacon of the church; he had assisted Father Pat in many Sunday Masses, and over the years they had become friends. They had a great deal in common: Father Pat was a veteran, too; he had served with the Marines in the Pacific in World War II, and his experience in war had led him to dedicate his life as a soldier for Christ.

It pained him terribly to see his friend lie suffering in that bed, but he knew it was God's will. He had been right to call in Father Antonelli. The investigator's own glances said so as he continued his examination.

This was a great miracle, but also a dangerous one. Father Antonelli paused as if he had had the same thought and said, "This man must not be left alone."

Father Pat nodded. "I'll make sure there's

always someone here with him."

"Good," Father Antonelli said. "I will of course notify the Vatican. I'm sure you already know what will happen to your friend."

"Yes," Father Pat said. "I know." He looked at the sufferer with great sadness, but also with great admiration. This would grant the Holy Man a place with the Divine in heaven, but nevertheless it pained him greatly to see his friend in such suffering.

Father Antonelli went back to his work, photographing Foley's right hand in its bandages, then handing off the camera to the younger priest who was in charge of it. He took Foley's hand in his and began unwrapping the bandage.

It was important, at least to the Archdiocese, to photograph all the wounds in one session. This would forestall any doubt and remove the possibility of documentation error.

The deeply punctured palm bled continuously. He laid Foley's hand on the bandage that he had removed, to catch the steady drip of blood, and held out his hand again for the camera. As he adjusted the lens, Brian Foley began to speak, but the words were too soft to understand.

Father Pat took the unbandaged hand in his own. Behind him, the window shade shot straight up and the window slammed wide open. A strong wind blew back the curtains and extinguished all the candles, gusting fiercely around the room.

The priests looked at each other in dismay and shocked speculation. A movement brought all their eyes back to the bed. Brian Foley sat up, staring out the window. His feet had bled through the bandages; blood stained the floor. He held his arms outstretched, palms up, like a priest celebrating the Mass.

He spoke clearly now, in Latin, in a strong and vigorous voice despite the pain he was suffering. A mourning dove flew through the window and landed softly on the exposed wound in his right hand. A second landed on the left, and a third came to rest on his shoulder. Others gathered at his feet.

The bleeding had stopped. Foley cupped the first dove in both hands; some of his blood had stained the soft gray feathers. He spoke to the dove in Latin, then flung it gently toward the window. The rest of the doves followed it: a dozen altogether.

Foley lay back down on his bed and said in English what he had been saying in Latin: "Seek the Lord and His strength; seek His face continually."

Then he lay quiet as he had since he was brought home from the hospital. Outside, the priests heard the flapping of thousands of wings and the sweet, loud, unspeakably sad cooing of mourning doves.

The priests gathered in front of the open window and looked up. The early morning sky was dark with doves in flight, as more and more and more of them lifted up from every tree within sight. They flew in a vast V or pointing arrow; it took them several minutes to pass by.

Almost too late, Father Antonelli remembered the camera and began to take photographs.

"'Seek the Lord and His strength,'" Father Pat said, echoing Brian Foley. "'Seek His face continually.' Psalm 105:4. Heavenly and Almighty Father, give us the strength to carry out Your Will." The other priests joined him as he began the Lord's Prayer: "'Our Father Who art in Heaven, hallowed by Thy Name . . .'"

#

Some time later, Father Antonelli and one of the younger priests came out of Brian and Rita Foley's house to find that the doves were returning in droves--literally thousands of them. They gathered everywhere a dove could gather: trees, electrical wires, chimneys, rooftops, shrubbery. Still more flew in giant circles above the house, as if waiting for their turn to land. The priests stood in awe.

#

I awoke to the distant wail of a mourning

spirit. The sun was shining brightly through my open window as I got my bearings and realized that for the first time, I had slept through the agony of pre-dawn.

The spirit's third and final cry faded away into the distance. It was the Boston Commuter-Silver line, I realized, bound for Framingham and approaching West Medford. My mind spun, trying to make sense of my latest nightmare.

A dove came to a landing on the ledge of my open window. His cooing song filled the apartment.

He was late. The dove usually came with his mate right before the sunrise and sang his song that was so similar to the owl's, but softer.

This one was an unusually large for a dove, and the colors of its feathers were unusually bright and crisp: gray, black and brownish red against the pure white markings. It perched on the windowsill, peaceful and calm, and its soft black eyes somehow reminded me of Jessica's.

It was singing straight at me, and its song

echoed in my head. I tried to sit up and shove it away, but my body ached all over. I sank back down with my eyes closed and my left hand hanging off the side of the bed, trying to remember what Grandpa had told me.

A cold wet nose poked at my hand. I jumped up in complete shock. "<u>Nika</u>!"

She wagged her tail and grinned at me like she always had, with her look that said, "Everything's OK."

Was I still dreaming? Was this part of my nightmare? Would I wake up and find her gnawed bones piled up on my floor?

My head tried to tell me one thing, but my heart knew another. Things had changed. Nika had been sent to me a long, long time ago. It wasn't by chance she'd found me at the bus station.

"She traveled a great distance to be with you," Grandpa had said. Just how great it was, I hadn't ever known before. But now I did.

I flung back the covers and looked down at my body. All the wounds and the deep cuts were healed. Fresh pink skin covered every scar. The wounds were real, but Grandpa had healed them. It was all real. My feet were filthy, as if I'd been slogging through mud and worse.

There was a whole flock of doves at the window now, and more in the trees outside, cooing so loud I could hardly hear myself think. Nika didn't bat an eye. This was right, her posture said. It was just as it was supposed to be.

I got to my feet, full of an energy I had not felt before. As I passed by the dresser mirror on my way to the window, my reflection stared back at me. My face was covered with the sacred symbols that Grandpa had painted on me during my resurrection. My whole body was a prayer.

There was something else about me, too. The look in my eye was different. Confident. Powerful.

My sense of smell was acute. I could smell the doves, a smell like feather comforters and green leaves and spring wind. My hearing was enhanced: I could hear people talking across the river.

I looked out the window. The trees were filled with cooing doves for as far as my eyes could see. Was I immortal now?

No, I thought. Not immortal. I was just a man still. But a changed man. I had a feeling I'd only just begun to understand how much I had changed.

The first dove, the largest of them all, waited calmly for me to approach. When I picked it up it cooed, trusting me, settling softly in my grasp.

There was dried blood on the outside of its wing. I brushed it softly, looking for the wound, but found none.

Nika watched calmly. That was not like her at all when she was around other animals.

I found myself doing something I had not done since the death of my parents: I was praying. I kissed the bird on top of its head and put it back on the windowsill. It had begun, just like Grandpa said, and there was someone I needed to see.

I pulled on a pair of sweat pants and

started to go out, but stopped short just inside the open door. My euphoria evaporated. The opposite side of the river swarmed with reporters, and the sky buzzed with news-station helicopters.

The last thing I wanted to do was leave the sanctuary of my apartment, but something made me step out into the yard. Nika's grave was open, as if she had dug herself out. The sight made me shudder slightly, but there was nothing horrible about the dog who walked beside me down to the edge of the water.

The river was dead. Fish, turtles, ducks and frogs floated belly up, hundreds of them, and I smelled once again the putrid stink that I'd smelled in my dream. Only two species of creature had survived the carnage: snakes of all kinds swam in and out among the carcasses, and flies gathered in force to feast on the bodies of the dead.

A voice echoed across the putrid water: a news reporter speaking into her microphone. "It's as if the entire river boiled overnight."

The river's death was awe-inspiring and

horrible. Grandpa hadn't been lying when he said this battle would not be easy.

My confidence had damned near crashed and burned. I knew what everybody all the way up to the Great Spirit expected of me, but I wasn't at all sure I could do it. I'd been chosen, supposedly, long before I was born-- but was I strong enough? Was I even right for this?

Nika was waiting for me in the jeep. She looked spooked, too, but she wasn't running away from what we both had to do.

I might be crazy enough to end up in J Ward, but I couldn't let my dog show me up. I climbed into the jeep and threw it into gear and pulled out onto the street. I didn't know exactly where I was going, just that I had to go.

A whole cloud of doves swirled around and above me and streamed ahead of me.

They were showing me where to go. West through Medford, down deserted streets and across empty intersections. I didn't know exactly what I was headed for, but that it was something, or perhaps someone, powerful and important--that I knew in my heart and soul. I even thought I might know who it was.

The doves guided me to a house on a quiet street, surrounded by trees. There were already thousands of their relatives in the trees. My guides flew to join the rest.

Two priests stood outside the house. The name on the box in front was <u>Foley.</u>

That was the name I'd been expecting, but he wasn't standing there waiting for me. Two priests stood on the step, frowning at me as I came up the walk.

"You can't go in there, son," the older priest said.

"He's expecting me," I said. Neither one of them moved aside to let me by.

I looked each of them in the eye. "With all due respect, gentlemen, there's a higher power at work here." I swept my hand toward the doves. "Now if you'll excuse me, I need to see Sergeant Foley."

The priests didn't look ready to end the standoff, but a new voice spoke from above their heads. It was another priest, a ruddy, white-haired Irish type like an older version of Brian Foley. "Let him in," he said. "Brian's expecting him."

#

The man in the bed looked nothing like the sturdy, broad-shouldered policeman I'd seen at the hospital and in my dreams. He was almost translucently pale, and his hands on top of the covers were bleeding through what looked like freshly applied bandages. His voice was raspy and weak as he spoke to me. "Jesus has known you and loved you since long before you were born."

Those were my grandfather's words, almost exactly, though they spoke in white man's language about the white man's God. Chills ran over my body as I realized: Foley was a good spirit and would help me in my fight against the dark one.

Our eyes met. "Could it be that our God is the same?" he asked me with a hint of a chuckle, but his expression was deadly serious.

"I don't know," I said, but actually I thought I did. One God, many ways of worshipping Him.

Foley held out something in his bandaged hand. It was a set of wooden rosary beads with a sterling silver crucifix. "There is only one God, and He is always with us. We have been chosen by Him to destroy demons, not fear them. See your way through the darkness, Barry. And may the loving peace of Christ always be with you."

I caught the rosary beads before his hand fell. He dropped back on the bed, his eyes falling shut, as if he had used every last bit of energy to give me this message. I wanted to cry, and to scream with an indescribable sense of power, both at the same time.

Resurrection

I know now that the hospital is alive. Not because of the patients and staff that inhabit it, but because it is a living, breathing, evil entity: preying on human fear and suffering and yearning for the destruction of humanity. Every inch of space tells its own story of horror.

Its long, pulsing hallways are like veins transporting mysterious howls and echoes of sadness and despair. Its endless miles of tunnels and passages and the winding staircases made from blood-red bricks never end; they lead down and down, narrowing as they go. You can go down, but the deeper you go, the surer you are that you can't go back up by even one step, as if your feet are nailed to an escalator descending into the abyss.

The damp, stale, oxygen-deprived air grows thicker with each downward step. You wonder who or what could have created such a place of misery, death and agonizing torture taking place just out of the public eye, under the guise of treatment, of healing.

The hospital consumes you. It sees you coming; it knows your fate years in advance.

It felt me coming. It felt my presence as strongly as I could feel Its. Standing at the top of Pine Hill, looking down into the valley, I could see the smoke rise from the chimneys as the Evil exhaled, breathing through Its lungs, expanding and contracting. From the pit of Its stomach, in the dark stale tunnels, through the nostrils of Its chimneys I felt its heartbeat echoing through the woods and vibrating through my body: cold, dark and hungry.

It was calling me--no, challenging me. Daring me to come back inside, where the tunnels waited, and a new death.

I knew I had no choice but to return. I looked toward the cross that poked through the tops of the trees. Even at night it shone bright golden through the dark branches.

Barretto's body was gone, along with the police and the fire department and the rest of the crime-scene circus. They had all moved on.

All but one. "Foley," I said aloud. Did he know what he was fighting for and what was happening to us?

I got the feeling that he had known all his life. Just as he had known that his Jesus and my people's Great Spirit were the same, or close enough, and that everyone should honor and respect life.

The ways we are taught are important. They matter to us, though it's all the same in the end. I would fight with all my heart and power to honor those teachings.

I snapped a cedar branch I had taken from the woods and sniffed its sweet, pungent scent before throwing it on the fire. The smell brought back memories of the reservation and my parents.

I watched as the flames licked toward the sky. The smell of burning cedar was just as distinct as the smell of the fresh branch-- different, but still the same. It was all part of the same thing.

I dropped a hit of purple microdot

mescaline I had scored at the Pit and waited for the effects to kick in. If I was going to fight, I needed the guidance of my people--of the spirit world.

One thing I knew for sure. My entire life, every step, every breathing moment, had been preparation for the battle that I was about to engage in.

I stared into the fire, searching for the path through the embers. Looking for strength and guidance from my ancestors and from my newly profound faith in the Great Spirit--and Foley's Jesus. It brought me great comfort in the face of the great unknown.

It was 2:00 a.m., and the mescaline was taking full effect. I felt numb all over, and yet I was full of euphoria. The woods were alive, watching, stirring in every crack and crevice, waiting to see what I would do next.

They knew why I was here: the crickets, the trees, the grass, everything that lives in the woods. They all knew. They had known for a very long time, for it had been written in the stars long before my birth.

They had witnessed much of the horror that took place at the hospital in the valley below. And now the time had come. In just a little while, dawn would arrive.

I touched the rosary beads Brian Foley had given me, that I had hung around my neck, and closed my fingers around the body of his Jesus nailed to the Cross. I prayed to the Great Spirit that this dawn would be different; I mourned the arrival of twilight.

The mescaline made me snicker at the irony of the thought. Mourn . . . twilight . . . Mourning Twilight. Those two words would never mean the same to me again.

I took the .45 from my knapsack and turned it in my hands. The night sights glowed even in the bright light of the fire.

It was almost time to go. I had everything I needed: the .45 with tracer rounds loaded, one extra magazine, a Bowie knife and a flashlight. Just like old times.

The Messenger's wings beat close by, virtually silent, but to my heightened senses as loud as a clap of thunder. He settled on a branch twenty-five feet below me, overlooking a path that led down the hill, and fixed the yellow fire of his eyes on me. "Someone is going to die," he said.

I raised my arms palm up and turned my face toward the sky. The moon shone brightly down upon me, turning the forest as bright as day.

The woods had gone completely quiet. No crickets, no breeze in the branches, nothing. It was like being in the hospital itself, buried deep and shut off from the outside world.

The Messenger hooted long and low. His voice echoed through the trees. It gave me strength and a surge of power that I had never felt before. Grandpa's voice spoke in my head, a memory from when I was small: "When an owl looks into your eyes, he is looking into your very soul."

The woods came alive again. My heart beat strongly; my breath came deep and fast. I was ready. Ready to die, ready to live.

Clouds raced across the sky. They wore the faces of my ancestors. I pulled the last, charred piece of cedar from the fire and drew on my face, painting myself for war.

The clouds covered the moon. The woods were dark again. I threw dirt on the fire and watched to see where the smoke would go.

A line of tiny lights ran down the path. Fireflies--thousands of them, traveling more or less straight, lighting my way to the battleground.

I left my empty pack and followed them downhill toward the hospital. It was time. Back to the tunnel wars, just like old times.

Who needed mescaline when I had adrenaline? I was tripping my balls off.

Gus was waiting for me by an open manhole parallel to the cemetery and almost directly under the largest pine tree on the grounds. His face glowed in the light of the fireflies that danced around his head.

The cemetery was full of people, hundreds of them. Some were children. Some were old. Some wore light blue hospital pajamas and some were wrapped in sheets. Some were wounded, still bleeding-- and I remembered the experiments Jessica had told me about and the tortured souls I had seen in the tunnel. Their screams still echoed in my head. Each of them stood on his own grave.

I acknowledged them with a glance. What I was about to do was for the good of all things.

Gus blessed himself in the Catholic way: "In the name of the Father and of the Son and of the Holy Spirit." Then he blessed me by drawing a cross in the center of my forehead. His touch was cool and comforting.

Everything around us was quiet, waiting. I went down first, with Gus behind me. Neither of us said a word.

The temperature dropped as we traveled through the tunnel, but somehow I was not cold. These tunnels were much wider than the ones I had hunted in when I was in Vietnam. Shadows by the hundreds walked past on both sides as if the tunnel was a busy city sidewalk, hurrying on their way to nowhere. Some walked right through me, and I felt a cold chill. It freaked me out a little.

Make that more than a little.

Gus's voice spoke in my head. "That's how they let you know they're there: by walking through you and making you feel the cold. But it's different for you now. You've been given the sight."

It really was different. All my senses were magnified tremendously. I could see easily down the tunnel, though I knew it was barely lit. The air was thick with the unmistakable smell of gasoline.

Sampson, I thought.

Gus nodded. "Sampson is here," he said, still in my head. Somehow I knew he would keep communicating with me in that way. We had moved a long way past ordinary human speech. "You must find him and destroy him."

Brian Foley had said almost the same thing: <u>We are not meant to fear demons. We are meant to destroy them.</u>

I nodded to both the memory and the presence beside me. "I will," I said.

The farther we walked into the tunnel, the stronger the stink of gasoline became.

After what seemed like a long while, Gus stopped in front of a gap in the tunnel, four feet square, like a crawlspace. Instinct told me it would lead nowhere.

"Not quite," Gus said with the hint of a wink. "Follow me."

We crawled into the unlit small space. Even in the dark I could see the brick wall at the end.

It was a trapdoor. Gus popped it. Over his shoulder I saw another tunnel leading down.

"Yes, and that's just the start. There are doors below this one and tunnels that go even deeper, seemingly without end. Deep into the bowels of the earth."

"A tunnel within a tunnel," I said. "One step closer to Hell." That's what we tunnel rats used to say in the jungle, right before we dived down for another hunt.

"Without a doubt," Gus said.

I had been trained to fire two rounds through any trapdoor we came to, before we went in.

"You do that," he said, "if you have the

ammo." His eyes were bright. He was as hopped up as I was.

I thought about firing the shots this time, but it was already open and neither of us was dead. Or dead again, at least. I'd save my ammo for the next one.

The secondary tunnel was narrower than the one above, but still much larger than the tunnels in 'Nam. This one was lined with steam pipes.

There were no lights. Gus sighed slightly, which I took as a hint to turn on my flashlight. Even my enhanced senses needed help to penetrate the absolute darkness.

My heart raced. I controlled my breathing, so as not to give our position away. In the tunnels you had to rely on sight, sound, touch and hearing, and even a deep breath could get you killed.

Gus walked ahead of me, not seeming to care how dark or dangerous it was. I heard running water echoing below, indicating yet another tunnel beneath us. That made it even more like the tunnels in Vietnam: never-ending, disorienting crawl spaces leading to dead ends, and often to someone's death--ours or the enemy's.

I was on high alert, and I knew we were getting close.

Gus turned to me. "This is as far as I'm allowed to take you. May God bless you and always be with you."

"Is this where I look the other way and you suddenly disappear again?" I asked.

This drew a slight smile from him. "Yes."

I closed my eyes. "Thank you," I said.

When I opened them he was gone. The smell of gasoline was so strong I choked on it. I was alone again, just the way I liked it.

Those who dwell in the wilderness will bow before Him, and His enemies will lick the dust.

Psalm 72:9

Rita dabbed her husband's lips with a damp facecloth. They were dry and chapped, and he was struggling to say something, a barely audible word.

Suddenly she realized what it was. It was a sacred word. "<u>Maranatha</u> . . ."

"The Lord cometh," she said, and her breath caught.

His hand brushed hers weakly. Tears trickled down his cheeks. "Yes," he whispered. "*Maranatha*. The Lord cometh."

Rita kissed his bandaged hand. The wrappings were soaked through again, like all the rest: his feet, his head, and most recently his side had opened too and begun to bleed. Her own tears flowed almost without her knowing it. The end was close; she could feel it.

Father McCarthy laid his hand gently

on Brian's foot and began praying in Latin. Rita bowed her head and tried to pray with him, though the words kept catching on sobs.

The priest blessed Brian with holy water, then dropped to his knees, unable to hold back the tears. "Old friend," he said. "Dear friend. The highest Power has blessed you. May It guide you gently home."

Brian Foley drew a deep breath and held it for a handful of heartbeats. Then he let it all out in one last, long sigh, his body visibly sinking into the mattress.

Rita let out a cry of pure pain. She could barely hear Father McCarthy's prayers droning on above her head.

She must not question why this had happened. Brian would want her to accept it. It was the work of the Lord, and he who had suffered greatly was now at peace.

But oh, even for her strong faith, it was hard. She had loved this man her whole life. Yes, he was the Holy Man; yes, he was needed in Heaven. She was glad for that.

But he was her soulmate, and she had lost him.

"Please, Father," she said. "Just a little time alone. Please?"

Father McCarthy stopped praying and nodded. She watched him go, while the votive candles flickered all around the room.

When he was gone, the flames slowly went still, as still as her husband's lifeless body. She laid her head on his shoulder and cried.

#

Father McCarthy trudged heavily down the stairs to the living room, where the other two priests sat, awaiting the inevitable. As he sank onto the couch, a strong wind shook the house and rattled the windows. It sounded like a million birds beating their wings all at once.

There was a knock at the door. "At this hour?" said Father McCarthy, pushing himself upright.

"Father Pat," Rita said. "Let me."

She was standing at the foot of the stairs. Her eyes were red and her voice was choked with tears, but her back was straight.

Father McCarthy half-bowed and stood back to let her by. She opened the door.

#

Rita recognized the visitor immediately. It was the soldier she had met at the shrine of the Blessed Mother, who had given her the rosary beads for Brian. He was in full Army uniform, and he seemed to glow in the light from the doorway.

She knew she should be scared. This Vincent Kelley had haunted her husband's nightmares--he had called the man's name night after night. But there was such peace in his face and such a light in his eyes that she reached out without hesitation and hugged him tightly.

He hugged her back. Behind him she saw mourning doves everywhere: in every tree, on every wire, on the lawn, on the woodpile--everywhere.

"It's time, Rita," he said.

"I know," she answered. The tears had come back; there was nothing she could do to stop them.

"What are you doing?" Father Pat asked behind her. "Who are you talking to?"

She glanced back at him. He was looking right through Vincent Kelley--frowning at what, to him, must look like empty air.

When she turned back, Vincent was still there, looking real and solid and alive, but in her heart she knew he was dead. This was a ghost, and he was speaking words of great comfort in this darkest hour. "You are a holy and just woman, Rita Foley. You and Brian were soulmates from the moment you laid eyes on each other. True love--and true love never dies. You will be with each other once again. Until then, know this. Everything happens for a reason--everything. You are exactly where you are supposed to be. Never question it. Some things are just not meant to be understood in this life."

His eyes left her face and lifted to something behind and above her. There was such light in them and such joy that her heart beat harder; her hands shook. She turned half in fear and half in anticipation.

Her husband stood on the stairs, dressed in the white deacon's robe he wore at Mass. He looked young and vibrant, healthy and handsome. A bright light surrounded him.

He showed her his hands. They were whole. The stigmata were gone.

She ran to him and flung her arms around him. He was warm--living. Breathing. "Brian! I love you. Please don't go. Please!"

"My darling and precious wife," he said. "You know I love you with all my heart and soul. I promise, we will be together once again--but for now I must go."

Brian hugged her tightly and kissed her. She clung for a moment, but then she gathered herself. She let him go. It was the hardest thing she had ever done, and the most necessary.

She stood on the stairs as he walked past the awed and silent priests. When he reached the door, Vincent Kelley took him by the hand.

#

Brian Foley did not look back once he had taken his old friend's hand, though a good part of his heart was still with his beloved Rita. Vinny led him down the walk past the woodpile. His ax was still there, sunk in a log. Several doves perched upon it. It glowed brightly, like a campfire in a dark forest.

He glanced at Vinny, who bowed his head. Foley reached for the shining ax. The doves rose in the air as his hand approached, as if surrendering it to him.

#

Rita watched them from the doorway. As Brian took the ax and the doves took to the air, a strong wind blew hard in her face. She squeezed her eyes shut against it and clung to the door frame.

When she opened her eyes, Brian and Vinny were gone. She turned and ran back through the house, up the stairs and into the bedroom.

Her husband's body lay on the bed, as still and lifeless as it had been when she left it. She threw herself on him and cried uncontrollably, while behind her the three priests began to pray.

#

A burst of flame shattered the darkness in the narrow tunnel. The flash and the heat rushed past me, but the source screamed for a few more seconds before the victim sucked the flames into his lungs and the scream cut off.

The body was still burning, the victim throwing his head from side to side, flailing his arms as if he could shake off the flames.

Another shape ran past it, big and wide and dark. Sampson. He laughed as he ran, his voice echoing off the bricks.

I fired two quick shots from the .45. The tracer rounds chased each other like lasers, straight and fast, one red line crossing the other. They seemed to travel forever.

I ran as fast and as carefully as I could. I'd forgotten what a pure, heady high adrenaline was--and mescaline made it even headier. I howled from the top of it. *"I came to kill you, Sampson!"*

Sampson's laughter bounced back down the tunnel, leapfrogging the echoes from my voice. "Come and fuckin' get me, Redcrow! I got a <u>nice</u> surprise for you."

I fired two more shots. They flew wide, blazing off into infinity.

That was the mescaline. Fucking up my aim, too.

I slowed down as I got closer to the burning body. It was one of the patients, with the light blue hospital pajamas fused to his skin. The smell of burning flesh was awful, and all too familiar. He was tied to the steam pipes with leather restraints, arms pulled straight out, ankles bound together, like Christ on the Cross.

My hand went to the crucifix that I wore around my neck. Brian Foley's face floated up in front of me. Was he still alive? What would he do if he were here?

I heard his voice in my head, as clear as if he stood next to me. *We have been chosen by God to destroy demons, not fear them.*

I left the burned body behind and ran down the passageway. A hundred yards or so past the dead man, a trapdoor lay open in the middle of the floor. I peered down into darkness and breathed cold stale air.

How deep did these fucking tunnels go?

"All the way to Hell," Gus's voice said. I looked around a little wildly, but there was no sign of him.

I got down on all fours and lined up two more shots. Down below, something moved. I aimed both my gun and my flashlight.

Sampson's mutilated face grinned up at me, with its ropy red scar tissue and the black hole where a nose should be. He had an old-fashioned copper fire extinguisher, the kind you only see in old buildings, that you have to hold upside down in order to get enough pressure for the spray, and you can refill it water.

He was aiming it straight at me. His bright blue eyes were wide and bright and completely insane.

He rested the canister on his shoulder and held the hose up high and pulled out a zippo lighter. I knew, looking into his eyes, that there was no water in the can. It wasn't a fire extinguisher, it was a flamethrower--and it was full of gasoline.

I backpedaled hard from the roar of the flames and jerked off a couple of blind shots. Sampson laughed; his bare feet slapped off the floor as he ran, echoing in the tunnel.

The echo faded. My face and hands

stung. I'd been just a hair too slow to escape the flames.

The last coiling blue flame shriveled up and died. The ladder was too hot to touch bare-handed. I pulled off my jacket to cushion my already stinging palms and went down as fast as I could.

I knew where he was leading me. To the Dark One. Foley's demon.

I didn't have a battle plan. Just my faith. I made my way forward cautiously. I had to keep my head in focus. One wrong step, and this time I'd stay dead.

Old lessons played through my head. Watch for trip wires, watch for spiders, watch for snakes . . .

Damn snakes. I knew they'd be here, waiting for me.

Flame erupted again in front of me. Again the scream of agony, and the fire so bright I had to shield my eyes. This one struggled violently, swinging like a pendulum. The stink of gasoline and then of burning flesh made me gag. Sampson laughed, far away on the other side of the screams.

The light was too bright for me to see past it. It could be a trap. I thumbed my flashlight off and shrank back into the darkness of the tunnel.

If I was going to get any rounds into Sampson, I had to think tactically. He must be watching from the other side of the burning body.

Patience.

I advanced a foot at a time, concealing myself in the shadows, as the flames died down.

Ghost soldiers are only friends with the shadows of their own nightmares.

Damn right, I thought.

I dropped down to a crouch and then to a crawl. The burned body loomed over me like a ghastly crucifix.

"Redcrow," it said in a demonic rasp. "He's gonna tear your soul to pieces."

Its eyes were bright. Its teeth were white. It skin was crispy black. It grinned at me; and then it crumpled in on itself, eyes melting, body collapsing--but its teeth, even dead, were still porcelain white.

I crawled past it, though my shoulders knotted up in anticipation of it reaching out to grab me. The air was stale, almost impossible to breathe.

Even my enhanced sight was useless here, but my senses of smell and hearing were as sharp as ever. I scanned for booby traps and sudden surprises.

Would I die here? That would be ironic. After years in the tunnels in Vietnam, ten thousand miles away, I'd come home safe and as sound as I was likely to be--and here I was about to be buried forever in the depths of a fucking insane asylum.

I shook off the horrors and crawled on. Ahead, something moved. I flattened myself to the floor.

Noise traveled down here. A drop of water a hundred yards away was as loud as the crack of a bat in Fenway.

Feet shuffled on the floor. Flames shot up ahead. Sampson's massive figure was briefly silhouetted against them.

I emptied the .45. Red tracer beams

flew fast and furious. A couple of them smacked into Sampson's body.

He grunted in pain. I heard his body hit the floor, but couldn't see where he had fallen.

I changed the magazine, working smooth and fast. The fire in front of me was different from the other two. It looked like dozens of snakes burning and writhing on the floor, colliding with one another and twisting away. None of them tried to help any of the others. They were snakes, and snakes trusted no one, not even each other, for they were independent, ruthless and merciless hunters.

I cheered silently as they burned. I had never loved snakes, but from the jungles of Vietnam all the way to what happened to Nika, I had learned to hate them.

I crawled forward again. Some of the snakes in the tunnel were still alive. They fled as I approached, pressing against the walls. They must be in no condition to attack, or else something or someone had ordered them to let me pass.

There were several dozen of them all told, alive and dead. I couldn't figure out why Sampson had burned them. They had to have been meant to block my access to this tunnel. Sampson must not be totally under the demon's control.

One thing I did know: he'd taken a couple of bullets. I lifted myself to my feet as I passed the snakes, not trusting them not to bite. They slithered slowly away from me. They were all sizes and species, but now they were all the same color: barbecue black.

When the last of them was well behind me, I got back down on my belly. A familiar smell prickled my nostrils. Fresh blood.

I shielded my flashlight to keep it from advertising my position and shone it on the floor. Blood trail. Sampson <u>was</u> hit-- and from the amount of blood on the floor, he was hit bad.

A fresh burst of adrenaline rushed through me. The trail ran straight ahead. I turned off the flashlight and followed the smell. There is no other smell like it. Once you've got a head full of it, you never forget.

The smell told me where to go. My sense of touch helped me find my way. I strained my hearing to its utmost, but there was nothing. No sound.

Was Sampson dead? Somehow I knew he wasn't.

My hands, groping ahead of me, found the outline of a trapdoor in the floor. Holy shit, this place went even deeper? I must be three levels down already since Gus showed the way in.

I fired two rounds into the opening and waited. Nothing. I sprang down, landing on all fours like a cat, then rolled to the side and flattened myself out. The stink of gasoline was strong enough to make my eyes water.

"Over here," Sampson said. His voice was weak and raspy, but it echoed in the tunnel.

He sighed deeply and coughed: a thick, gurgling sound. His throat was full of blood. He was dying.

I belly-crawled toward the sound of his voice, flashing a quick beam from the flashlight down the tunnel. Sampson was a black lump midway down: curled up in a fetal position, with the trail of blood leading toward him like a river to the ocean. The smell of gasoline was almost overwhelming.

"The snakes were for you," he said. "Apparently I wasn't supposed to burn them." He snickered. "I was running out of things to burn, and it seemed like the right thing to do at the time. You understand."

I rose to my feet and inched closer, shining the light down on him. His eyes stared straight into mine. Could he see in the dark, too? Had he seen every move I made?

His body glistened. He'd doused himself in gasoline. The extinguisher lay beside him--empty, I guessed, judging from how much he'd used and how much was on him.

"I understand," I said.

His breath came short. He pushed out

words in snatches. "The Master . . . was not pleased . . . but being . . . obedient servant . . . I said I would . . . make it up . . . to him. See you . . . in Hell . . . Redcrow."

He opened his massive fist, baring the zippo lighter. He flipped the top.

I threw myself backward away from his thumb on the flint wheel, his face smiling, the whoosh of flame down the tunnel.

It caught me. I covered my face as best I could. It seared my exposed skin, singeing off the hairs on my arms. The pain wouldn't start for a while, but I knew it would be bad when it came.

The fire was gone as rapidly as it had come. Down the tunnel, Sampson burned, smiling as if in bliss. If he could have laughed, I was sure he would have.

I sank down in the darkness and watched him burn, and did my best to assess the damage to my body. I was hurt, but I still had strength to gather.

The flesh burned off Sampson's body. My lungs were full of the ash. I did not try to stop it. Sampson was a part of me now, and would always be. It was meant to be-- and some things are not meant to be understood.

The flames died down. The tunnel grew dark once again. This was the last barrier, the only one left, but I did not know if I could keep going. I thought I might just have had enough.

Brian Foley's voice spoke in my head. *Fear not Evil. Fear not Death.*

Slowly I got to my feet. I thought I might turn around and go back, but I walked forward instead. Toward Sampson's burned body.

I stepped over it carefully, more than half expecting him to reach up and grab me, but he didn't move. He was really and permanently dead.

I stayed on my feet once I was past him. There was no point in crawling. The Thing that waited for me knew exactly where I was and what I was and what I was doing.

I flicked the flashlight on. The .45 was steady in my hand. My mind was clear.

Foley's words had given me the strength I needed, the courage to go on.

The air grew colder even through the heat of the flash burns on my body. The smell of death crawled into my nostrils. I bounced the beam of the flashlight up and down, back and forth.

Wings flapped hard, somewhere ahead. Flies buzzed toward me: fat, black, nasty flies, the kind you find around death and decaying bodies. Only a few at first, but in the silence of the tunnel their buzzing was loud and clear.

The flashlight's beam caught something up ahead. Then I went flat. The cold, the smell of death, the flies--they were all much stronger.

I waited, listened, sniffed the air as deeply as I could stand. After a minute or two I crawled forward. I could hear nothing but the flies humming like electrical wires.

A lump leaned up against the wall. I shone the light on it. A body, I thought. Dead.

I stood up and moved toward it,

slapping flies away from my face. Disgusting bastards. I fucking hated them.

The body was male, dressed in light blue psych-ward pajama bottoms, mostly covered with blood. His chest was split wide open, and his entrails lay next to him. His heart was missing. Eyes missing.

My eyes darted in both directions. Nothing else was in the tunnel with me as far as the light reached, but there was something just beyond it: a shape, hard to make out, but it might be a steel door.

The body rose slowly and stiffly, its guts dragging on the floor. I watched it without surprise. Nothing could shock me by this point.

"You don't need eyes to see where you're going, Redcrow," it said.

My knife slashed down across its neck. The head spun clean off and thudded to the floor, rolling down the tunnel. The body slumped back against the wall.

I strode past the body. "Hell's a-rolling in," the head said. "He is waiting for you, Redcrow."

I kicked the thing viciously out of my way and braced for more eerie mocking, but the head had said all it was going to say. It thumped against the wall and lay still.

The cold was brutal now, the sound of wings louder, banging on the steel door like something trying to get out. The flies grew thicker, their buzzing stronger, but even through all that noise I heard voices whispering, the same voices I'd heard the night the Dark One came to me, the ones I'd heard before I'd found Joe and the nurse dead in the tunnel.

There were hundreds, thousands of them, talking all at once, overlapping:

Don't go in there.

"He's waiting for you."

Don't go in there. Don't go.

"He'll steal your soul."

Don't go in.

"He'll cut your heart out and eat it."

Don't go.

"Your eyes, too."

Don't.

"He'll cut out your eyes."

Don't go.

"He'll steal your soul. You'll be bound here forever."

Don't go in. Don't. Don't go. Don't. Don't go in there. . . . He'll cut out your eyes . . . and eat them . . . bound here forever . . . cut your eyes out . . .

I'd seen them when I was with Gus, the tortured souls, crowding around me, walking through me, filling my body with cold and hopelessness to let me know they were there.

I laid my hand on the steel door and recoiled. It was so cold it burned.

A huge sliding deadbolt held the door shut. The sound of wings on the other side was deafening. Flies crawled out from underneath. The voices around me were frantic, whispering and hissing. <u>Don't go, don't go, don't go!</u>

I slid back the deadbolt. The voices fell abruptly silent.

The door burst open and slammed against the wall. A swarm of bats and flies poured into the tunnel. I dropped to the floor and buried my face in my arms. They bounced off my back and butt and legs, battering, biting, stinging.

As quickly as they had come, they were gone. Only a cloud of flies remained, watching me. Seeing so that He could see.

I pushed myself up. I was hurting all over--burned, beaten, bitten. But somehow I wasn't scared off. Not any more. I was fucking pissed.

On the other side of the door, stairs led downward. Of course they did. Arched ceiling, red brick, twisting and turning--the belly of the snake, again. Always with the damned snakes.

I wouldn't have thought there were enough bricks in the world to build a place like this, but obviously I was wrong. I went down slowly, with the flashlight pointing the way.

The smell of death was so horrible I covered my mouth and nose with my hand. I braced for something to leap up at me, but so far nothing did. I was falling deeper and deeper into a brick-red Hell, with the flies for escort.

After a long, long time I reached the bottom. The tunnel stretched off in both directions. I had no idea which way to go.

I was going to die down there, just as the voices said. Bound here forever.

A familiar voice snapped out to the left. Ramirez. "Delta Bravo Six! Delta Bravo Six! Under heavy fire! Repeat! Under heavy fire. Numerous casualties! Request immediate Medevac!"

I hit dirt--or brick--and flashed my light toward the voice. Ramirez sat in the middle of the tunnel in a cloud of flies. One of his arms was blown off. It lay in front of him, its fingers still moving, as if it tried to crawl on its own towards me.

There were dead bodies all around him. He had the field radio in his remaining hand and was speaking into it.

He ducked when my flashlight's beam caught him--then he saw who it was. "Barry!" he called out. "We're hurting real bad, man. The whole team's dead. It's just me and you, bro. Me and you. The gooks are everywhere."

I aimed the light away from him to keep from exposing him any further to the enemy and low-crawled toward him. He was babbling into the radio again. "Request immediate fire mission at my coordinates . . ."

I crawled faster. When I was almost upon him, Gus's voice yelled inside my head. "No! Go back!"

I stopped dead. "Barry!" Ramirez sounded desperate and near tears. "Over here, man. I'm hurting real bad."

"Look again," Gus said.

I shone the light on Ramirez again. It wasn't my old Army buddy, it was the demon, glaring at me out of its scarred pale face, lying as still as a hunting snake. Flies swarmed all over its body.

I could feel its hatred like a hot, stinking wind. Its roar echoed through the tunnels. I sprang up and fired the .45 at point-blank range.

The red tracers disappeared into the

demon's body. I fired until the hammer clicked empty, threw the gun at the demon and pulled my knife from its sheath.

I was ready to die. Bound here forever? Seriously, I didn't give a shit.

The demon stared at me. I hoped it was awed by the balls I had.

"Run!" Gus snapped in my head. "Topside!"

Something in me snapped.

I didn't stop to think or argue. I turned and ran into the blackness, my knife in one hand, flashlight in the other, my skin burning from the flash fire. I was in deep-- literally.

I ran on pure instinct, back up the stairs as fast as I could. But it wasn't fast enough. I was stuck in a nightmare, running and running but getting nowhere.

I could hear the flies closing in. I knew the demon was with them.

Would I make it out? Was it still dark outside--topside, like Gus had said?

I didn't know. I didn't care, either. I just ran. Back the way I had come.

The flies followed my every move. Watching and reporting back to their Master.

I ran past the headless corpse. "May your soul rest in pieces!" it rasped at me.

I hurtled over Sampson's body. I was starting to flag, to lose momentum.

"You must make it topside," Gus urged me. "You *must.*"

There were more flies the farther I went. More eyes for the demon.

Up a level, past a burned body in the shape of a cross. Flies tried to crawl into my nose, my mouth and ears. I swatted them frantically, scanning the ceiling for the next trapdoor.

There--right above me.

I dragged myself up and through, surrounded by flies. My whole body hurt.

I ran, sucking wind, every muscle screaming with exhaustion. The next body hung motionless, its white eyes visible long before the flashlight beam caught the rest of it.

There were so many flies I could barely

push forward. The next trapdoor had to be close. By the time I found it, they surrounded me like a buzzing tornado.

I pulled myself up, each rung a greater effort than the last. Any super strength I'd had was long gone.

Almost out. Almost topside.

The trapdoor was right above me. I balanced on the last rung of the ladder and pushed.

Nothing. Buzzing vibrated from it through my hands and arms. Flies swarmed on it, holding it shut. Despair dragged me down.

I gritted my teeth and shoved with all my remaining strength.

The trap flew open. Clouds of flies swirled around me. A hand reached down and got hold of my wrist and pulled me up and away.

Gus dumped me in the cramped crawlspace and slammed the trapdoor shut and stood on it. The flies buzzed furiously, but they were all on the other side.

"Go!" he barked. "Topside!"

His voice was as impossibly strong as his hand, pushing me through the crawlspace and into the main corridor of the tunnels.

Almost there. A few flies had got through after all, but not enough to stop me or even slow me down. I staggered another fifty feet, to the ladder that had brought me down into this outpost of Hell.

The buzzing of flies was suddenly, enormously louder. I looked over my shoulder. A wall of them came at me. In the center of the wall was the demon.

I threw myself at the ladder and scrambled up it. The manhole was open. I dragged myself out into the cold, clear, blessedly fresh air.

It was still dark. The faint hint of dawn brightened the eastern horizon. All I wanted to do was lie on the ground and let the morning find me, but the flies were already thick around me.

I dragged my aching body away from the manhole toward the tall pine tree that stood close by. Behind me, the demon rose up out of the hole in a whirlwind of flies.

They deposited him lightly on the ground and drew back. He strolled toward me, in no hurry. Why would he be? We both knew I was no match for him.

I crawled backward, and almost screamed at the shock of cold water on my burned skin. I'd fallen into a puddle left over from the rain. I was going to die, and the water felt good.

Step by step and foot by foot, the demon closed in.

Close by, a coyote howled. Then another, and another, until they were all howling in unison--loud, strong, ferocious and powerful.

The demon stopped, head up and tilted, listening.

Wings flapped above me. Fucking bats, I thought--but when I looked up, I saw thousands upon thousands of mourning doves descending into the tree under which I lay.

A coyote broke out of the woods and

ran toward me. Others followed it one by one, picking up speed as they came closer. They spread out in a circle around the demon, running faster and faster.

One last, lone coyote walked calmly out of the trees and approached the circling pack. It was a female, and she passed through the circling pack as if it had been made of air, never taking her eyes from the demon.

The demon stood perfectly still. So did the coyote. Unable to move? Unwilling? I couldn't have said.

Off to my right, a bright light welled up in the woods. A glowing figure stood there.

"Foley," I said.

He left the trees and came toward me. His eyes rested on me; his voice spoke in my head, steady and calm. "God sent me. Your part is done, and well done. Now let me do mine."

He carried an ax that glowed as bright as he did. It looked hot in his hands, like leashed lightning. He passed through the circle of coyotes as the female had, as if they had not been there at all.

The female and the demon were still locked in their battle of stares, oblivious to everything else around them.

Foley raised the ax two-handed, high over his head. "By the power of God," he thundered, "cast into Hell Satan and all the other evil spirits who prowl the world seeing the ruin of souls!"

He smote the demon between the neck and the shoulder. Blackness sprayed out of the massive wound--buzzing loud enough to wake the dead, swirling into a funnel of absolute darkness.

Flies. Swarms and swarms of them, pouring out of the demon's body.

The doves in the pine tree took wing. Thousands and thousands of them, swooping down upon the vortex of flies, chasing them down, catching and swallowing them.

The demon fell to his knees. Foley struck again with the ax, severing his head. New swarms of flies streamed out of him, straight into the doves' waiting bills.

The swarm flattened and spread sideways away from the birds, but ran head-on into the coyotes' circle. Not one of them could pass that boundary. They pulled back together and whirled upward, higher and higher. The doves followed--a tornado of birds feasting on the tornado of flies.

The demon's body lay motionless, but its severed head still blinked and its lips moved as if it were still alive. Its eyes darted back and forth in confusion. It seemed to be trying to speak--some curse, maybe, or some mockery of us or our God.

Foley shattered it with the blunt end of his ax, hammering it to bloody powder, while the coyotes ran and ran in the circle, and the wind cranked higher with each lap.

When the head was completely gone, Foley hacked the body into pieces, none of them bigger than one of the fat black flies that had all vanished into the maws of the doves.

Then finally he stopped. He got down

one knee, blessed himself and began to pray.

The first hint of sunlight glimmered through the trees. Morning twilight was upon us.

The coyotes closed in on the demon's body and began their own feast. Only the female stayed aloof. She walked toward me with a proud and confident air.

Water lapped around me: the puddle into which I had fallen. I splashed some of it on my burned face, closing my eyes for a few seconds with the relief of cool water on scorched skin.

When I opened them I couldn't see her, but I could feel her behind me. The water had gone still. I looked down into it, at the reflection of what stood behind me: the most beautiful sight I had seen in this world. "Momma," I said, and began to cry.

#

Jessica Choofane looked out the first floor window of A Ward and watched a man in a priest's robe destroy the Dark One while an American Indian woman in full ceremonial dress stood close by. Others of her tribe danced in a circle around the priest as he destroyed the Preacher with a shining ax.

The priest was the policeman she had drawn from her vision with an angel on either side, embracing him. They would make a statue in his honor from that drawing.

Barry lay on the other side of the circle in a pond of rain water. The Indian woman went to him, and Jessica began to cry.

It was his mother, and she folded him in her arms as his shoulders shook with deep sobs.

Jessica had to get out. She had to see him.

#

My mother held me tight. "My son," she said, "I love you. I would never leave you. You will never be alone. You have done great deeds in this generation, and done great honor to our people."

I had not cried since my parents died. Not for my grandfather, not for my buddies in Vietnam, and never for all the people I had killed there. I gasped for breath now, trying to speak but unable to, with the tears running freely down my cheeks.

I would not cry again. Nor would I ever be alone.

"I must leave you now," my mother said, "but I will never be far. In time we will be together again."

I clung to her, but I knew I had to let her go. I forced my arms to open. "I love you," I said.

She stood up and held out her hand, saying goodbye--for a while. Then she turned and walked toward the feasting coyotes. She shrank as she moved, going down on all fours, and vanished into the pack.

As if they had been waiting for her, they left the feast and ran off together toward the woods.

A red-tailed hawk screeched above my head and swooped toward the coyotes. As it reached them, it dropped down as my mother had and disappeared. They all ran under the trees, their yellowish-gray coats flashing among the dark trunks.

Jessica ran out of the main door of the hospital with a handful of staff members in close pursuit. She flung herself into my arms and hugged me tightly. "Your mother?" she asked. She was crying.

"Yes," I said. "You could see that?"

"I could see. She's been with you the whole time."

"I know that now," I said. "And so have you. Haven't you?"

She didn't answer that, but she didn't need to. We held each other for a few minutes, though my body hurt all over. I could see the nurses and the orderlies over her head, standing in a huddle, not sure if they should intervene, or how.

"Stay with me," I said to Jessica.

Brian Foley's voice spoke softly in my ear. "Fear not Evil. Fear not Death."

I looked up. He stood in front of the gate to the cemetery. There was a flock of children around him, clinging to his hands and his belt and his robe. Adults of all ages surrounded them.

The lost souls, I thought. No longer tormented; no longer disfigured. Their faces were full of peace.

"They have been delivered to God," Foley said, "by a man who has once again found his faith. Seek the Lord and His strength. Seek His face continually."

"I will," I said. "I will."

Coyotes yipped and wailed in the distance, one by one and then in chorus.

I cherished the sound, as it dissipated and the sun began to rise above the red brick of the hospital. No more mourning twilight. Here was beauty, and here, finally, was peace.

EPILOGUE

The Preacher woke to freezing cold. He lay naked in a dark forest. Nothing lived there. Even the trees were lifeless, their bare branches hanging low, bristling with thorns.

He shivered violently, not only at the cold but at what it had to mean. He hadn't felt anything like it since he pledged himself to the darkness.

It wasn't only the cold, either. The putrid stink that accompanied it was so bad he covered his mouth against it, but it still seeped in, so strong his stomach kept wanting to turn itself inside out to get away from it.

The ground under him buzzed, vibrating through his body. Its surface was crawling.

He raised himself up slowly, eyes darting in all directions but one. He dared not look up.

Something was watching him. For the

first time in a very long time, he was afraid. Afraid of what he would see.

The sky was very dark. The clouds were thick enough that Whatever looked down, maybe It could not see him after all. That made him feel safe, for the moment at least, despite the feeling that someone or something wicked was peering at him from a few inches away.

Safe. Yes. He was safe.

A woman's voice cried out up ahead. He caught the flicker of light through the trees and headed toward it.

The way was far from easy. Sharp, cold sticks and jagged stones covered the forest floor. His feet were already aching with cold; now they stung and burned.

What had the Holy Man done to him? Where was he?

The woman's voice was a little louder now. It was calling his name. "Tommy. Over here."

Then a man's voice joined it. "Hey, Tommy! Come on!"

They were friendly voices. They sounded

as if they cared about him; they made him feel just a little bit warmer. That drew him toward them, though his feet hurt like holy hell. There was something familiar about them.

The light grew brighter, flickering through the trees. A dark purplish-gray fog crawled around his feet. That was where the horrible stench was coming from.

He lifted his foot up above the fog. It was swollen and blue with cold and covered with cuts. The feeling of being watched was stronger and more ominous. "Don't look up," he told himself. "Don't let It see you. If the clouds have cleared--if It can look down--"

The woman's voice was thick and slurred, as if she was drugged, but the words were getting urgent. "Tommy. Hurry. There isn't much time."

He picked up his pace. The power that had filled him and fed his glorious rage was gone. That frightened him. He was all alone, weak and vulnerable. His feet hurt terribly. He was cold, and sick with the smell that refused to leave him.

He could still see reasonably well in the dark, which gave him hope. He was, after all, a faithful servant.

#

After a long and torturous time, the source of the flickering light finally revealed itself. It leaped and flashed and struck at the ground and the trees like lightning, but the bolts were made of flame.

Soft voices spoke to one another nearby, but he couldn't see who they were. He peered through the trees, careful not to look too high up into the sky; then he looked behind him, but all he saw was cold and reeking darkness. He had nowhere to go but forward.

He speeded up as much as he could, limping and hobbling as he was. Just ahead, the path turned to the right. It seemed a little less dark there, and the fog began to lift.

Those were not sticks and stones that he had been walking on. They were human skulls and bones, millions and millions of them as far as his eyes could see. Some of them were intact, and others were shattered. And everywhere, crawling all over them and causing the ground to vibrate clear up through his own bones to the back of his skull, was a swarm of pallid and glistening maggots. They fed on the bones, then twisted and knotted and transformed into flies, which buzzed and crawled and bred new multitudes of maggots. The sound and the smell were both theirs.

For the first time that he could remember, he despised the filthy insects. The flies had always been his allies, but now, somehow, they were different. He had come to the birthplace of wickedness and unseen evil, and he could only hope that it meant he was about to be endowed with greater power.

He had never been so frightened. He stood frozen, unable to move or think or plan. Was he dreaming? Would he wake up a king again? Or had everything changed? The Master was obviously not pleased.

Tommy bent down and snatched up a piece of shattered bone. Maggots dripped wetly from it. All around him, flies rose and circled, distracted from their feasting.

The bone was jagged and plenty sharp. Tommy jabbed it deep into his wrist--deep enough to see the white bone underneath. But no blood came out.

He lay down on the cold and putrid path among the bones and the maggots and began to weep softly. He was scared beyond death, but a fierce and audacious anger had risen up in him. "Please! I beg of you! Please! I deserve better than this!"

The cold dark forest swallowed the sound of his voice. He raised it to a scream. *I did everything you asked!*

"Tommy," the woman's voice said, very close, very clear. "Tommy, you're almost there. Just another little way. We're waiting for you."

He could make it that far. She would

take him out of this place. He was absolutely positive of that, because he knew exactly who she was. "I'm coming, Mom!" he called to her. "I'm coming! Please, Mom--wait for me!"

He ran as fast as he could, though his feet were in agony. As he ran, the dark made its way gradually to the light. It was the time of day or night that he knew best of all, when darkness and daylight fought for dominion.

He tripped and fell, got up, tripped again, fell again, but he kept on going. His feet were shredded. So were his hands and knees, and his body. The skin was stripped from the bones.

It didn't matter. He had to get to the bend in the path. The light was much brighter--and to his amazement it did not frighten him.

He turned the corner, eager to see his mother and his brother Paul. Instead he only saw more darkness and more trees. He sagged in disappointment.

Something moved up ahead. A man in

full military uniform stood among the trees in a soft chatter of voices.

It was his brother Paul, and it was the most beautiful sight Tommy had ever seen. He stood tall and proud in the uniform of the United States Marine Corps. Bright, shining metals hung on his chest. He was smiling so brightly Tommy raised his hand to shield his eyes.

He looked exactly as Tommy remembered. Next to him stood what he had long missed and yearned for: his mother, wearing the dress she had worn at her funeral. He would never forget that dress or that day.

She smiled and held out both hands. Tommy wept openly. He had not felt such happiness since he executed his father.

At the same time, he felt more cold and frightened than he had since he first arrived in the waiting room of Hell. He knew what he had done, and what the price for it had to be. Yet, looking into the faces of the people he loved best in the world, and who had loved him, he knew there was still hope.

Hope was a word and a feeling that Tommy had long since forgotten. It was foolish to hope for anything. Anyone who hoped or prayed was foolish and weak. Hope was a bad thing.

When Tommy was young, hope had treated him without either mercy or compassion. After his mother and his brother, the only hope he had ever contemplated was to rule in Hell. That hope had been fulfilled--but now it was nowhere near as important as being with his family again.

He needed hope. Blind hope. He refused to pray for what he wanted, for God had let him down hard, early and often.

"Tommy, please!" his mother said.

Tommy felt a glimmer of hope, just a glimmer. But he refused to ask God for anything.

The end of the path was close now. The flames licked around him, as if trying to hold him back. His whole body shook violently, convulsing with shock after powerful electric shock.

The path ended in a footbridge over a black and bottomless abyss. His mother and Paul waited on the other side. If he crossed that bridge, he gambled it all--win or lose.

For the first time he looked up to the sky--if that was what it was. Dark purple clouds spun across the whole of it like a vast whirlpool.

The bridge was all of three feet wide, made of railroad ties and rope. He clutched the rope railings, holding on as tightly as he could with his torn and bleeding hands.

It seemed sturdy enough, he told himself. He stepped onto it.

The putrid stink was gone. So was the cold, and the pain in his feet and body. Even the sense of being spied on by some small and petty malice had disappeared.

All he had to do was cross the bridge, and everything would be all right again. He looked across it into his mother's eyes, and his brother's.

"All you have to do is ask Him," she

said.

Ask God, she meant. Tommy's jaw set. He shook his head. He would not ask God for anything. Not. One. Thing.

"God forgives everyone, Tommy," Paul said. "Everyone! All you have to do is ask for forgiveness."

Tommy inched forward. He could sense that he was not alone. Both sides were watching: both Good and Evil.

His mother and brother stood silent. This decision was his to make, whether to ask God to forgive him, or risk it all to be a ruler in Hell.

Was this a joke or a trap?

To that he got no answer, except silence. It was all up to him.

He took another step, and stopped. One quick dash, he thought, and he could make it across, into the arms of his family. Thinking about that gave him the same heady adrenaline rush that filled him when he sacrificed his "collection," as he liked to call it.

That thought brought him back to

reality. He hadn't thought about his collection since he woke in this forest of death. What had once consumed him was now the last thing on his mind.

Even the flames seemed to be awaiting his response, and the clouds seemed to pause. He tightened his grip on the railings and eyed the rest of the distance to the other side, plotting his next move.

Planning was everything. He had never failed in anything as long as he had a good plan.

He launched himself across the bridge. His mother and brother knelt on the far side, stretching out their hands. He could almost feel their touch.

A bright light rose from the trees behind them. It radiated peace and kindness.

Then something terrible happened, the most unspeakably cruel and treacherous thing that Tommy had ever known. Slowly Mary Neveska and Paul Neveska lowered their hands. Their eyes on Tommy were full of terrible sorrow. They wrapped their arms around each other and stood perfectly still.

Tommy's feet, so swift just an instant before, grew immensely heavy. His hands weakened; his grip on the ropes slipped. He was almost to the end--close enough, by just a few more inches, to touch his mother and brother.

If they had reached out, they could have caught him. But they knelt instead and folded their hands in prayer and bowed their heads. "Our Father Who art in Heaven, hallowed by Thy name . . ."

A crack of thunder overwhelmed their voices, but Tommy could see their lips moving. They were still praying.

His body was a dead weight. He could not move his legs, or even pick up one of his feet. The only part of him that would obey was his head, which turned to look over his shoulder.

The darkness behind him was complete, but he could feel the daylight coming. Deep sorrow struck him, and self-pity, and the compulsion to mourn a great loss. He crumpled on the bridge, gathering just enough strength to look up at his beloved mother and brother.

They were on their feet again, but still with hands clasped and still praying. "Mom!" he pleaded, as if he had been an innocent child. "Paul! Please help me! I want to come with you! Don't leave me here!"

Tears rolled down his face, while part of him recognized the irony. The last time he had shed a tear for anything was when he killed his father.

The floorboards of the bridge began to crack and splinter under the suddenly tremendous weight of his body. Through the rolling of thunder he caught snatches of prayer: ". . .burdened with the weight of sin . . . Forgive him, Lord, for he knoweth not what he has done."

Mary and Paul Neveska looked down at Tommy one last time, turned their backs on him and walked slowly arm in arm toward the light in the trees.

"No," said Tommy. "No, you can't be doing this. You can't! I won't believe it! It's a trick! Everything I lived for--everything I loved--you can't leave me here!"

Paul did not pause or turn, but his voice spoke clearly in Tommy's ears. "What about God? What about Jesus?"

Tommy stretched out his hand, clawing at the crumbling bridge. *"Please!"*

Paul turned at that. His eyes were full of tears. With one arm still around his mother, he reached for his brother's hand. "I know it's forbidden," he said to someone--or Someone--that Tommy couldn't see, "but I have to try. This is my little brother. Life was never either kind or fair to him. I know You will forgive me for trying to save him from what lies below. All I have to do is ask. But," he said, and this time he spoke to Tommy, "Jesus can't save you unless you ask Him. This is the law of God, and God's laws are not meant to be broken."

Tommy stretched out his arm with all his remaining strength. It felt as if he was fastened to the bridge with hooks that tore through his skin.

Despite the tremendous pain, he

persevered. He could feel the warmth of his brother's fingers as Paul dropped to his knees and caught Tommy's hand in a strong grip.

It was the most wonderful feeling Tommy had ever known. It was warm and kind. It filled him with peace.

He looked into his mother's eyes. She smiled through her tears.

His body was heavier than ever. The board beneath his knees groaned. Paul pulled with all his might, and Tommy forced himself as far forward as he could.

Paul's hand was hot enough to melt Tommy's flesh. The tighter his grip, the worse it was. Tommy's hand swelled and smoldered, and his body sank through the splintering boards of the bridge.

Paul sobbed with the effort, but Tommy's hand crumbled like the boards and slipped away. With terrible and irresistible slowness, Tommy fell into the abyss.

"God's law," Paul gasped, "is not meant to be broken. Tommy, you should have asked. <u>You should have asked.</u>"

Then he turned his back, he and his mother, though they both wept. For as long as there was light to see, Tommy watched them walk away--slowly, stumbling, bent over with grief, but never looking back.

Darkness rose up around him, with cries of pain and sorrow and terrible torment. Winged shadows surrounded him as if to escort him down below. Thunder cracked; lightning flashed.

Far above him, the bridge was whole again, and a continuous flow of colors approached and attempted to cross. Some were bright and some were dark. His was dark, he realized--but he had always known that. The bright ones who made it across--what was it like for them? Was it the exact opposite of this?

He could wonder, but he would never know.

The cries grew louder as he fell faster. The sides of the pit were lined with souls in torment, bound with red-hot chains, beaten with whips of fire, attacked without mercy. His body twisted in agony.

The bottom raced up toward him. Sharp, cold teeth gnawed at his flesh and bone, and swords of fire slashed through his body. The tortured spirits around him, sensing his arrival, climbed on top of one another like a makeshift ladder, fighting to be the first to get a taste of the freshly fallen soul.

Tommy had finally returned to serve in Hell--but this time as a slave. Chains of red-hot iron bound his hands and feet. Vipers sank their filthy fangs into his flesh, striking his face and piercing his eyes.

There was no God in this forsaken place, for that is Hell: the eternal absence of God. Tommy's arrival in the first depth of Hell was only the beginning of eternity. There were many depths below, so cruel, so torturous and unforgiving, that even Holy Scripture did not mention them.

He had failed his Master, and Satan was always watching, and always unforgiving. The Master of deceit and creator of all lies had claimed another soul.

#

The morning after that fateful night when so much changed, Sharon Corcoran had been committed to the ward in which she once had served as a nurse. A few weeks later, when it became apparent that she was pregnant, no one knew or would admit to knowing who was the father of her child. Because of that, hospital policy required that she not be allowed out of the ward without female escort.

Sharon showed no sign of either knowing or caring what happened to her. Her face was blank, catatonic, staring off into the distance, with pasty white saliva dried to the corners of her mouth: the mark of the heavily medicated psychiatric patient. Every thirty seconds or so, she blinked.

Nurse Fletcher was the only one who took the time to care for her, to comb out her dry and brittle, snow-white hair and try to make her look at least a tiny bit like her old, attractive self.

One day as Nurse Fletcher escorted Sharon through the tunnels to the medical building for her checkup, Sharon said barely audibly, "I know just the name for him."

She hadn't spoken since the day all Hell broke loose. Nurse Fletcher bent down toward Sharon's face. "Sharon! You're talking. That's wonderful. I've been praying for--"

"I know," Sharon said.

"How can you be so sure that it's going to be a boy?" asked the orderly in charge of the gurney.

"I know it's going to be a boy," Sharon said. Her voice was stronger now, and clearer. "Of course it's going to be a boy. What else would it be?" The orderly, her tone said, was lacking his fair share of intelligence.

"Forgive me," the orderly said sarcastically. "How foolish of me."

"Yes," Sharon said in the exact same

tone. "How foolish."

Nursing Supervisor Fletcher pressed her lips together and said nothing. She had been going to reprimand the orderly, but Sharon seemed to be holding her own.

The general presumption was that Sharon had been raped. By whom, no one knew. There were more than enough candidates in this place, God knew, and far too many instances of patients and even staff raping catatonic or incapacitated patients. After all, who were they going to tell? It was a sad, harsh reality in every psychiatric hospital Marie Fletcher knew about, and even a Nursing Supervisor could do very little about it.

The baby was healthy, in any case, and developing extremely rapidly. It was miraculous, some of the doctors and nurses said. Marie Fletcher was not so sure that a miracle was what it was-- unless the other side could work them, too.

"So," the orderly asked, all too obviously humoring the crazy lady, "what are you going to name him?"

"I'm not supposed to say," Sharon answered, "until he's born."

The orderly snorted. "What's the difference? You know it's a boy, right? Why not tell?"

"The baby's father told me not to," she said.

"Well then," said the orderly, "sounds like you've got it all figured out."

"Oh yes," Sharon said. "His father went to great lengths to see that everything was properly taken care of, right down to the last detail."

"Well, in that case," the orderly said, "you're in good hands. Go on and tell us what his name is. Something nice and *special*, right? Like Rip van Winkle. Or Rumpelstiltskin." He snickered.

He really was not very bright, Supervisor Fletcher thought. She had heard him calling the patients "loonies" and "nutbars" to their faces, and referring to this hospital as the "cookie factory."

Good staff were hard to find.

"Go on," he said, as he pushed the gurney from dim light into shadow and back into flickering light again. "What's the harm?"

Sharon was silent. The gurney's wheels squeaked. The air in the tunnel was chilly and faintly putrid.

"Come on," said the orderly with a big, false smile. "We're waiting. What are you going to name him?"

Sharon looked up, not at him but at Marie Fletcher. Her eyes were cold and unblinking. She smiled.

"Preacher," she said.

Kevin F. Branley is the son of immigrant parents from Ireland. He is one of five children born and raised in the Greater Boston area. He has earned a Master's Degree in Criminal Justice at the University of Massachusetts/Lowell, and a Bachelor's Degree in Criminal Justice from Northeastern University.

He is a member of the Law Enforcement community currently assigned to the Investigation Section of a police department within Greater Boston.

On his off time, Kevin enjoys fishing, mountain bike riding, rollerblading, hiking with his brothers and running with his Staffordshire Terrier "Lula."

"Mourning Twilight" is his first novel, and he is currently working on his second novel, which is a sequel to "Mourning Twilight."

Visit: kevinfbranley.com or
mourningtwilight.com

Contact: info@kevinfbranley.com

540